MEXICan Eskimo
Book 1: Exmikan

This is a work of fiction. Names, locations, and events—even when portrayed as historically accurate—are either the product of the author's creativity, or if factual, are used fictitiously.

First edition. First printing.

Frankoni, Anker
"Mexican Eskimo Book 1: Exmikan"
Library of Congress Control Number: 2014905241
ISBN: 978-0-9960285-0-9

Book design by Schipper Design :: www.SchipperDesign.com
Printed in the USA by Think, Inc. El Dorado Hills, California

Published by Anker Frankoni
PO Box 902
Carnelian Bay, CA 96140-0902
www.MexicanEskimo.com

Anker Frankoni is part Joker, part Thief, part Joyful, part Grief, but strives above all to be a Defender of the Right & Pursuer of Lofty Undertakings.

Dear Claire,

what wonderful work you do:
bringing books to the world!

If you find my story and its
cause worthy of furthering, please
allow "Mexican Eskimo" a little
shelf-space in Bellingham

thanks!

Arthur

I dedicate this to my wife and children, my mother and father.

Saying "Thank You" seems almost like insult on top of injury.

"I'm Sorry" is much closer to what I feel I owe you all.

Contents

I was an Eskimo
heading south to get me warm
to be born in Mexico.
Floating past the San Francisco Bay
I got confused by the fog and
the fumes of Texaco...
and got lost in the body of a white woman.

Forward

WHEN writers say that names and places have been changed to protect the innocent, what they are really saying is that they are protecting themselves. In this book, which begins the story of my unlikely existence as a Mexican Eskimo, I have changed nothing, for even if I counted myself amongst the innocent, no one can harm me more than I have already harmed myself. If this seems a rash jab at my duty to behave responsibly, and uphold my obligations to the rules of the society in which we live, I confess it's nothing new. Time and again, year after year, those with whom I was closest urged me to face reality. Instead, I ultimately chose to face that infinitely more beguiling and enduring realm which I believe is the real crux of our shared human experience: Fiction.

In the greatest realms of our world's fictitious histories, pure-hearted pursuers of lofty undertakings valiantly slay all that is rapacious and despicable in the name of honor and duty. There, true lovers are forever made blind to all but their lifelong devotions to each other at the instant of first kisses, and dear lost brothers, separated by a decade and ten thousand miles, become reunited in the final hours of their honorable father's blessed passing into Heaven.

But here in the reality-based history that forms my current incarnation's family roots, drunken sailors abuse their own daughters, respectable gentlemen teach their sons to lie, cheat and steal, and once devoted husbands and wives vainly seek solace for pain in a murky stream of open bottles and open legs, sucked to the dregs under the very noses of their own beloved children in desperate repeated attempts to escape their own helplessness against the dying, and the thieving, and deception all around them.

For the record, I take full responsibility for having born myself into this. Still, I must beg you to pardon the necessity of my self-deception, for the cold hard truth of my current existence, told between the bookends of my birth and coming death, is not a reality I can bear to face. Instead I offer a tale of two lives, separated by the one I'm currently occupying. Through them all weaves a love story: a true to life story about finding forgiveness, trust, and hope amidst generations of anger and neglect, substance abuse and suicide.

This is my *real* experience of this existence, delicately fashioned from piled up pieces of my falsely remembered facts, and gospel-truth fantasies. If charges of fictionalized autobiography are brought against me, ultimately know this: I am finally speaking the truth of all my lies, the awful facing of which made possible solely through this application of a snot-thin varnish of rickety self-respect and quasi-honor, liberally applied from a can of the only finish lustrous enough to cast a fair sheen on my present life story's tarnished surface: Fiction.

And who am I to speak so knowingly? To deem myself worthy of flourishing Fiction's brush, and dare dissect the truth from lies? A certifiable professional of the highest degree, of the most deeply burnished pedigree. Even before assuming this form, I crafted the first lie which introduced this story. I laid out a plot to write my own conclusion to the last life, but the abrupt ending to the chapter that bore witness to my quitter's attempt to flee the cold, the drunkenness, the rending of my culture, was merely a new beginning of life's demand: before I would get what I want, I must get what I need. So as from frying pan to fire, I was flipped from there into this conflux of lies, the stinking fluids of its blood-and-spirit-born recipe measured into a pitted leaden cauldron, then stirred by masters of this dark cookery until I was ready to ladle up the poisons from its oily depths on my own.

Now, midway along the journey of my life, desperate for a magic box of truth that I might open up to flood with light the overflowing black broth of stagnant lies pooled in my lowest recesses, I find myself lacking. There is no golden chest at hand, no pill I'd still willingly swallow to help me take this stand. Rather, I must weave a delicate gauze of threadbare explanation over the whole stinking mess, from words I strain to pluck from the thin air of this life and others prior;

trusting blindly in the slim possibility that—like the glistening drips oozed from the frightening eight-legged monsters of childhood dreams—the poisonous black spider in me will secrete something a thousand times stronger and more luminous than itself, and that by spinning and spinning and spinning, I'll craft a worthy yarn in which to wrap its dangerous, slimy, stinging larvae, and then by some miracle, find my soul is nourished and not poisoned by draining off the venom I must suck from it once and for all.

***

My first steps into this wiry thicket where I'll unravel honesty from lies, must begin by confessing that this book is really a love letter. This is a love letter to my wife and children, a love letter to my parents and generations of grandparents, and ultimately, a love letter to you. But this is the love letter you almost didn't get to read, as at several periods during the writing of it I became convinced that it was my own lengthy suicide note. In the most painful stages of the process of self-examination, when placing each word after the next felt as draining as if I were writing it with my own blood, I got too fixated on what I believed was the looming inevitability of the act, rather than the importance of fully explaining what had brought me to it. Then I nearly drove myself to trash this form of careful explanation altogether, and instead simply lay it all out in one fell swoop as a big, red, impressionistic mural on the bathroom wall for those left behind to divine my message.

But in my steadfast determination to beat my lifelong rap as *quitter* just once, I kept on, word by word, drop by excruciating drop. In a dozen terrifying attempts to leave behind something significant, something complete, something that would irrefutably prove that I wasn't all talk, I wrote and re-wrote draft upon draft, praying all the while that I might not burden my children with one single question as to why I had ultimately chosen such an unnatural and violent, self-terminating act to end their father's story.

Perhaps due to the power of hard work, as I did my best to make something excellent of my last communication to the only people who had ever believed in me, the very message I designed to explain what had brought me to the ultimate act of self-loathing, became its own love letter to myself. As I wrote more than just excuses for the character that I had become, and the road that he had travelled, I found the perspective and empathy needed to understand him, love him, and forgive him, which I had lost the ability to feel for the writer. Through some alchemy of my attempt to describe what I thought was the reality of my life, blended with the fiction that was unavoidably created by trying to accurately remember and explain it, the writing became on its own that which I had been striving so desperately to create—*something worthy of leaving behind*—and by the blessing of its fictional creation, saved me from the self-judgment that had convinced me that I must.

Smells are surer than sounds or sights
To make your heart-strings crack--
They start those awful voices o' nights
That whisper, "Old man, come back!"

Rudyard Kipling, *Lichtenberg*

Chapter 1: **I'm Ahltok**

WHERE I wish I could tell this story to you is right where you are. Just you and me as we exist in the present, which is where the truest tales unfold. If only we could sit and talk of here and now; let the past take care of itself — fill in its own blanks! But those days are over. I suspect that if you really want to know about it, you will dig. And we people can not bury our trash deep enough anymore. Not here, where too much now talk is tweet. No snow ever falls to hide our trails now, and incomplete or ugly clumps of our sacred stories are too easily dug up by anyone curious enough to spend an hour sifting through the cast-off piles we have dumped all around, and ultimately into the very center of our lives: alternating mounds of pearls and poop, ever larger heaps piled moment to moment, growing out of the shards of our most deep or dear or ridiculous, electronically encapsulated musings. So if you really want the dirt on me, put your googly shovel away, and let me start by telling you about the me that came before — the me with no face, from a place with no book.

My dream-travels to the past have revealed only ghosts of memories: my name; my people; my purpose. The visions paint a rough sketch of where I came from. They tell me that last life must have begun about a hundred years back. I can not tell you just where it started or where it ended, or define an exact name for that heritage — Inupiat? Aleut? Unangan? An exact determination of which tribe of Arctic people I belonged to has no real bearing, so: Yup'ik.

One thing I know for certain is, I was born in a time when talk held in it everything on which our lives depended. Generation upon generation of talk laid the rules for where and when we moved, what we ate, how to respect the past and the present; how to stay alive. In that I ultimately failed. I became too impatient for death.

***

Truth is, I was impatient more than once. The first time it happened when I was stricken very young by an attack of burning fever. My father's mother tended me as I slipped between life and death, and back and forth between worlds farther apart than the planets. On ours, I traversed centuries and continents, visited ancient cousins in lands of sultry green and orange heat. They lived atop monuments to the strength of Earth's inner fire, carved from the solid stone congealed from the upwellings of her deepest, hottest liquids, and piled a hundred times higher than the paltry dome of snow and ice in which my body lay.

A craving as strong as a fish feels for water, born of an ancient instinct left in me from some still earlier existence, compelled me to dive into my vision of that steamy jungle, full of the rich spice of hot life. But as I shook in my sweaty delirium, to escape the aching chains of my dying flesh, Grandmother blew smoke over me again and again; an anchor to the people and place of that birth, preventing my departure from our frozen northern lands.

Like a salmon fighting to swim upstream, my spirit thrashed against the currents of space and time rippling over a tantalizing scene of raw human beauty: a young royal Aztec warrior, his perfect naked, jungle-hardened body freshly scented with the musky sweet oils of their marriage ceremony, leaned tenderly over his anointed princess bride. Petrified with the thrill of her gut-wrenching longing for his rock-hard staff's first cleaving of the pristine tunnel walls leading to her warm, soul-nurturing womb, she could at first open only her mouth. Patiently, her tender new master lovingly pushed morsels of ripe mango past her trembling lips, sweetening her slowly yielding virginal body's willingness to succumb to her yearning, as the sticky yellow juices mingled with the glistening drips of sweat running down her heaving breast in a scene of tropically heated ecstasy.

The sweaty lovers were as much aliens to the fur-clad people of my frozen world, as the brightly-plumed jewels of the lush canopy's jungle birds that whistled and cooed high above the thatched roof of that conjugal palapa were to the black ravens of the tundra, but every fiber of my projected self urged my enraptured spirit to take root in the beautiful maiden. Struggling to wrest the last vestige of my errant soul from the sick boy cocooned in tight rolls of ash-spattered seal fur atop the dirty mound of packed snow back in my grandmother's dark igloo, I fought a desperate battle for the new life which lay so tauntingly close to my grasp. Instinctively, I knew that my sense of smell—the most subtly attuned of our human input receptors, and that most closely tied to memory and the foundation of our largely untapped ability to travel through time—was the channel my grandmother had been jamming to keep me from breaking the last tenacious grip of the physical body tying me to our shared genetic destiny.

Striving desperately to open a split-second of physical communication between the two worlds, I strained to catch a whiff of that sweet mango scent and trip the circuit breaker of Grandmother's noxious smoke. Each time she exhaled, it mixed with the bitter stench of her putrid brown nubs of rotten teeth, worn nearly to the gums by decades of chewing stiff hides to soften the leather for countless pairs of moccasins. Sucking puff after puff of a thick gray fog from the hollowed ivory stem of her shaman's pipe, its rancid mouthpiece long dyed a blotchy purple from greasy lips stained a permanent dark bruise color by the mash of pounded seal fat and dried animal blood that had long since replaced the meat she could no longer chew, she rocked and chanted and blew. Doggedly, she disgorged endless rhythmic layers of a cloudy straight-jacket of stink, laying its sooty, clinging moss on top of the invisible part of me struggling to free itself from the feverishly convulsing body.

In my attempt to escape the net, I strained nearly to the breaking point of her pipe's transdimensional tether. Frantically I groped for some purchase on the aery folds of space and time, desperate to push my formless self into the last drips of gooey mango nectar mixing with the musky lovers' perspiration, which ran in delicate rivulets down the fresh young bride's perfect chestnut-hued skin, and through the iridescent patch of glistening black jungle hair gently grinding atop the entrance to her now ecstatically open spirit catcher.

I needed only one breath of the lovers' perfume to infuse the very molecules of my being into the syrupy nectars being pumped so lovingly in and out of her, to become one with the crashing tide of his white-hot warrior milt, that would push the flickering whip of my spirit's tale deep into the fresh new egg, immediately to begin dividing and dividing and dividing and dividing... and then after nine moons and a billion cellular divisions, bear the next and better version of my eternally evolving self into the arms of my young jungle-queen mother, whose first sweet mango-scented kiss would wipe clean the last traces of memory of a short, bitter-cold life in that world where every mother's breath smells only of the thousands of animal souls sacrificed to provide the only food available on those permanently frozen stretches of the Earth's farthest northern curve.

But Grandmother's magic was too powerful. Like an old mother White Bear she waited, poised like a wound spring beside the sea of thick smoke she sent pouring over me from the well of her pipe, until sensing the exact moment in which my spirit gathered all of its last departing strength in preparation for its leap through space and time. The instant my glittering, star-scaled essence exposed itself, cresting up from the rushing current of the Life Stream, she struck. Slashing through the thin fabric of a thousand years from where my dim body lay ready to expel its last breath, she hooked her black claws deep into the underbelly of my naked soul with a perfectly timed swipe of her enormous paw.

An inhuman roar jerked me back from the instant prior to my splash into the sweet water of new creation, and I came to with a shudder, fever broken, looking up through the frame of grandmother's cascading ropes of greasy white hair hanging down nearly into my face. Looming over me with the huge bulk of the bear spirit she had assumed to capture my slippery soul, I stared into her eyes. She had me locked in the predator's glare, her victory proved not by my death, but in preventing my embrace of it. Before the bear receded completely, she used the last of its force to hypnotize me into accepting my life again, as all who return from the dead inevitably must. Still echoing her spirit animal's ursine grumble, she addressed me in a low growl, speaking a name I'd never heard: "Welcome Ahltok. You have travelled far to return to us."

If you don't go far enough back in memory or far enough ahead in hope, your future will be impoverished.

Ed Lindeman

Chapter 2: **POP!**

POP! A familiar sound for pretty Anne Allerfeldt. POP! It marked the celebration of another successful man's hard-won victory. POP! The sound always included a flash of her well rehearsed smile and a slight bend at the waist, purposefully designed to show a few extra inches of her wholesome Scandinavian bosom; a surefire way to pad the tips. POP! Released under just enough pressure to ensure the audible mark of the special event, another precisely controlled cork, expertly guided by her practiced hand. A master of control, never had Anne allowed even the least splash of precious star-nectar to bubble over prior to tipping the first delicious sip of Veuve Clicquot or Dom Pérignon into the winner's outstretched glass, his eyes self-assuredly fixed on the alluring substance of her milky white cleavage.

POP! How many now — five hundred? A thousand? Enough so that she'd long since begun uncorking champagne bottles in her sleep, on the rare nights when her dreams were good. No matter. What part of her life wasn't an act? In this as with everything else, Anne somehow retained the ability to fake it, make that sparkling smile never plastic, but seem always real, just for him: the next Big Winner. The one who might finally extend the tip to end all tips, and lift her out from the ranks of the other waitresses at the Buckeye, every one of them batting their pretty eyelashes, leaning their sculpture-perfect busts into the middle of the dinner-table conversations, and hoping to be the next in an impressively long line of young businessmen's wives, trained for elegant poise and servitude in the exclusive dining room of the Buckeye Roadhouse.

Since 1937, the Buckeye Roadhouse had sat tucked up against a slope of pine trees on a quiet curve of the road between Mill Valley and Sausalito, in privileged defiance of the progress and development spinning rapidly all around, yet still out of sight of its valet attended parking lot. Its privacy, culinary excellence, and regular rotation of playmate-grade waitresses made the Buckeye one of the most jealously guarded secrets of San Francisco's elite professional class. At the time Anne worked there, it was especially favored by a tight-knit cadre of very successful antitrust lawyers, climbing to prominence and bucketing riches during the rise of the last major consumer-rights movement that began in the late 1960's.

Anne hadn't arrived at the Buckeye with dreams of marrying a lawyer. Generally speaking, Anne didn't dream of acquiring, or becoming: Anne dreamed of escape. Slowly but surely, the notion of marriage had simply become in her mind the most logical means of the next escape. She had started working at the Buckeye to put herself through college, but nearly two years after graduation from San Francisco State University, had done nothing with her degree in history beyond mentally charting the long line of bottles she opened for other people's celebrations. With some help from an analyst early on, Anne might have realized that college itself was an escape from her life as a World Airways stewardess, flying ceaseless loops between California and the Orient during the early 60's, when a trans-Pacific flight aboard the propeller-powered DC-6s used at that time meant upwards of 20 hours in the air. More therapy could have helped her understand that becoming a stewardess was simply the most direct form of escape from her childhood, which she spent growing up on the USA's largest overseas military base, where she lived until she was 18 years old after her father moved his family there following World War II. Something in Anne made even the conscious thought of self-analysis almost impossible, however, and she certainly wasn't thinking of it on the night of the champagne accident. Her attentions were entirely fixed on the slim possibility that lay in the perfect execution of the job at hand: serving Marco.

***

Marco Frankoni was a closely watched favorite of the Buckeye waitresses. Only 28 years old, this quintessential son of San Francisco was the direct descendant of an intermarried network of tight-knit

Sicilian families that lay claim to a large slice of the California boom-pie starting in the mid-1800's. The families made lucrative inroads into the state's rich timber-zones and fisheries, real estate, restaurants, and just two generations later, law and politics. Marco came of age at the peak of their wealth and influence.

The third generation in a pure Italian lineage of first sons of first sons, Marco was born November 11th, 1941, and baptized six weeks later on the morning of Christmas Eve, in front of a crowd of nearly a hundred relatives and well-wishers at Saints Peter and Paul Church in the heart of North Beach. There, in a public display of both her generosity and her enviable success, his paternal grandmother presented a check in the amount of twenty thousand dollars to fund his educational trust account.

***

Once Marco came into the world and made her a grandmother, she became henceforth and forever known to everyone in the family as "Nona." Of all the lives that contributed a piece to the genetic puzzle that put Marco's together, hers is the only one with no traceable history tied to it. Vita Volterra was born poor in Sicily, and arrived in New York alone as a young girl, probably before she was even ten years old. Whether or not she started her journey with any other family members is unknown. Vita was extremely secretive about her past, and very few things about her childhood were ever extracted from her by her son and grandchildren. Even the year she was born is questionable: all of her records list her date of birth as January 1st, 1900, but the earliest document with her name and birth date printed on it is a ship's manifest from her entry to the United States through Ellis Island on August 13th, 1909, upon which all the information was recorded simply on her say so, and as her son pointed out more than once after she died: "Mother really liked round numbers."

Unlike most of the Sicilian immigrants who came from coastal fishing villages to San Francisco at the end of the 19th and beginning of the 20th centuries, Vita had apparently been born in the mountains, though exactly where she never told. During the year leading up to her death in 1986, she told her son a series of stories about "our simple life in the shadow of the great volcano." This could only be Mount Etna, and therefore puts her birthplace in or around one of the villages above the foothills of Catania or Messina. The memories Vita relayed to her son that year were more like sketches than stories. She never put a name to the few people she mentioned, or hinted at her relationship to any of them, yet the intricate details of the scenes she described—peasants beating ripe olives from the trees with long poles in the fall harvest season; children playing atop centuries-old ruins of tumbled rock walls; searching for mushrooms on the slopes of the volcano in the light of the full moon—filled his head with a gallery of rich images that he treasured for the remainder of his life.

As Vita's memory and tongue loosened at the end of her life, her only son, Francis, sought to satisfy his curiosity about how she came to San Francisco from

New York all by herself when she was so young. Though he rephrased the question repeatedly in his attempts to get her to open up, she responded the same way every time, closing her eyes and leaning back in her rocker to indicate that nothing more would ever be spoken on the matter beyond the single word she always gave in answer: "Nebraska."

Francis had also hoped to press more of the information about his ancestry from her before she died, and asked her repeatedly during his daily visits to her home about his grandparents. But even as she drew so close to the line between life and death that she seemed to no longer even know exactly which of her memories existed on either side of it, her tight-lipped response was always the same: "Brother Treuzzo and Sister Concetta say it's safest not to speak of them."

Regardless of her humble beginnings, or what potentially damning mysteries lay in the close-kept secrets of her past, nothing seemed to impact Vita's financial success or social standing in America, and by the time her grandson Marco was born, she was very likely the wealthiest businesswoman in San Francisco. Granted, there wasn't much competition for that title in those days, as the door to her pathway to success was not one that would have been open to most women of her time. Like many lives in this story though, hers was greatly affected by fate.

Late in the summer of 1924, her husband Onofrio Frankoni was killed in a crash while driving his new car to show it off to his favorite cousin in Pescadero, a small farming community a few hours south of San

Francisco. Less than an hour away from the city, the almost brand-new convertible he had purchased in June that year overturned as it rolled off the highway and down the cliffs into the sea just north of Pacifica. The car was one of the last of Studebaker's entry-level models named the "Light Six," which was renamed the "Standard Six" in August of 1924. Although the car was the least expensive model offered by Studebaker, made even cheaper since it was being cleared to make room for the rebranded models, Vita was not at all pleased about the additional eighty-five dollars Onofrio spent on the convertible model, instead of the hard roof version. Had he lived, she certainly would have never questioned her husband's decisions again. Were it not for the convertible roof, left down on that beautiful summer afternoon when Onofrio was to proudly show off both his new automobile, and his fast-growing young boy to his country cousin, Vita would have lost both her husband and her son: Francis was thrown clear of the shiny new Studebaker just before it overturned and crushed his unlucky father.

Following the accident, a chorus of voices from the elder heads of the many branches of her late husband's family urged Vita to remarry, tend to her boy, and let a new man—several of Onofrio's cousins were specifically suggested—run her restaurant. But Vita's new status as a widow conveyed to her a range of certain legal and social privileges that she was loath to squander, and in a move almost completely unheard of at the time, she quickly had her maiden name restored to further distance herself from any financial claims on the restaurant by her former in-laws, and devoted herself almost entirely to her business, and her son Francis.

Vita Volterra never remarried or had another love relationship, as far as anyone in her family ever knew. Within a very short time, she grew her first small restaurant into four large ones, and by the middle of the 1930's her kitchens were supplying the cruise ships that docked in the San Francisco Bay during that time, with weekly hundred-case orders of her restaurants' famous hors d'oeuvres and cocktail-hour foods. By the time Marco was born, Vita had invested her profits in a half-dozen rapidly appreciating parcels of prime downtown San Francisco real estate, and could have easily given much more than the twenty-thousand dollars she set aside for her first baby grandson's future education.

Never one to hand over the reins to anything she had a vested interest in, Nona herself managed Marco's college fund investments as successfully as she did her restaurants, and that gift multiplied greatly in the 18 years that followed. Late in the summer after high-school graduation, with funds in his college coffers worth in excess of a hundred and thirty thousand dollars, Marco Frankoni set off for an intensive seven-year period of study in Washington D.C., culminating in a degree from Georgetown University's law school.

With his intellectual capacity and his grandmother's backing, Marco might have pursued life as a scholar indefinitely, and for a while it seemed that his insatiable thirst for education and classic literature would steer him towards that course. His breeding and grooming had awoken other tastes in him as well though. The house he grew up in was a posh five-story, four thousand square foot home, custom built in the Spanish Colonial Revival style to his father Francis Frankoni's specifications in the late 1930's. The proceeds of the extremely generous salary Francis earned as general manager of his mother's restaurants allowed him to build on a lot situated for the best view of the lake at The Palace of Fine Arts on San Francisco's Baker Street, just a five minute walk from the prestigious Saint Francis Yacht Club, where Marco spent weekends developing his skills as a young sailor of fancy racing boats.

Following his schoolboy days at Stuart Hall, Marco joined the rest of San Francisco's most privileged Italian teens at Saint Ignatius College Preparatory, where the fierce competitor which sprang from his Scorpio spirit pushed him to the top of his academic classes, as well as into the lead position on the school's renowned varsity golf team, whose players gathered several times per week on the exclusive fairways of the Robert Trent Jones designed Olympic Club golf course. When he wasn't acing tests, sailing on the bay, or sinking birdies, the remainder of Marco's extracurricular free time was primarily devoted to developing a connoisseur's appreciation for the finest fresh pussy on supply from the city's best Catholic girls schools, which his movie-star good looks, young athlete's body, and enviable pedigree compelled even his most respectable dates to offer up to him in spite of the prevailing sexual conservatism of the 1950's.

While he kept his head in the game during all of his years at college and law school in Washington, Marco's heart always remained in San Francisco. By the time he graduated from Georgetown, Marco had laid out a carefully crafted plan to create a life of his own self-made wealth and power back in his home town. He would begin laying the foundation for that life by joining the antitrust law firm of his uncle Hubert Lunardi, immediately upon his return from Georgetown.

**

In addition to Marco's own smarts and ambition, it was Nona's seemingly clairvoyant ability to place her bets on the winners that had set the wheels in motion that would help ensure Marco of a position with the future State Senator's law firm, long before her grandson—or even Hubert Lunardi himself—was even born. Following her son Francis' early psychic trauma from witnessing his father's tragic death, Vita Volterra made it her constant responsibility to keep her family members from further harm, and pave their way to easy lives as best she could.

Even at the peak of her activity, as she labored 14 hours or more a day to guard her independence and build the fortune that helped ensure their successful futures, Vita always made it her second job to know everything about anybody who mattered in San Francisco's Italian community. She stitched the most intricate details of the complex fabric of her city's social network into a constantly updated mental card catalog, which she used to her benefit at every major juncture of her personal affairs and business dealings. When selecting the locations for her new restaurants, Vita chose properties in North Beach, Fisherman's Wharf and Pacific Heights, not only for the locations' street traffic and favorable lease terms, but also for their proximities to the home addresses of the wealthiest and most influential Italian families. To these addresses—decades ahead of the science of direct marketing—she mailed a steady stream of postcards and handwritten notes to her fellow Italians, enticing them in to try an array of exquisitely prepared old-world standards, presented alongside an eclectic offering of delicious new foods she called "Early Californian."

Borrowing from the Sicilian tradition of marrying complex Mediterranean flavors from land and sea, Vita tapped a vein of even bolder spices and ingredients that had been simmering in California's culinary melting pot since Junipero Serra and his fellow Spanish Catholic missionaries travelled north with their indigenous cooks when they established their colonial foothold on the West Coast through the Alta California Missions. A full 50 years before the term was even invented, Vita's masterful translation of the city's unique blend of cross-cultural food heritage established her as San Francisco's top fusion chef, and for nearly as many years a loyal stream of patrons fed generations of their families at her tables, not only on the city's best Minestrone soup, but on such never-before-tasted creations as her poblano-chile spiced squash blossom and Dungeness crab tamales, the rough textured corn masa of the traditional Mexican variant replaced with creamy Italian polenta to suit her clientele's more refined tastes, then ingeniously steamed to perfection in a large stainless steel cup, which when upended on the platter-sized terracotta colored plates that were a hallmark of her restaurants, presented the tamale like an exquisite little savory bundt cake, free of the messy corn husks that would otherwise stain a lunching businessman's shirt cuffs.

A close examination of Vita's story and the moves she made to ensure her bloodline's success makes clear however, that both her innate business sense and culinary expertise paled in comparison to her astounding ability to actually foretell human destiny: in tracking and memorizing the intricate details of dozens of San Francisco's most successful Italian families, her tightly-focused attention on one in particular seems to best illustrate her uncanny gift.

***

The two Italian families most central to the story of San Francisco's 20th century history shared ancestral roots in the tiny fishing village of Porticello, Sicily, just east of Palermo below the Cape of Zafferano along the coast of the Tyrrhenian Sea. Incredibly, neither of the family histories point to a connection between the Guariso and the Lunardi clans prior to their first members' emigration from Sicily, but just as much as fate, timing and circumstance are likewise key players in this story of complex, interwoven destinies.

Before dawn on the morning of April 18, 1906, San Francisco's hard-working fishermen were preparing for the day's catch. In his home on Telegraph Hill at the end of Filbert Street, a few short blocks away from his growing fleet of fishing boats, one of the most successful of the second wave of Italian fishermen that had begun monopolizing California's exploding seafood business, Antonio Guariso, owner of the Pacific Fish Company, was enjoying the fruits of his success by sleeping in past 5:00 AM — a treat only a well-established boss could afford in his business. At almost precisely 5:12, the first violent shock of the great earthquake that rocked the city that day blasted Antonio from his slumber and into action. During the twenty-five seconds or so of calm between the initial shock and the devastating shaking of the main quake, he rushed his wife, Angela, and his son and four daughters out of bed and into the front of their house, where they crouched terrified below the monstrous Romanesque arch and columns separating the parlor and living room that Antonio himself had designed into the plans.

Just as any proud Greek might have announced his success to the neighborhood by gracing his front yard with a garish marble statuary installation, Antonio insisted on the obtrusive status symbol, despite Angela's loudest protests. In an ironic nod to the staying power of bad taste, it was probably due to the additional engineering required in designing the building to accommodate the weight of Antonio's solid granite trophy arch, that of the nine lavish homes on their prestigious block of Filbert Street, their newly constructed, Italian-villa-inspired mansion was one of only two left standing after the first minute of the Earth's incredible seizure.

As soon as the rumbling stopped enough for her to be heard over the shrieking of her five terrified children, Angela quickly huddled them together in the parlor, the air thick with white dust from the still crumbling plaster ceiling. As devout to her word as she was to God, even in the terror of that moment, Angela upheld her rule of speaking only English to her American-born children: "Let us all kneel and a-pray my children!"

But Antonio was a man of action: "We nobody of us gonna rob-a the time for pray when God is knockin' down-a the house! We are a-gettin' outta here!" Once outside, Antonio could scarcely believe his eyes as waves a full two feet high rippled across the bucking asphalt surface of their street. Any man with as much salt water in his veins as Antonio would have chosen to face the ocean's worst storm, rather than the nightmare of waves crashing across what should have been solid ground, so between the ominous aftershocks that continued to shake the homes all around them, with the sidewalks cracking under their feet and Antonio barking orders as if to a crew of deaf sailors, he rushed his family safely down to the dock, where they jumped aboard his largest boat just as another brutal wave of aftershocks began buckling the heavy timbers of the pier to which it was moored.

Angela would forever insist that it was her prayers—which she shouted all the while in Italian to Jesus, Mary and Joseph despite being denied the right to do so in a kneeling position—which saved them. But what of the next twist? Was it destiny? Fate? Coincidence?

Surely it was one of these, or some other independent universal force ignorant of the most urgent prayers of any individual—even one as devout as Angela— which crafted the next turn of the screw that would ultimately wind up binding the two families together so completely.

Thirty seconds behind the Guarisos, another Sicilian fisherman was running for the safety of his boat. This younger man had only recently leveraged his hard work and determination into the purchase of his first Felucca—the graceful little one or two-man fishing boats common at the time—and Antonio just vaguely recognized the fresh faced newcomer racing by him as he helped the last of his children down to Angela in their much larger boat. Moments after Antonio leaped down from the pier, cast off the mooring line and gave his boat a mighty shove away from the precariously swaying pile to which they had been tied, he heard the man's anguished cry. He looked up to see him stop dead in his tracks, his escape cut off from his own boat by a huge gap in the pier suddenly created from a rift in the timbers as the whole middle section shore off and crashed into the bay.

"*Salta Giovanotto — Salta!!* (Jump young man — Jump!!)" Antonio yelled up to the stranded fisherman. With his escape route cut off, and the entire structure now threatening imminent collapse, he was only too happy to follow the order. Sprinting back towards the trembling edge of the pier, Lodovico jumped. He jumped with all his might, all his faith; and all his certainty that he had just died and gone immediately to

Heaven, for as he leaped from the last standing board of the shuddering pier beneath him, hurling his body towards the deck of Antonio's boat, the slow-motion tunnel-vision created as a side effect from the intense boost of adrenaline shot into his bloodstream to create the supernatural strength for the almost twenty-foot leap, focused his gaze directly on the face of an angel.

At the end of however many seconds or minutes of frozen time Lodovico hung suspended in mid-air enthralled by her beauty, a voice celebrating his sudden acceptance of fate, circumstance, and God's benevolent will, rang joyfully from his throat like a golden trumpet, crowning the arc of his fantastic swan-dive with the impromptu shout: "*Mi dono di Dio per la tua gloria e la protezione!* (I give myself God to your glory and protection!)" And even before he'd crashed onto the deck of the boat to discover first of all that he was still alive, and second of all that the girl whom he'd mistaken for an angel was in fact the Guariso's 13-year-old daughter, Domenica, Angela already knew for certain that one day this high-flying, God-praising young man would be her son-in-law.

Lodovico Lunardi and Antonio Guariso would shortly discover that they had much more in common than just the good luck to ride out the aftermath of the great earthquake in the same boat that morning. The older man grew more and more astounded as Lodovico related his story, and could scarcely believe that with all of the similarities to his own, their paths had never crossed before. To learn that the young Sicilian who had just dropped from the heavens into his boat was also from Porticello was a cause for as much celebration as possible, given their view from the bay of the terrible fires rising up all over the cityscape in front of them. To discover that they were both the first-born sons of large, poor fishing families there seemed a simple enough coincidence, but by the time that their conversation revealed that they each had mothers who came from the tiny mountain village of Cefalà Diana to marry fishermen in Porticello, and that both of those mothers had distant relatives in the Northern Italian city of Ancona, Antonio felt as if someone were playing him. Were it not for the earthquake, he would certainly have concluded that he had been made the butt of some elaborate hoax. The last layer of synchronicity was revealed as Lodovico recounted the circumstances leading up to him coming to America:

The first of nine children born in his mother's bed in Porticello (Antonio had been first of eight), Lodovico Lunardi was only twelve years old when he arrived in San Francisco in the summer of 1896. With too many mouths to feed, the boy had been shipped off to California by his well-meaning parents upon the recommendation of a wealthy branch of his mother Stefana's distant northern relatives, the Albertinis of Ancona, whose son Nunzio had created a unique opportunity for Italians wishing to immigrate to the United States.

***

The Albertini family's riches and social standing in one of the most prosperous areas of Italy in the mid-

1800's were not enough to temper the wanderlust of its adventure-prone middle son, Nunzio Albertini, who—questing for a story beyond that of his birthright—set sail for America in 1858. Within a year of his arrival, the young Italian's yearning for wide-open space and discovery had sorely disenchanted him with the already overpopulated metropolis of New York City. Determined to find the real frontier of 19th Century America, Nunzio signed on as boatswain of the famous clipper ship Andrew Jackson. His nautical skills had been developed over many years of captaining his family's large yacht as a teenager on the Adriatic Sea, and his natural leadership abilities were clearly evident as he oversaw her crew during the Andrew Jackson's record-setting 89-day run around Cape Horn from New York to San Francisco. This experience added further spit to the already polished proof that for the well-born Nunzio Albertini, the greatest of successes were not simply possible, but practically inevitable.

Late one spring afternoon, shortly after arriving in San Francisco aboard the world's fastest sailing ship in March of 1860, Nunzio was fishing in the bay from a natural rock outcropping jutting from the northeast edge of the city. While patiently awaiting his supper, Nunzio gazed transfixed at nature's sad air show over Alcatraz Island, as thousands of stubborn Brown Pelicans glided through the lengthening golden rays of the late afternoon sun, circling a shattered memory of their ancestral nesting grounds, vainly seeking a solid place to roost in the ghosts of trees clear cut by the platoon of Federal Army engineers busily expanding the military fortifications there to house Civil War prisoners.

Well read in both Italian and English, Nunzio's exploring personality and constant curiosity about his world had led him to study as many of the first written accounts of the West's early history as he could find, and he was in those moments contemplating the freshly inked chapters in the story of California, which had been made a part of the United States only 12 years prior to his arrival as a result of the defeat of Mexico in the Mexican-American War. His attention drawn towards Alcatraz by the pelicans, Nunzio's mind was particularly absorbed in recollecting reports he had lately read detailing the career and character of John C. Fremont, an impetuous, passive-aggressive social climber who managed to overcome the moral stigma of his illegitimate birth by marrying the daughter of Senator Thomas Hart Benton, Democratic Party leader in the Senate for more than 30 years, and the earliest and staunchest advocate of the country's expansionist movement.

Fremont borrowed trappings of the respect that was never his own to command by marrying into the Benton family, and the Senator gained a puppet son-in-law from the bargain. Through his power and influence, Senator Benton obtained choice military and political appointments for Fremont, then sent him off as leader of a series of important expeditions to chart the boundaries of the continent and advance the borders of the United States. It was during the Mexican-American War in California that Fremont, as acting Military Governor of the region, negotiated in 1846 for the purchase of Alcatraz in the name of the United States, a full two years prior to when the signing of the Treaty of Guadalupe Hidalgo had even marked the end of the war.

As the pelicans drifted over their stolen breeding grounds, Nunzio's contemplations mused particularly around his understanding of the premise of "Manifest Destiny," a tenet upon which it seemed the single-minded Fremont based the majority of his actions. In Washington, those who pitched the Manifest Destiny agenda were spinning more political dogma than specific governmental policy, but the basic precept embodied in the term Manifest Destiny was one that would come to irreversibly alter the social landscape and physical geography of the United States, especially during an intensely concentrated period of national expansion during a roughly 20-year span between the 1840's and 1860's. In those two decades alone, war victories, political conquests, and the outright refusal to recognize the poorly defended colonial claims to the last chunks of land bordering the already established states, nearly doubled the country's land holdings through the addition of Texas, California, Oregon, Nevada, Washington, Utah, and other vast tracts of the continent as states and territories. By the time Nunzio arrived to cast his line into the San Francisco Bay in 1860, proponents of the Manifest Destiny doctrine had succeeded in pushing the boundaries of the young United States from "sea to shining sea," and efforts by the ideology's most extreme advocates to force their fledgling republic's novel new version of free government on every soul in the continent by annexing *all* of Mexico, after California, New Mexico, and Texas were already taken as the spoils of war, had only recently lost momentum.

For Nunzio Albertini, the term "expansionism" meant simply expanding his own world view, and in this regard he'd attained great success since leaving the shelter of his well-to-do family in Ancona. A true humanist, Nunzio's appreciation for the individual beauties that he saw in the myriad examples of mankind that he had observed since crossing the Atlantic and landing in the multi-cultural melting pot of America, made him a natural opponent of the Manifest Destiny camp, whose philosophy in a nutshell is probably best summed up in words by John Quincy Adams, who was cranking the wheel that would give power to the movement via the lever of Continentalism, long before the term Manifest Destiny was even coined by the media of the day. Adams opined that "The whole continent of North America appears to be destined by Divine Providence to be peopled by one nation, speaking one language, professing one general system of religious and political principles, and accustomed to one general tenor of social usages and customs."

How nonchalantly Adams described the crushing wave of cultural homogeneity that would flood the continent during the next 150 years! Though this flood was still just a minor swell in 1860, somehow the latent augur in Nunzio—laid deep in his ancestral psyche by an ancient Roman auspice from which his Italian bloodline descended—subconsciously divined a dreadful eventuality in the hopeless circles of the distant pelicans that he watched fly over Alcatraz that evening, which would soon be nearly wiped out and displaced forever by the crass and inelegant gulls that would effectively blanche out the diversity of the area's native birds, as surely as the all-conquering droves of *Humanus Europeas* would methodically eradicate or dispossess 95% of the more than five hundred unique tribes of native people living upon the land that their invaders would call "The United States of America," and eventually cause to become covered coast to coast by a not-so-shining sea of Walmarts.

But Nunzio Albertini was no Nostradamus; magical doomsday herald, mysteriously channeling visions of the 21st century future that would come about as a result of the American Experiment's craving for territorial expansion and societal conformity. Rather, he was a free thinker, embracing of the beautiful complexities of form and spirit that grace Earth as a result of Mankind's and Nature's diversity. In the celebration and protection of that diversity, Nunzio saw a future of wisdom and abundance. In contrast, the premonition he read in the thinning spiral of displaced pelicans, vainly attempting to return to their namesake island, spoke to him of the tragedy of possibilities lost even before becoming known. The Alcatraz pelicans, still-living harbingers of their own endangered species, somehow conveyed to Nunzio some misty understanding of a distant future he would never want to see, and he was saddened by imagining it.

Lost in these contemplations, his fishing pole was nearly jerked clean into the bay as his meditations were shattered by the surprising force of whatever it was that suddenly hit the bait at the end of his line. Per the habits of his offshore fishing roots, Nunzio had tied multiple leaders onto his main fishing line in order to put more hooks in the water. For the next ten minutes, the drama of his struggle took center stage in the lengthening rays of the evening sun, as Nunzio and the unseen force at the end of his line pitted the survival of the one, against the dinner of the other.

An appreciative audience of two successful gold-miners recently come from the Sierra Nevada mines had paused to enjoy the calm hours of the evening near the spot where Nunzio was fishing. As soon as his contest with the force in the water exploded into action, they too shifted their attention from the pelicans coursing over Alcatraz, to Nunzio's masterful handling of his rod and reel, as he carefully played out and recovered lengths of line over and over again in the delicate dance required to land whatever had taken the bait at the end of a set of tackle obviously meant for much smaller catch.

The crazily erratic sweeps of the line extending out from below the water were finally explained once Nunzio had tired his catch out enough to reel it in close to the rocks. Upon reaching into the foamy tide to claim his prize, he discovered at the end of his hooks not one, but two magnificent fish. The onlooking miners had more gold-dust in their pockets than food in their bellies, and when they saw Nunzio's delicious surfeit of dinner in the two glistening Lingcod he held aloft as he stood ankle-deep in the water and took a bow to acknowledge their cheers of support during the fight, they offered to buy the larger of the two to satisfy the sudden hunger for fresh fish that was brought on by the sight of them.

If all events in history made a noise equal to their impact on the future, the exchange of Nunzio's surplus catch on the shore of the San Francisco Bay that evening in 1860 would have sounded a thunderclap of adumbration, for the sale of that fish created a ripple that become such a powerful wave in the economic and political development of California, that it is still felt 150 years later. Even the type of catch itself was a clear indication of Nunzio Albertini's future destiny, as Lingcod have a most bizarre trait: once cooked, their meat is like that of many other similar cold-water, white-fleshed fish. Prior to cooking, however, the fillets of the Lingcod fairly glow with a muted emerald-green color. Though Nunzio received gold dust as payment for that first fish, its deeper meaning was clear: if greenbacks were fish-flesh, they would be Lingcod; it's the fish that's the color of money.

Had the magic fishes been the catch of a greedy man, the effect of their sacrifice as a catalyst upon the future may have been entirely different, so perhaps it is no irony that they gave themselves to Nunzio Albertini, a man who had never wanted for money. He grew up surrounded by his family's wealth in Ancona, was blessed with a generous allotment of it when he set off to see the world, and was paid handsomely with it for his role in crewing the Andrew Jackson's famous Cape Horn run. Furthermore, since his needs were simple and his material aspirations modest, once money found its way into his pockets it tended to stay there. So it was not personal wealth and power that guided Nunzio from the sale of the first Lingcod, down a path that would create a company that would become the West Coast's largest wholesale seafood distributor; his success growing until Nunzio became officially known across the Western United States as "The Fish King."

Nunzio's crown sat lighter on his head than most. From the first exchange, when the price the miners were willing to offer for his extra Lingcod made clear the scarcity of good fresh seafood in the growing city, Nunzio realized the potential that existed to leverage the creation of an industry, not just for his own benefit, but for hundreds of his fellow Italians, who by their arrival would imbue a distinctive wave of Mediterranean color and culture to California's growing population — his clearly intended contribution to the anti-homogenization of Anglo-settled America.

Within a week of selling the first Lingcod, Nunzio procured a small boat and crewed it with three Italians who had sailed under his direction aboard the Andrew Jackson, and then remained in San Francisco to seek their fortunes rather than treasure-hunt the already thinning gold of the Sierras. By mid-summer of that first year, Nunzio and his fishermen had been so successful on the water that he worked himself out of his favorite job: fishing.

From that point on, Nunzio remained onshore to oversee the processing and distribution of their daily catch, having made a co-op style arrangement with his three fishermen to work towards ownership of the boat by forfeiting half the value of their take until the cost of the vessel had been recouped, and then agreeing to sell only to him for at least two seasons afterwards. This arrangement worked so well for everyone involved—mainly because Nunzio was never underhanded, and always paid fair market rates for his fishermen's catch, even during the time they had promised to sell only to him—that he replicated this system of fair-trade for ownership on more than 20 additional boats between 1860 and 1863, and at least a hundred more before the end of the century. Back in Ancona, the Albertini clan circulated news of the opportunity through a network of friends and family that extended all the way south to Sicily, and a stream of Italian fishermen and their families rode their way into California on the wave of Nunzio Albertini's cooperative business model.

***

It was that fish-powered portal of Nunzio's generous design which allowed both Antonio Guariso, and Lodovico Lunardi ten years after him, to make their way into California. Hearing this last parallel to their stories was the clincher for Antonio, who was by then just as convinced as Angela that Lodovico had dropped into their lives for a distinct purpose. Before the end of that first day of their seemingly ordained meeting, as the two men watched the raging fires burn all across the San Francisco skyline from the deck of Antonio's boat, they hatched a partnership that formed the Guariso-Lunardi Fish Company, and took such well-timed advantage of the opportunities created in their industry in the wake of the earthquake and fires, that their success would grow to dwarf that of their original backer and mentor, Nunzio Albertini, and eventually cut their family members in on a major chunk of practically all the fishing trade on the California coast north of San Diego and south of Eureka.

Those days in the Italian community, business was done first and foremost with family. With the volume of business the experienced Antonio Guariso and his aggressive new partner Lodovico Lunardi were soon doing together, it only made sense that they would seal their mutual interests by uniting their family ties as well as their business dealings. Antonio (who had been prodded incessantly in this direction by Angela during the previous four years) finally declared his beautiful daughter Domenica marriageable when she reached her 21st birthday, and she and Lodovico were wed in the Saints Peter and Paul Church in San Francisco on April 14th, 1914.

During the eight years leading up to the marriage, Lodovico's reports of the Guariso-Lunardi Fish Company's success back home to his parents and siblings were so compelling, that they eventually all came to join him in San Francisco. As the business expanded through all this wonderful nepotism, so did the family bond between the clans, and all told, three of the Lunardi brothers and one sister eventually married three of the Guariso sisters and one brother between

1914 and 1927. If the accumulation of money and blood meant power, this new dynasty was the family to watch in San Francisco. And no one watched them more closely than Vita Volterra.

***

The oft-recounted story of Antonio Guariso's and Lodovico Lunardi's first meeting and subsequent partnership did not take long to become a thing of legend in San Francisco's Italian-American community. In the most embellished versions of its telling, Lodovico's leap from the capsizing pier to the deck of Antonio's boat had grown to a distance of 50 feet or more, and the angelic face in the story was attributed to an actual otherworldly winged figure, which under God's direction, swept Lodovico from the crumbling pier across the impossible distance to the deck of Antonio's boat. In actuality there was nothing at all supernatural about Lodovico Lunardi's abilities or blessings, and if any cat's cradling of his futurestring was at work behind the scenes, it was not God, but Vita Volterra that had singled him out for the extra attention.

By the time Onofrio had died and Vita was left to single-handedly run the first restaurant and raise little Francis, Lodovico and Domenica were already a well-established family with four children of their own. But even before any of the children were born, when Lodovico Lunardi was just coming in to his full stride as a community power broker in San Francisco, and Vita was still only Onofrio's helper, she insisted that her husband deal exclusively with the Guariso-Lunardi

Fish Company as his restaurant's seafood supplier.

Vita was both famously generous (witness Marco's baptismal gift), and an incredible penny-pincher. She would pit three competing produce suppliers against one another to save a penny per pound on the dozens of sacks of onions that were delivered to her restaurants each week, then if the lowest bidder allowed a single rotten one to sneak into her kitchens, she would short-pay the invoice by ten percent, claiming the deduction as a "food safety inspection fee." From meat to potatoes, cutlery to tablecloths, constant re-negotiations and haggling helped her squeeze every available penny in her favor from her wholesale suppliers' already thin margins, but she maintained one hard and fast exception to her rule, and never haggled price, nor skimped or fudged on payments to the Guariso-Lunardi Fish Company. Over time, Vita made herself Lodovico's single most favorite customer. She not only absorbed the largest volume of any of his company's restaurant accounts, but also personally hand-delivered her payments directly to his office, never neglecting to bring a specially prepared, hot lunch for him along with every check.

After Onofrio was killed in the car crash, Vita engineered a series of carefully staged collisions between the Lunardi family members and her son that never appeared anything but coincidental, but ultimately created exactly the outcome she had designed for a future that benefited not only Francis, but also her yet unborn, but already favored grandson, Marco.

***

Vita knew from the start that the life she would create for her boy as a restauranteur would never lead to greatness. Perhaps to vicariously share in a measure of that greatness which she had somehow read in the Lunardi boy's cards, she guided Francis onto a parallel track to that of Lodovico's son at the first opportunity. The two boys were born within several months of each other in 1916, and when little Hubert began his early studies at the Saints Peter and Paul School, Vita enrolled her son in his class a week later. After they finished grammar school, Vita followed the Lunardis' lead again, and sent Francis to Sacred Heart High School to ensure her son remained in Hubert's shadow.

During the four years leading up to graduation, the boys became fast friends, and Vita was content to let Hugh go off to St. Mary's College, and take over her own son's education in the restaurant business personally, as Francis would need no diploma for his career path as far as she was concerned. Vita by then also felt certain that the friendship established between Francis and Hubert had properly tilled the ground at the Lunardi household for what she and every other Italian of her time knew was the most important connector of all: family roots.

By 1934, when the two young men turned 18 and went their separate ways—Hubert off to college and then law school, and Francis to work full-time in the restaurants—Vita had created enough financial success for herself to finance the construction of a set of four Art Deco styled apartment flats in San Francisco's fast-developing Marina District, where just a few years earlier Lodovico Lunardi had built his own stately home when the most successful families of the time first started spilling over from the traditionally Italian neighborhood of North Beach. When Vita followed suit, she selected a property just a few blocks from his. Once construction on the apartments was complete, she and Francis moved into the finest of the four spacious units, and the trick of grafting her genetic stock onto the Lunardi family tree began in earnest.

As Nona grew older, Francis Frankoni usually spoke of his mother's idiosyncrasies with a little twinkle in his eye; the kind of twinkle a secret makes when it is held tight. Years after her death, perhaps when the recollections loosened from his deepest memories towards the end of his own life pushed him closer and closer to the truth of the matter, he would avert his gaze altogether from the listener, and say things like, "Vita was a witch without a wand," or, "Mother's crystal ball was hidden in the dining room chandelier."

As a young man, Francis—always the loving and dutiful son—simply followed the path laid out for him. The few times he wondered at his mother's wisdom or the choices she made on his behalf, it was never to question major issues, such as why college would not be part of his plan. It was the logic behind the smaller puzzle-pieces of her instructions to him that he sometimes struggled to understand.

***

One evening in mid-December of 1935, just prior

to the arrival of the waitstaff for the dinner shift at her newest and largest restaurant on Hyde Street near Ghirardelli Square, Vita suddenly announced that they would remain closed that night. Francis, who was busily stocking the bar for the early supper crowd, happened to glance across the empty restaurant where she sat verifying the starting count in her cash register when he saw it happen; similar to other brief spells of inattention he'd witnessed in her before, but nothing quite like this. As if his mother had suddenly realized she'd been sitting on a tack, she sat bolt upright atop the leather upholstered stool on which she was perched, then with a sudden full-body jerk, sprang three feet clear of her seat to stand stock-still next to the hostess station, her eyes locked on the ceiling, staring intently into the middle of the dining room's central light fixture — a brilliantly cut Romanian crystal chandelier that was the single most expensive item Vita had selected in designing the splendid interior of her flagship restaurant.

Without taking his eyes off her, Francis walked out from behind the bar and across the dining room. "Mother? Mother what is it? Is something wrong?" he said, approaching her with concern. During the five seconds or so it took him to cross the expansive room, she remained frozen, staring motionless into the facets of the glittering crystals.

"Mama? Mama answer me!" Francis strode crisply towards her, real worry in his voice now. As he reached out to take her gently by the shoulders and draw her attention back to the moment, a faint crystalline chime sounded behind him. The mysterious sound seemed just soft enough to be imagined, but distinctly real enough for Francis to stop in his tracks and turn around to look for its source, which his intuition more than his hearing told him could only have come from the center of the brilliant chandelier, though it hung absolutely motionless in the windless room. Another second ticked past and Francis turned quickly back to face his mother again, suddenly perplexed about the barely perceptible breeze that seemed to blow the hypnotic haze from her deep-set eyes. Had it come from the rapid turning of his own head? Or had his motion coincided exactly with another aery figment of the imagined emissions that he was almost certain couldn't possibly have come from the chandelier?

As if the breeze were the snapping fingers of a hypnotist, Vita's full and alert attention returned as quickly as it had disappeared and she said: "We must go home immediately, Francis, and I'm afraid that the new assistant manager is not experienced enough yet to manage with both of us gone. Please go dismiss Rosito and the kitchen help — we will not open tonight."

"Close?" Francis could scarcely believe what he was hearing. "It's Friday night Mother. This is the busiest night of the week — we cannot close tonight!"

His protests meant nothing: "We must be home within the hour," she said. "Go at once to send the men away now while I finish things here, Francis." And with that command she took her astonished son by the elbow, turned him around to face the kitchen doors, and after giving him a gentle shove in that direction returned to the hostess station to secure the register.

It took Vita less than five minutes to lock the front door, shut down the bar, turn off all the dining room lights and join Francis in the kitchen, where the still fairly inexperienced 19-year-old was having a difficult time convincing the kitchen staff to follow the instructions he hardly understood himself:

"...I *know*, Rosito," Francis was insisting to their sous chef. "I can't understand it myself, yet she's standing out there telling me I'm to send you home!"

"This is some-a joking!" Rosito scoffed. "If in twelve years I am once told 'Mrs. Volterra wants to not make-a the money tonight' I would say to him, 'this is the craziest talk inna San Francisco!"

The two prep cooks and dishwasher paused in their activities to watch the exchange, but Rosito Simonelli turned back to his pots, shaking his head and chuckling at the preposterous notion that Vita Volterra would keep her cash register closed on a Friday night.

Bustling into the kitchen minutes after Francis, Vita quickly applied her authority to seeing the marching orders carried out: "Come now Rosito! I have told you to follow Francis' instructions as you would my own. He and I must return home at once. You and the men"—she gestured to the prep cooks and dishwasher—"are to have the night off."

"But..." began the flabbergasted chef.

Slashing her finger briskly through the air to cut short his protest, Vita continued: "Have no worries about your weekly pay, any of you." She said as she maneuvered her way around the big Italian cook to shut the burners off underneath his bubbling pots. "Your full pay for the week shall remain intact, but you are all to have this evening off."

The prep cooks and dishwasher needed no further prompting. With a "Yes, Mrs. Volterra. *Thank* you Ma'am!" they quickly put their tools and towels down, grabbed their coats, and hurried out the service door. Poor Mr. Simonelli—faithful member of her kitchen staff for over a decade—could simply not fathom his employer's unprecedented behavior, and was now seriously concerned about her condition.

"But Mrs. Volterra, if you are ill then-a you must—"

"Shush Rosito!" She had already taken his coat from the hook by the door and was now helping him to put it on while she continued: "You are a good man and I appreciate your concern, but I am not ill," she continued, "and you must not try to understand anything more than that Francis and I simply must return home at once. Now go home yourself to Carmella and the children, and spend a free evening together with my blessings."

Before she was even done speaking, Vita had finished helping Rosito into his coat, and guided him by the elbow to the door almost without his noticing. With a kind smile, and gentle but firm nudge she emptied the restaurant of the last of her workers, and then with an odd look of measured anticipation turned to face Francis, who was standing in the middle of the kitchen struggling to fathom just what it was that *he* should be trying to understand.

Before his mother could utter another word, Francis waved his arm in a wide sweeping motion to indicate the entire kitchen: "Just what has gotten in to you, Mama? Half-cooked soups and sauces upon the stove, a double-batch of polenta ready for the tamale cups, tubs of unwashed salad greens and a crate of fresh chickens left out of the walk-in; and now only the two of us here to manage?! If you intended that we spend the evening at home," he went on, "this is certainly an odd way to arrange it — we'll be here half the night!"

Vita spoke soothingly to Francis: "Come now my son, nothing left in this kitchen tonight will not remain here to be dealt with tomorrow."

"But Mother!" Francis was aghast: "You can not *seriously* mean to leave the—"

"Chicken out?" She finished his sentence for him before he could even point an accusing finger at the unrefrigerated crate of plucked birds. "Certainly not, Francis. While you go bring the Packard around to pick me up, I will return the meat to the cooler." Having led Francis to the door unawares by distracting him with her calmly spoken directive, she nudged him out the kitchen's back door just as she had Rosito a minute earlier.

By the time Vita put the chicken away, locked the empty restaurant's rear service-door behind her and walked up the alley to Hyde Street, Francis was standing on the sidewalk with the car's engine running, waiting to open the door for her. Sliding herself into the passenger's side of the stately car, she settled back with her purse on her lap, opening it up just enough to slide her hand into it and gently finger the rosary beads she kept there — without which she would not ride in an automobile.

Often the fear of something imagined can be much worse than the impact of an actual experience. Although Francis was the passenger in the car that killed his father, Vita still regularly imagined the last seconds before her husband rolled over the edge of the cliff in his Studebaker, while Francis had already stopped replaying scenes from his memory of the terrible accident long before. As much as his mother hated riding in it, he loved driving the big Packard Super Eight. Purchased as an aesthetic companion to her newly completed apartment building, the long sweeping front fender and tasteful embellishments of the 1935 Super Eight "Phaeton" embodied the essence of Art Deco styling more perfectly than any other car of its day. Never one to flaunt luxury, however, while she was not above modestly praising her own good taste in selecting such a car, Vita always concluded by saying of her Packard Super Eight: "It possesses the Twelve's great looks for considerably less money."

Despite her appreciation of the beautiful machine, she was clearly much less fond of the car while riding as Francis' passenger in it, than she was when it was safely parked. So during their short trip from Fisherman's Wharf to the Marina District on the night the restaurant stayed closed, Francis was quite surprised to sense an air of relaxation in his mother that he'd never before detected while driving her. She kept her fingers on the rosary in her purse out of habit of course, but her body was not tense as it normally was. As if she were a moviegoer watching a favorite Myrna Loy and Clark Gable film for the third time, she sat in the moving car with a mysterious, knowing smile on her face. Looking as comfortable as if she were in a theater seat, she watched the cityscape go by as if it were the storybook scenery leading to a happy ending she already knew by heart.

***

As soon as Francis pulled the Packard up to the curb in front of their building at the corner of Beach and Cervantes Streets, Vita skipped her last habitual Hail Mary whispered in thanks to the Virgin Mother for delivering her safely through another car ride, and was out the door and climbing the front steps before he had even shut off the engine. She had already entered the flat by the time he ascended the stairs in the waning evening light. Instead of waiting to take his coat to hang in the entry-parlor closet, as she had done every evening since Francis had begun working in the restaurants, she had gone into the living room, then disappeared through the dining room into the kitchen — another odd move since normally she would have entered the main part of the house through the parlor's back hallway, instead of through the undisturbed elegance of the formal rooms. Determined to get to the bottom of his mother's bizarre behavior, Francis shut the front door behind him and traced her path through the well-appointed dining room.

Any other time, Francis would have paused as he walked through that part of the house to puzzle at the very presence of the antique Chippendale table, centered atop an intricately detailed Persian rug, over which hung a twin to the gleaming Romanian crystal chandelier in the restaurant; though Francis had never once seen her switch the power on to illuminate this one. Around the enormous expanse of darkly gleaming polished wood stood 14 matched scroll-back chairs, ready to seat — who?

That was the constant question Francis scratched his head at on the rare occasion he passed through the sumptuous, dimly-lit dining room. Although Vita would occasionally receive solitary female visitors, with whom she would sit and talk quietly behind the closed doors of the front living room, despite the near constant flow of birthday and anniversary cards she mailed to so many of her fellow San Franciscans, in the short time they had occupied the new flat, and in all the years spent living in their home in North Beach before that, Francis had never known his widowed mother to entertain a group of friends, or feed any guests outside one of her restaurants. Eventually—having heard the extended version of the legendary first meeting of Antonio Guariso and Lodovico Lunardi as many times as the best childhood friend of Hubert Lunardi would have been expected to—Francis decided that just like Mr. Guariso's ostentatious granite arch, the costly dining room decor was the little vanity that his mother allowed herself to show that she had truly *arrived*, even if she was the only one that knew it.

Forty-five Christmases later, Francis would grant himself a silent pardon for thinking such ungracious thoughts about his mother's ego, as she beamed at him from the head of the full table and offered a toast to the longevity and prosperity of her assembled grandchildren and their spouses, as the sound of her happy great-grandchildren playing in the living room brought smiles to all their faces; a cherished moment in time created from the direct human extensions of the course of events that would begin that very night.

What with the currents of magic flowing through the air around him in that moment, perhaps Francis would have preceived outlines of the joyfully assembled spirits of his future kin, had he paused as he usually did to ponder at the vast, empty table, but he was intent on getting to the bottom of his mother's strange actions.

Things only got stranger once he walked through the dining room door into the kitchen. His first surprise came at finding the room empty. A moment later, his heightened attention was jolted again by a chilling sliver of a distant, otherworldly chanting sound, as if several far-off voices singing an octave beyond the tonal waves detectable by humans, slipped for just an instant into the audible spectrum of his hearing, then ceased the instant he called out: "*Mother?*"

Besides the door from the dining room, there were two other ways to exit the kitchen. To Francis' left, the main door led to the bedrooms, bathrooms, library, and large west facing solarium, all reached by way of a central hallway. In front of Francis, at the opposite end of the tidy geranium-yellow tiled kitchen, a smaller door opened in to a large pantry, that in turn led outdoors to the private yard behind their building where Vita grew seasonal edibles and exotic perennial herbs in her meticulously tended garden. The pantry's ceiling was lined with hooks used to dry braided garlands of garlic, a variety of common herbs; rosemary, marjoram, anise, sage, oregano and the like, as well as a few precious plants and funguses whose names were known only to Vita and a few others like her, faithfully propagated for nearly three decades from cuttings and spores she had brought with her from Sicily as a girl.

Along the walls of the pantry room, floor to ceiling shelves contained baskets of freshly picked squash, burlap sacks filled with onions and potatoes, as well as jars of jams and preserves, home-pickled cucumbers and onions, and jugs of fermenting teas and herbal tinctures. In the center of the widest middle shelf, cleared of any of the other stored food-stuffs, canned goods and assorted concoctions, Vita kept a large hand-wrought rectangular copper tray. Roughly 30 inches across at the diagonal, its sides were a full four or five inches high. The piece appeared to have been crafted by a master artisan from the Southwest or Northern Mexico, probably dating back to a time when those regions were still one land. Its walls bore intricately hammered designs reminiscent of ancient symbols of the Hopi or Tarahumara cultures, and was obviously the product of hundreds of hours of meticulous work. Along the upper rim, a band of highly polished mother of pearl inlays cut in the shape of the Christian cross adorned the inside. They seemed to be spinning cartwheels around the inner lip of the copper walls, as each of the long sides' thirteen crosses, and each of the short sides' six, alternated orientation from 12 to 3 to 6 to 9 o'clock as they danced around the rim. The piece was beautiful enough to grace an elegant table laid for an exotic feast. It was fine enough to display as art in any natural history museum. But it never left the pantry — Vita kept snails in it.

***

The terrible shock of witnessing his father's gruesome death in the automobile accident that he miraculously survived himself, wiped away most of Francis' earliest boyhood memories. As he recovered emotionally from the trauma and started to file away sets of new ones, the earliest among them was that of catching snails for his mother. Since he'd begun the practice so young, the peculiarities of this exercise never struck him as odd. It seemed to Francis as if he had always been catching snails, and in fact he was still catching them as a young man of 19 years old, and had collected a small pail of nearly two dozen of them from the garden's beds of winter chard and broccoli on the evening of the full moon the week before.

Whenever his mother asked Francis to catch snails, she instructed him to place them gently, one by one, into the fine copper tray, arrayed in a circular pattern on top of a one inch thick layer of finely ground cornmeal that she sifted into the bottom, then carefully smoothed, leveled, and raked into fine lines as neat as a sheet of college-ruled binder paper, with as much concentrated precision as a Zen monk might practice the Tao of sand-gardening. Any time after Francis set a new batch of snails into the carefully prepared cornmeal, Vita would stand in her pantry in front of the great copper tray each morning, and examine the snails' work from the night before.

"How do my snails know where to go, Mama?" As a young boy, Francis was intensely curious about his mother's attentions to the snails, and the time she spent silently examining the lightly sparkling tracks they left upon the carefully prepared matrix spread across the bottom of the copper platter.

"They know," was her only explanation.

During the course of the six days that she left the snails to their work, the sooty-tinged mucousy film that would harden in the shallow channels left behind them would slowly turn crystal clear, as the cleansing cornmeal that was ingested replaced the stain of garden soil they ejected: "Why do the trails change color Mama?" Francis would ask.

"The dark trails show what came before; the light, what lies in store," was her vague reply.

***

Just as Francis was preparing to turn and exit the kitchen into the hallway to search for her in the back rooms, she suddenly emerged from her pantry as he called out again: "Mother? Mother, where — *Oh!*" He jumped at the shock of her unexpected appearance from the pantry.

"Shhhh — shush my son, do not be alarmed," she cooed caringly to him, brushing a few grains of cornmeal from the palms of her hands as she approached to take both of his. Looking up into her young man's worried eyes, she smiled gently, and calming him with a hypnotic, soothing voice she said: "This is the perfect evening for a walk, Francis. Come back to the parlor and let me help you with your coat."

In something like a daze, Francis allowed himself to be led back to the entry-parlor, where he realized as she opened the closet door: "Mother — I'm still *wearing* my coat."

"You shall walk this evening in your good coat, Francis." Vita was already taking his everyday coat off his shoulders as she said this. She hung it up, then removed the one normally reserved for church or formal evening affairs, and helped him on with it while she continued nonchalantly: "Take a nice walk around the Palace lake my dear, then pass by way of Hubert's house before returning here."

"Hugh will not be home from college for Christmas until next week, Mama. Do you *not* remember asking me about this on Tuesday?" A hint of suspicion broke through Francis' voice again, as if his focus were beginning to return to the strange behavior his mother had been exhibiting during the past hour.

Ignoring his question, she continued guiding his steps towards the front door, speaking now to him in a low, almost trance-inducing, rhythmic tone: "Walk now to the Palace my son, then twice 'round the lake before you're done. Don't come home soon, but dally rather — seek your dearest friend once clouds thick enough to block the moon are gathered."

Just before she opened the front door, Francis snapped back to a moment of clarity: "Aren't you coming with me Mama? I *don't* think you should be alone right now!"

With a wave of her fingers, his worry was gone: "This is your time, Francis—there's a good fella—now walk; and don't forget your umbrella."

With these strange words, she lifted his plain black umbrella resting next to the silver-handled purple one she kept handy in the genuine elephant's foot bucket in the corner by the entry door, pressed it into his waiting hand, and before Francis had a chance to utter: "But Mother, there's not a cloud in..." she gently shut the door behind him.

The spell remained intact once Francis stood alone upon the terracotta-tiled landing in front of the apartment door. Vita had emptied her son's mind of all concerns, and he stood for a few moments at the top of the front steps to enjoy the deepening magenta of the last rays of twilight in the crisp, clear December sky. Her influence upon his perceptions that evening had been so deftly cast, in fact, that Francis felt for all the world that he had invented the plan for a walk to the Palace of Fine Arts himself. Like nearly all young men, he never doubted for a moment the assumption that he alone was the master of his own destiny, and with the easy confidence of youth, strode forward unwittingly to meet it.

Quickening his pace to warm himself in the cooling night air, Francis soon covered the eight blocks between the apartments and the Palace of Fine Arts, one of ten monumental, Greco-Roman inspired pavilion halls and grand palladiums constructed to house the 1915 Panama-Pacific Exposition, the grounds of which originally covered 635 acres at the city's northeast corner. The site was made buildable by landfilling the natural marshes and sand dunes bordered by the Army Presidio, the Navy's Fort Mason, and the shores of the bay — a minuscule engineering project in comparison to the Panama Canal, the completion of which was the focal point of the expo named to celebrate that incredible feat of modern man's ultimate defiance of Earth's preference for the physical shape of herself.

After the exposition, city planners elected to preserve only a handful of the original pavilions, and demolished all but the finest of the lofty arched buildings designed by Bernard Maybeck, situated around the serene man-made lagoon which formed the centerpiece of the expo grounds in the heart of what would afterwards be renamed the Marina District. Had Francis a fold-out map of his own future in hand that evening, he could have easily spotted on the recently cleared stretch of the north side of Beach Street, the spacious lake-facing lot upon which he would build his own lovely home just a few years later.

Half way around his second circuit of the Palace lake, Francis' contemplations were strictly in the present as he thought about one of the loveliest of the neighborhood's recently constructed homes, and more specifically, one of its even lovelier residents. Since the beginning of his high school years with Hubert, the Lunardi house had held a secret draw for Francis that he was always very careful not to let his boyhood friend suspect, since he knew so well how protective Hugh was of his sisters, even the one two years older than them, who plucked hardest at Francis' heart-strings.

Francis (son of Onofrio) and Hubert (son of Lodovico) represented the first generation of their heritage whose fathers broke with traditional Italian names for the christening of their boys. Both successful, forward-thinking entrepreneurs, they nevertheless recognized that the bulk of their fellow immigrant Sicilians in California were looked upon then as second-class, menial laborers. They wanted to create open doors for their American-born sons, and the reasoning behind the anglicization of the traditional Italian baby names was to help prevent them from being held back by social prejudices still festering in the business and social circles of their time.

Lodovico Lunardi held no such notion in regards to his daughters. The road to be paved for each of them led to becoming the wife of a successful Italian husband, and he named them for maximum appeal to just such a character. A rose by any other name might smell as sweet, but to Lodovico's thinking, any fine young man worthy of the salt of his roots would turn his nose at a plain Mary, Jane, or Sue.

Estefania ~ Angelina ~ Antonina. The very cadence of their names was indeed music to the ears of Francis Frankoni's soul. From the first years of high school, when the mellifluous reverberations began playing their seductive songs to his awakening manhood, Francis sought any occasion to spend time at his friend Hubert's home, in order to simply be in the company of his lovely sisters, to hear the sweet sound of their names and voices, and steal surreptitious glances at them while pretending to focus on the homework subjects he'd ostensibly come to seek Hubert's help with. His greatest pleasures were achieved whenever Antonina—a great lover of Romantic literature who could recite reams of Wordsworth and Longfellow from memory—saw fit to rescue the works of Shakespeare or Chaucer from the boys' stammered orations, and instruct them herself on the finer points of elocution and dramatic delivery.

Walking along the rows of Corinthian columns fanning out on either side of the central rotunda of the Palace of Fine Arts building on the far side of the lake that evening, Francis was as oblivious to the clouds gathering overhead as he had always been of the algebra equations or Latin phrases Hubert struggled to explain to him whenever Antonina sat in study with them, or passed in view of the Lunardi home's library or drawing room in which the boys worked on their lessons.

Lost in the familiar throes of what he had always felt sure was an impossible fantasy, Francis raised his face skyward to the Palace, gazing up at the sculptured frieze encircling the entablature of the rotunda's great dome. In the design of its three repeating panels, the artist Bruno Louis Zimm crafted a magnificent visual theme entitled "The Struggle for the Beautiful." Interspersed between them, a series of weeping women by the sculptor Ulric Ellerhusen adorning the tops of the colonnade dividing the panels, symbolize *Contemplation, Wonderment* and *Meditation*. With her sweet name on his lips, and a hormonally-induced hallucination of her lovely face superimposed upon the classically robed Mediterranean beauty of one of those curvaceous stone women far above him, Francis breathed her name aloud—*"Antonina"*—just as the first fat drops of rain from the rapidly gathering clouds he was still too distracted to have noticed, hit his cheek.

His suddenly lubricated imagination easily transformed the raindrops into lover's tears. Quickly stitching together an elaborate fairy tale of pent-up young love from the fabric of his years-long crush on his friend's older sister, then embroidering it with the golden threads of his youthful imagination, and the creative residue of half-forgotten Shakespeare exams, Francis cried out to *Wonderment*: "Weep not, fairest Antonina! For I too shall love you always... though unto thine... skyey perch in Heaven, my earthly bonds prevent me from ascending to kiss... to kiss... the breath thou art!!"

Once the clouds let their rain begin falling in earnest, in order to sustain his fantasy worship of the divinely merged *Antonina~Wonderment* figure perched high above him, Francis would have had to imagine her blessing of holy tears had thickened to a shower of angelic piss upon his upturned face.

But this was 1935, a full three generations before the effects of the Internet would coax that level of kink into a typical teenager's romantic fantasies. Instead, the splashing rain snapped Francis back to the clear and present awareness of his circumstances that had been missing ever since his mother had appeared in the kitchen through the pantry door some 45 minutes prior. Somewhat puzzled to find himself dressed in his best overcoat, and equally pleased to discover that he was in possession of his umbrella, he raised it just in time to prevent a drenching, and set off in the direction of home. The very last effects of his mother's earlier hypnosis kicked in as Francis exited the park grounds, causing him to subconsciously head down a block leading home not by the most direct route, but by the most familiar—past the Lunardi residence—wondering as he strode briskly through the pouring rain if Hugh would have returned home for the Christmas holiday yet.

Francis reached the Lunardi house and was about to open the heavy ornamental iron gate separating the entry courtyard and front steps from the sidewalk when a taxi pulled up to the curb. He looked back over his shoulder through the sheet of water streaming off the backside of his umbrella to see who had arrived, and heard the lovely voice that had been missing from the motionless stone fantasy of his weeping *Antonina-Wonderment* figure sweetly cry his name as the passenger door swung open: "Francis! Francis Frankoni — is that you? Do be a darling and help me stay dry; I'm sure I don't know where in Heaven this sudden rain has come from!"

Before Antonina Lunardi's finely sculpted, silk-stockinged calves had even swung out towards the sidewalk, Francis sprang immediately to her side. Sheltering the cab door with the full expanse of his umbrella, he reached out with his free left hand perfectly on cue to receive the thin-walled, pink cardboard pastry box tied shut with a smart bow of white cotton twine that she handed him, then—every bit the classic example of a perfect gentleman—offered her the crook of his right elbow for support as she alighted from the cab.

As Francis selflessly shielded Antonina with the full width of his umbrella from the now torrential rain, she poured an overflowing bucket of heavenly burble into his ear as they walked through her gate and up the long flight of stairs to the front door: "What a blessing you are Francis! Not that I would have melted away in this flood to be sure, no! I dare say this tiramisu would not have survived past the courtyard with this drenching, though, and then where would I be? I had assured Papa of my return in time for dinner this evening, and when I missed the 4:45 ferry back from Oakland I realized the only possible chance I might have of staying in the old dear's good graces would be to get at his sweet-tooth with his favorite from Liguria bakery. I suppose all of my attempts to butter him up are just force of habit these days, for the good it's done me to win him over to my ulterior motives, Francis — three years! Indeed, it's been three years now that I've been wheedling at him for permission to live during the week at Stebbins Hall, to avoid this perfectly awful ferry commute! Well, but you know Papa; I suppose I thought that at least once Huey went off to college as well he might relent, but once his mind is made up, that's it — "*Girls; they-a live-a at home until they-a marry!*" This last bit Antonina spoke with the gruff comical gusto of her best "making fun of Papa" voice, as she and Francis reached the top step, though to detect a hint of real malice or disrespect in it would have been as impossible as finding even a trace of wickedness in her deep-set shining brown eyes, or the slightest fleck of ugly in her graceful face.

Antonina's delicate nose, spared the hawkishness so often inflicted by their genes upon Italian women, was set perfectly above her full, pouting, rose-petal lips. Her radiant, unblemished cheeks and neck, framed by the cleanly elegant bob cut of her dark chocolate-sheened hair, were crafted of the loveliest, Mediterranean shaded complexion, like the delicious bronze-tinged ivory skin of a peeled Marcona almond. As if displayed upon a delicate pedestal that was the single strand of impeccable pearls looped just above her clavicle, were Francis the hungry curator of The National Museum of Rome, the face of an undiscovered Botticelli Angel would have looked no more delicious than hers.

Worshipfully, not wantonly, the perfect young gentleman still sheltering her at the top of the steps gazed intently into her eyes, his attention held rapt by her frivolous chatter as Antonina continued: "But it has all been a minor inconvenience to exchange for the right to pursue my studies at Berkeley you know, Francis — at least in that he did relent: "*There are no opportunities that you will-a miss to serve-a as a good wife without-a the college degree!"* Antonina parodied her father again. "But I just kept taking the high road, Francis. Over and over I simply kept insisting 'Education for its own sake is laudable, Papa, and certainly you know better than anyone that a good man is only as good as the woman who serves him,' and..."

Antonina's voice trailed off as she and Francis stood out of the rain now, face to face under the sheltered entryway at the top of her front steps. Meeting his adoring gaze with a fondness she'd always held for her younger brother's best friend, she confidently held his stare as she examined his handsome face. The playful smile, the plumply rich lips that hinted at the infusion of North African genes and soul into their Sicilian bloodline in the first century, his thick, wavy black hair combed neatly back to highlight the truthful eyes made all the brighter by gazing back at her own beauty; Antonina had recognized all these aesthetic pleasantries of Francis' physical character many times before. Now for the first time, the rising soul of the developing woman within her, surging up from under the last surface layer of the sheltered girl she was about to break free of, saw past the familiar veneer of the boy she'd grown up with, into the heart of the adult that Francis had become: a fully realized, strikingly good-looking, self sufficient man, set on a path of worldly success, and—though he was not yet even consciously aware of it himself—ready for a mate.

The awakening woman within her knew just what to do: "But my goodness, Francis! Just look at your lovely coat — it is simply drenched!" A more willing co-conspirator there never was. As Antonina turned to open her front door, she outlined the tasty plan: "Besides, Papa would never dream of scolding me with a guest present, especially one that he likes as much as you, Francis, so there is no chance of your escaping now — you shall be my shield! And anyway, why should Papa eat the lovely tiramisu that would have been nothing more than a ruined mess were it not for you? No indeed. The sweet shall be the spoils of your chivalrous umbrella's well-timed rescue of the maiden and her treat! But there is a stipulation!" Antonina warned as she swung the door wide open to him, her inviting smile glowing more brightly than ever: "You must share it with *me*."

Francis thought a better bargain had never been proposed in all of history, and like history before him—though his step across the threshold into Lodovico Lunardi's home was but a tiny fraction of the great space covered when the master of the house performed his amazing long-jump onto the deck of destiny, fate, or coincidence on the day the Earth shook so violently nearly 30 years before—Francis' future was sealed the moment his foot hit the floor.

Several hours later, after Francis walked the few blocks back home under the twinkling stars of a now beautifully clear winter night's sky, he quietly unlocked his front door and entered softly, expecting the house to be dark and his mother long asleep.

Instead, he followed an intense glow of light into the dining room. There, grandly illuminated under the brilliantly lit chandelier, he found her seated at the head of the dining room table. Laid out formally in front of her, as if his mother had set the table for the dinner at an awards ceremony at which she were both honoree and audience, was a place setting of her finest china, silver, and Waterford crystal stemware. On the otherwise empty plate, a scattered pile of snail shells gave evidence of the late supper she had consumed. To Francis, still basking in the glow of his heavenly evening spent in innocent conversation with the girl of his dreams, none of his mother's outlandish behavior seemed at all out of place. "Oh Mother," he sighed. "I had a lovely time at the Lunardis. Hugh is still away at college you know, but I bumped into Antonina as she was returning home. We shared a tiramisu, then played Gin Rummy and simply had the most wonderful time."

Lost in a sweet cloud of love, Francis barely even heard her as Vita raised a crystal glass to her son's happiness, took a sip of the very expensive Rothschild Mouton Pauillac Bordeaux she had opened for the occasion, and with the faintest shadow of a smile playing on her lips said simply: "I suspected you might."

***

Throughout her life, Nona's own certainty of the outcome of the long string of wonderful events that stemmed from the path she had laid out for Francis and Antonina to fall in love that night, only seemed to become clearer as she aged. Twenty-eight years later, at the end of the summer just before the first beloved grandson they made for her returned to Washington D.C. to commence his postgraduate studies at Georgetown University Law Center, Nona calmly welcomed the news Marco brought to her following a dinner with his parents at his uncle Hugh Lunardi's home: in recognition of his nephew's intelligence and intense personal drive, as well as the almost religious obligation that the Italians felt towards their custom of supporting family members, Marco was promised a privileged position within the future State Senator's firm, to begin the first Monday after he arrived back home after graduation from Georgetown Law. When she heard the good news, Nona's lips curved slightly with the same subtle smile Marco had become so familiar with over the years since his childhood (when he'd first started asking questions like: "But how do my snails know where to go, Nona?") and she said once again: "I suspected you might."

But the strength of the ambition that filled Marco was nearly as superhuman as the uncanny powers of perception and influence that his grandmother possessed: Marco was not a man to wait around for Monday. When he returned home from D.C. in June of 1966, he arrived back in San Francisco on a Thursday afternoon. By 7:00 PM the very next evening, he had already logged his first 12 hours at the helm of the leather-topped mahogany desk in his new office, burning through two packs of unfiltered Camels while studying several hundred pages of trial briefs relating to his first case assignment as the youngest member of the Lunardi Law Firm.

***

The path that led Anne Allerfeldt to the Buckeye Roadhouse was not nearly so direct. Anne was the last of four children, and only daughter of a low-bred Dane born in Copenhagen in 1904, who fled home at the age of 14 to escape a psychically crippled young mother and sadistic aging alcoholic father; a former whaler who for almost 15 years was part of the small army of Danish sailors who hunted the waters between Greenland and Northeast Canada in the mid-1800's.

On the day he left them, young Anker Allerfeldt hoped to find asylum with extended family, but instead of being sheltered by the aunt he begged to take him in, was instead forced out of his homeland and into a life of work the same day he ran away from his parents, after his uncle sold him into service as a cabin-boy aboard a merchant ship, in exchange for five bottles of Cuban rum. Anker would eventually circle the globe several times aboard a series of vessels over the course of more than ten years before landing in New York during the midst of the economic turmoil of the Great Depression. But although he was uneducated, there was nothing stupid about him: Anker had seen what an entire life spent at sea did to men, and even no opportunity at all in New York, seemed a better opportunity to him than slowly whittling his best years away in the company of the surly old seadogs he shipped with.

A small man in so many ways, Anker's early experiences at home, and throughout the formative years of a youth spent bound to the rough-and-tumble life of crewing oceangoing cargo ships, filled him with a hardness barely containable in his five-foot, two-inch frame. Earning the nickname "Anker the Angry" from his fellow sailors, he bragged that he could whip any man under two hundred pounds regardless of his height, and in the early Thirties earned the title of Welterweight Boxing Champion of New York City. With hardly any money to his name when he arrived, and not a single friend or family member to help him start a life on land, Anker weathered the Depression years in New York using his fists and a plumber's toolbox, offering handy-man services door to door in several Scandinavian populated pockets of the Bronx, especially in the area called Throggs Neck, where he found that the above-average vocabulary he had picked up from years of reading any books he could get his hands on during the slow times at sea, tended to open doors for him.

A well-regarded beach and social club in Throggs Neck, Askov Hall, was founded by the Trinity Danish Young People's Society in 1920. Although Anker presented himself without introduction or personal references, he was nevertheless accorded the warm welcome and kind respect automatically due to a lonely fellow countryman, and he soon became a regular fixture on their beach and in the men's cocktail lounge. There, Anker's newfound acquaintances soon noted episodes of his sporadic bouts of heavy drinking, but though they sometimes marveled at the prodigious amounts of whisky and rum the little ex-sailor was able to put away, for years his behavior and manners never seemed really amiss, even during one of his deep benders. That he would eventually do such a poor job of repaying their respect, would come as a great shock to their community.

Away from the decorum he long feigned so well at Askov Hall, Anker's habitual pursuits ran seedy, and he spent long hours alone poking for the darker parts of the underbelly that ran along the wharves between Coney Island and Atlantic City's Steel-Pier. The carny-style sideshows and back alley tricks that pock-marked those decaying boardwalks during the tail end of the Depression years were a perfect haunt for the likes of Anker, who scuttled along the dirtied shores, eyeing half-open doors with bad intent.

***

Of all the types of men luck would have had her avoid, Anker was tops, but little Joy Berg had no use for luck. The first and most precocious of three daughters born in New York to a Swedish Anglican deacon and a Danish Red Cross nurse, her pious father's determination to do all he could to help the poor his church ministered to during the Depression, eventually cast his own family deep into their ranks.

Joy had been born into the bustle of progress and promise of the developing Flatbush area of Brooklyn in 1916. Five years later, his church relocated to Throggs Neck near Askov Hall, and to reward Deacon Berg for faithfully leading their congregation, a small, empty lot in the seven hundred block of Vincent Avenue was gifted to him. There he built one of the very first of the new 1922 models of Sears Roebuck kit houses: The

Sunbeam. The cute-as-a-button, five-room bungalow had an open air sleeping porch that let the fresh air from the beach just four blocks away add sparkle to the happy family's dreams. Joy would remember the new house as the first one in the area with steam heat and hot water plumbing: the future to her must have seemed warm and bright indeed.

Joy would effortlessly retain the spirit of her name far, far longer than any normal reason might possibly imagine. By the time she was 13, her father's unflagging dedication to his soul enriching, but financially ruinous life's work had meant the loss of the house on Vincent Avenue, and his family ultimately spent most of two years during 1929 and 1930 living in the Anglican Church's basement, while he preached salvation and generosity to the congregation in the pews above on Sundays, and worked all week to help the many people of his community who were even poorer than he and his family. By then, Joy's mother was also caring for two much younger daughters beneath the church hall floor, and finally insisted that all available resources be leveraged to provide the family with a suitable home once again. This meant the end of school for Joy, and new responsibilities to help earn money for the struggling family, a proposition that Deacon Berg was unable to insist against as long as he continued to place the importance of his religious calling above the needs of his own wife and daughters.

When school broke for the holiday in November, 1930, Mother Berg informed Joy that she would not return to classes after Thanksgiving, but would instead immediately join the some dozen or so girls working in the shop of a parishioner lucky enough to have retained the bulk of his tailoring and shirt-making contracts with several of Manhattan's long-established Fifth Avenue menswear stores of the type that were little affected by the depression. "Pay attention and work hard for Mr. Grundvig," Joy's mother instructed her, "and with a little luck you will move up from the irons to the sewings in a year."

After two long days of her sweaty apprenticeship stuffed into the pack of embittered girls working under the shrewd tailor's constant watchfulness, Joy returned home with fire in her eyes. "This is *not* the kind of luck I wish for myself, Mother," she spoke firmly. Shaking her wild red hair back from her soot smudged brow, cocking hips all too curvaceous for her diminutive height and tender years, she placed her balled up fists atop the rounded outside sweep of her swelling young buttocks and delivered her pronouncement: "What I *need*, is to make an acquaintance with a better sort of man."

Powerless to insist against her bull-headed daughter's will, and with no help from the Deacon, whose constant obsession with humanity's salvation seemed to always lie just outside the circle of his own flesh and blood, the soul-weary Mother Berg stood aside as the blossoming young Joy shaped her destiny in a flurry of hasty decisions.

During the brighter years in the little Sunbeam house on Vincent Avenue, the Berg family had also frequented Askov Hall's beach club, where Joy spent many long summer afternoons outdoing the older girls in acrobatic dives off the high wooden pier. One of the girls Joy was friendly with had a cousin from New Jersey, who during her occasional visits to Throggs Neck would keep the girls at Askov Hall enthralled with stories of her school-free life as a young dance starlet performing under the stage name Skippy Blair, who was the star of Daddy Dave's Kiddie Review on Atlantic City's Steel-Pier. The day after her escape from the sweatshop, Joy looked up her old friend from Askov Hall. Unable to convince Joy that her younger cousin's stories of life as a child star weren't all they were cracked up to be (the girl's reality was like that of an ultra-low-budget Shirley Temple or Judy Garland), she reluctantly put her in touch with Skippy for an introduction, who by then was performing 12 shows per week for Daddy Dave, and hadn't seen the inside of a book in several years.

Daddy Dave thought he'd found his new diamond in the rough with Joy. Wowing him with an impromptu dry version of the self-taught leaps and twisting flips she'd perfected off the Askov Hall pier, her audition— just six days after fleeing Tailor Grundvig's coal-heated irons—seemed to swing the gates wide open to her start in the exciting world of show business. If she thought she had cleverly avoided the trap of hard work however, in that she was mistaken, as the grueling hours of intense rehearsal Daddy Dave heaped on Joy in his attempts to prepare her for a lead part in his upcoming holiday extravaganza, meant that the main difference between Joy's experience on the stage in Atlantic City and her job with the tailor's work crew, was that instead of an iron, she hoisted a baton.

The other essential difference between the stage and the sweatshop was that her job with Grundvig would have allowed Joy to return home at night, and contribute somewhere in the neighborhood of five dollars a week to her struggling family. Accepting Daddy Dave's invitation to join the Atlantic City based Kiddie Review so far from her home in the Bronx, meant that Joy became not only a cast-member, but also a paying guest at his spartan boarding house run by two strict matrons who'd lost any fondness they might have once had for their young charges years prior. By the time Daddy Dave calculated room and board charges against her unglamorous earnings, there was just enough left of her take-home pay to take herself home with empty pockets about once a month.

The problem was not to last very long though. Joy had that rare combination of athletic poise, childish exuberance, and vague air of impending sexual maturity that Daddy Dave knew appealed to the widest range of his paying audience, but she was sorely lacking two essential ingredients: rhythm and timing. No matter how much repetition or reprimand was heaped upon her, Joy simply could not keep step with the other dancers. Attempting to solve the problem by making all her acts solo numbers was fruitless too, as the only music Joy seemed able to keep time with was that which must have been playing only in her own head.

Daddy Dave was not one to readily give up on his investments however, and he pulled his hair and gnashed his teeth for nearly six months trying to get the gem-stone he first thought he'd seen in Joy to shine. But besides her missing talent, Joy's presence behind the curtain ultimately created problems that Daddy Dave would not have tolerated even from the most gifted of his performers. Though she was still only 14 years old, he strongly suspected that the "impending" aspect of Joy's budding sexuality was verging closer and closer to an abrupt ending. As superstitious on this matter as any Mayan high-priest, Daddy Dave was religious in his insistence that every young soul thrust into the sinkhole of his Steel-Pier Kiddie Review be a virgin. The increasing attentions being paid to Joy by one of the show's key stagehands—made even more suspect by two reports from the boarding house of Joy's attempts to find an unlocked door hours after curfew—gave Daddy Dave no choice. It was to be the can, rather than the Cancan for her.

Contrary to Daddy Dave's suspicions, Joy was still a girl in the truest sense of the word when she made a final visit home to Mother and Deacon Berg while still carrying the last intact membrane of her childhood in early May, 1931. Back in the Bronx, the Bergs had managed to scrabble out of the church basement and into a one-room brick tenement. The tiny rented apartment's ability to lift the dampened spirits and bruised pride inflicted on Mother Berg by all those months in his church's basement was a mystery to the Deacon, as in every other respect their new quarters seemed inferior to his sense of things. Men in his line had a certain deep-rooted respect for mysteries though, and he did nothing to dissuade his wife from thinking their lot had somehow improved. Joy too was baffled at her mother's apparent happiness with the situation, but those years in American history had a way of lowering expectations. Joy immediately reconsidered the possibility of trying to elbow a space back into her own family as soon as she saw the cramped quarters, however, and used four of the last seven nickels from the Steel-Pier left in her pocket after leaving that morning, to make her way back the very next day.

***

Though the first six months there had done nothing to teach her to dance, the consistently typical examples of human behavior she witnessed in Atlantic City taught Joy to do two things that already came quite naturally to her: take care of herself, and take advantage of connections. The logical sum of the formula created by combining the two elements formed the crucial third lesson: take advantage of other people to make connections. When she returned to the Steel-Pier, Joy sharpened up all three prongs of this barbed trident and had it hidden behind her carefully cocked hips while she stood waiting behind the stage doors of Daddy Dave's five minutes before the cast and crew would be released from the day's last show.

Pat Connors the stagehand had to pinch himself when he saw Joy standing in the alley behind the theater that evening. In the two years since his older brother Liam had helped him land a spot with the crew, he had proven himself to have an equal knack for lightning fast set changes. Daddy Dave's famous variety show called for no less than half a dozen major scene changes in one performance, and Pat shared his brother's monkey-like ability to shinny up the heavy stage rigging ropes and quickly solve any problem with the complex system of counterweighted line sets cramming the vertical space above the curtain that was required to pull them off.

Pat also copied his older brother's incurable show time habit of flirting with any of the girls that stood close enough to hear their salacious whispers in the darkened shush of the stage wings, but since neither of the young men ever made more than a half-serious advance towards any of them, and they were each capable of the work Daddy Dave would have needed two sets of hands to replace, he habitually ignored behavior he would never have otherwise allowed. Notwithstanding the job's pretty distractions and his employer's preferential treatment, Liam had left the act a few weeks before Joy arrived to put his skills to their highest use as the technical manager at the Steel-Pier's top draw: the aerial and acrobatic diving show of the Carver family's world-famous, diving horses.

Despite his skills, without big brother Liam around to keep his increasingly inappropriate attention to the young performers in check, Pat edged closer and closer to the limit of Daddy Dave's nuisance to usefulness ratio, and was unaware of just how near the chopping block he'd come by constantly hounding the girls. This changed the instant that Joy arrived. Like a recurring dream that is continually forgotten at the moment of awakening, then finally kindled into full bloom by a daylight spark of déjà vu, Joy awoke a passion in young

Pat Connors that he'd been unconscious of prior to his first heart-rattling glimpse of her. As if hooked to a toggle that Joy controlled, his constant trolling advances towards the other girls instantly switched off the moment she first caught his eye.

Pat's effect on Joy's spark—if her heart was even capable of firing one at that age—was zero. But while her total lack of experience automatically categorized her as a novice in the ancient game of man vs. woman, she instinctively knew it was good strategy to keep a pawn or two close at hand. So like an expert angler, she hooked Pat at the end of an eyelash-thin line of suggestion, just long enough to be sure there was no risk of having to touch anything slimy, but short enough to give him the false impression that he held the rod, and would very soon discover the correct combination of flattery and boastfulness that would impress Joy enough to scoop her into his net.

So great was Pat's elation upon seeing Joy again just one day after he thought her gone forever, he didn't stop for a second to puzzle on which of them might have been the other's catch — though if he actually thought she had returned to claim him as her prize, he must have been a whale-sized fool. In fact, Pat was merely bait; the expendable scrap of bait Joy needed to get to Liam. As susceptible as his younger brother to Joy's red-headed sorcery, Liam would also swallow the lure, but well before realizing that her ruse of hanging around the pier waiting for the brothers to knock off work had nothing to do with either of them, he'd given her exactly what she came for.

Joy's prize was a direct introduction to Liam's employers, Al and Sonora Carver, son and daughter in-law of William Frank "Doc" Carver, the originator of the famous diving horse show which toured around the country for three decades starting just before the turn of the century. Following Doc Carver's death in 1927, his son Al established a permanent home for the act on the pier, where Sonora and her sister Arnette gained a kind of cult fame as the daredevil beauties who rode astride the horses as they leaped from a platform towering four stories above the surface of the pool below.

Al and Sonora had only to watch Joy spend five minutes leaping, twisting, turning and diving as she joyfully relived the ghost of her happy summers at Askov Hall, before inviting her to become the youngest member of the small team of acrobatic divers they employed to warm up the crowds prior to Sonora's or Arnette's big horseback finale. Joy saw the Carvers as the stepping stone to what her limited worldview deemed the ultimate in success: top billing in Atlantic City's most popular entertainment attraction. From the first week of her performances on the aerial tricks diving team, Joy was scheming up ways to get herself on top of one of those horses. As adorable as she was cunning, Joy took every opportunity she could find to get herself closer to both the horses and the famous sisters. By the middle of the summer, her precocious sweetness had both the equine and human stars eating sugar from her outstretched palm, and Sonora and Arnette adopted her as a kind of foster-sister, whose attentions she in turn devoured as their most ardent fan.

In August of 1931, performing her eighth year of the horseback dive that had become so routine she could have by then done it with her eyes shut, Sonora Carver rode a dive in which she should have. Her horse, Red Lips, misstepped in the crucial last moment at the end of the diving ramp, plunging them off-kilter more than forty feet into the tank below, where Sonora struck the surface face first. The water's smashing blow to her open eyes caused her retinas to detach from the impact, resulting in her immediate, permanent blindness.

From their vantage point next to the diving tank below, Arnette and Joy knew the instant Red Lips slipped off the platform so far above them that something wrong was about to happen. As soon as the water stopped boiling from the horse-sized cannonball splash, they both dove in to help the dazed and sputtering Sonora to the side, still unaware of the enormity of her terrible accident. Placing Sonora's hands on the ladder, Joy and Arnette sprung lithely out of the water on either side of her, then reached back to help Sonora struggle out of the pool. As they looked down into her already bruised and swollen face to do so, they uttered two gasps as one, upon hearing Sonora sob: "I can't see!"

Though their two gasps sounded almost exactly alike, the emotions behind each were entirely different altogether. Without having to speak a word, Arnette's gasp clearly said: "Oh my dear sister! How your tragic pain makes me ache for you!" The crooked sentiment that propelled Joy's sudden exhalation was one she also voiced only inside. With her true feelings disguised behind a well-faked mask of love and concern, her inner voice hissed: "*Yes! This is my chance!*"

And well it might have been: the introduction from the strung-along brothers she'd used so well; her skill as a diver; her crafty cultivation of the horses' and the sisters' affections. Quickly adding up the successful elements of her methodically orchestrated plan to elevate herself to the Steel-Pier's highest tower, Joy hid her face behind hands shaky with excitement as she feigned grief for Sonora, while inside she fairly burst with anticipation at what the accident seemed to mean for her. In those few short moments of self-absorbed darkness, Joy's head blocked out the commotion of the shocked crowd all around her and screened a mental movie, written, produced, and directed just for her, in which she portrayed herself as a leaping orca: a relative killer whale of stardom in her little universe, propelled by her mighty flukes, about to plunge into a great and glorious splash that would wash away all the ridiculous seals bobbing around her, bumbling in their pitiful circus-clown attempts to shine half as wonderfully as she.

But in a frozen drop of time, just as Joy's inner vision pulled back to savor the slow motion crest of the liquid hallucination of her imagined future as the next and most spectacular of the famous horseback divers, her distracted consciousness briefly left her worldly flesh floating unprotected in the sea of humanity rippling all around her. In that fated moment, a cruel, self-serving hunter of sordid diversions and broken spirits, his beastly heart made even stronger and more bold by the crowd's collective burst of psychic pain whizzing through the air above the dramatic scene around him, took a fix on the bulls-eye of fiery red hair atop what had suddenly become his next target: the very soul inside little Joy Berg's nearly bare body.

Standing in a skimpy sequined bathing suit, dripping next to the tank of her dreams that would soon evaporate forever, Joy was totally unprotected from Anker Allerfeldt's spontaneous decision to chain the hapless girl's destiny to his own. In an instant, he shot his will, like a razor-sharp, chakric harpoon of determination, propelled hard and fast from the charge of lust at first sight created in the angry black space behind his cold blue eyes, and sunk it precisely and inextricably into the 14-year-old's tender gut.

***

Thus were the players staged to conceive the epic tragedy that would become Anne Allerfeldt's life, and set the wheels in motion to place her at Marco Frankoni's service the night of his celebration dinner with Hugh Lunardi and his cronies, one inauspicious night in February, 1970. But between August, 1931 and then, a few things had to happen to get her there.

First, Joy Berg had to be shanghaied by Anker Allerfeldt. After leaving the dressing room where she had changed out of her wet swimsuit following the shocking last act of the show, Joy went to the Carver family's office, where she very carefully maintained her downcast expression as she delivered one last round of condolences to Arnette, who was anxiously waiting for news of Sonora's condition from Al, who was with her at the hospital.

From the moment Anker let fly his invisible harpoon, he kept his attention fixed on Joy, never once losing track of her in the crowd, or when she moved from building to building once all the public drama of Sonora's accident had died down. She had only walked a few yards up the empty covered breezeway after exiting the back door of the office when Anker stepped out from the shadows in front of her. The 27-year-old lecher remained silent for a full five seconds, staring directly at his teenaged prey while she stood frozen, transfixed by his bright blue eyes, and the shock of his sudden appearance. None of his own inspiration jumped to mind quickly enough for an opening line to break the silence, so Anker dipped haphazardly into his memories of the hundreds of books he had consumed at sea, and blurted out the first words in English that his swelling tide of lust for her pushed up through his lips, without even checking with his own logic to determine if they would translate well for the occasion: "Come little child, the time's come to play here in my garden of shadows."

The shadow of dread that passed over Joy as Anker's raw intention was laid bare by the sinister words so alarmed her, that she would have turned and sprinted away, had he not already stepped forward and taken her by the hand. Lucky for Joy, at that very moment

Pat and Liam Connors rounded the corner on their way to express their sympathy over Sonora's accident to Arnette. Unlucky for them — the hapless brothers would never forget the treacherous Joy, or the merciless beast who whirled around to face them when they ran to her aid. Not ten minutes after Pat received the broken jaw, and Liam the dislocated hip which Anker so easily inflicted during their botched attempt to keep him away from the girl they thought was their friend, she walked away from the Steel-Pier for the last time, arm in arm with the older man, who—in a last-ditch attempt to say anything that would both excuse his violence against the Connors brothers as self-defense, and impress her with his situation—had serendipitously blurted out the key to unlock her instant return of his twisted affections: the promise of a home back in Throggs Neck, and the return to the sunny beach of her beloved Askov Hall, where Anker was pleased to be regarded as a member in good standing.

To throw a lock on the trap his young prize had walked into, Anker made good his word. He set Joy up in a little rented cottage just a few blocks away from the house her father had built, and with a rough pat on the rump each morning, sent her off to pretend to be a girl at Askov Hall for one last summer. Anker himself stayed absent from the club for some time, for though Joy was legally an emancipated minor since her parents had given up responsibility for her, and the cunning little boxer had quickly married her to legitimize their socially distasteful arrangement, he hadn't taken nearly enough shots to the head over the years to make him imagine that the respectable gentlemen of Askov Hall would pay more attention to its legality, rather than the appearance of the thing, were he to start parading his budding little teenage bride up and down their beach.

The fantasy of Joy's re-wound life lasted about a year. By the start of the following summer she was all of 15 years old, and had filled out her hips and breasts enough for Anker to risk owning up to her as his properly grown wife, and though there was definitely some eyebrow raising, they were not blackballed from the club. Before the weather cooled that year though, Joy's diving days were through. She slowly faded away from Askov Hall herself, as her own intuition told her that to be the less than respectable teen bride of the club's resident tough-guy was one thing, but to lay around on the beach being all that and clearly quite pregnant too, would simply push her presence there past the limit of tolerable.

Once she became a mother, Anker no longer saw his young wife as the precious little Lolita who'd captured his attention. Blaming her for the mounting expenses brought on by his first two sons, Anker's insistence that she earn their keep meant that Joy's free ride was over. Back in Atlantic City, Sonora Carver never gave up her dream, and for a full ten years after the accident that blinded her, continued her amazing flights of daring, guided only by gravity and the horses that carried her. Joy's dream was all dried up however, and there was no splash of fame or applause for her when she landed in the typists pool at Garson Plumbing Supplies over by the Bronx Zoo, where Anker bought the materials for his growing business.

If a positive thing can be said about Anker Allerfeldt, it's that he never failed to leverage his resources to improve his lot in life. Unavoidable suspicions planted much later, as more of the story of Anker and Joy comes to light, will make it very difficult to believe that her crimp turned husband didn't actually pimp her as well. If it did in fact happen this early in their marriage, that secret has been buried in death and senility by the only ones who might have told it. What we do know is that as soon as she started working in the accounting office at Garson's, Anker's service business profits shot way up. Whether his teenage wife was part of some deal he struck with her new boss, or he had simply instructed her to doctor the invoices to his account, the truth of this particular matter will never be known. Either way, after establishing Joy as a working asset, Anker ambitiously leveraged his shot at the American Dream by turning the labor of his expanding plumbing business over to a handful of underpaid employees, and once his time was freed up, used the next several years to study municipal and industrial water supply systems, then eventually acquired a degree in hydraulic engineering from the recently established Monroe College, not ten minutes from where Joy was working whatever kind of trick it was at Garson Plumbing Supply that allowed him to be there.

Notwithstanding Anker's single-entry list of questionably positive human qualities, the story of the American reinvention of the Allerfeldt family, as it was unfolding when the 1930's came to an end, might have appeared to hold real promise for Joy and her children. Somehow managing to spend a couple years at a time unpregnant, only three sons had been born to Joy by the time she was 22. With the financial successes she'd helped create for Anker, he was able to purchase a home to accommodate the expanded family even closer to the shore breezes than the little Sears Sunbeam house her father had built when she was a girl. Though he insisted Joy remain on as a bookkeeper at Garson's even though her wages bought nothing he couldn't easily afford by then, Anker loosened the reins a bit on her by allowing a part-time maid to help with her housework and the boys, and treated the family to leisurely summer weekends spent back in the good graces of their fellow members at Askov Hall.

By that time, any evidence that Joy had still been a teenager only a few years prior had faded as completely as the other members' memories of the summer she first returned to the club as Anker's barely legal catch. Playing in the sand with her children, she'd acquired the respected status of every other married woman on the beach, and if any of his fellows still paused to reflect on Anker's 13-year seniority over his wife, it was only to envy him and the spirits of their own fading youth, made all the more apparent when looking out from the shady vantage point of their cocktail lounge stools onto the sun-bathed scenery in front of them, forced to silently compare their own mates' sagging butts and wrinkled elbows to the buoyant rump and taught skin of his 22-year-old baby machine.

Anker's ship certainly seemed to have come in: three healthy sons; a rapidly expanding business now employing a half-dozen service plumbers to which he'd begun adding commercial construction contracts thanks to his new engineering license; a sexy young wife that obeyed him. Didn't he have it made? He especially enjoyed the new found respect he was accorded on the strength of these successes at Askov Hall, where he basked in the egoistic glow of his sense of integration with the other Danes there. For the first time in his life, his feeling of belonging transcended the notion that he was being merely accepted—that his very existence was simply recognized and tolerated—and he swelled with the self-assured pride he felt at finally considering himself a full-fledged member of the establishment. To savor the strange and wonderful new feeling, Anker began spending longer and longer hours there than ever before. Most evenings found him holding court in the men's cocktail lounge, where he enthralled his fellows with endless stories of his years at sea, discussed business and the real estate development deals picking up speed all around them, and toasted himself and anyone within earshot with more and more Cuban rum, in an ongoing attempt to celebrate what others believed he had become. But each time he drained his glass in another rousing *Skål*, he was also quaffing another blind chaser of his desperate, subconscious attempt to destroy his memory's ghost of the abused, unloved, and rejected child that clung to the core of his actual vision of himself.

But Anker kept the broken parts stuffed deeply away inside, and wore his inflated pride and robust, self-satisfied and mostly affable personality like a medal upon his chest, the impressive muscles of which were still full and hard from his life of work and fighting. He was certainly the fittest father of the dozens of families associated with Askov Hall at the time, and despite the near constant insobriety that characterized his hours spent at the club, while most of the other men his age limited their exertions to the shuffleboard, Anker held his own in the friendly competitive beach games favored by their athletic children.

***

Of particular interest to Anker was the rising fad of volleyball. Although the game had been played since the beginning of the century after its invention in Massachusetts, it wasn't until its inclusion in the 1924 Olympic Games in Paris garnered press attention that its popularity gained much momentum. Following this exposure there was a much greater awareness of the sport, and a beach volleyball phenomenon was quickly triggered in Southern California, but the depression years slowed down its eventual burst onto the East Coast recreation scene.

By the summer of 1941 the leanest years of the depression had faded, and with the attack on Pearl Harbor just six months away, but still entirely unforeseeable, there was no rationing of the rubber necessary for the Spalding Company to pump out the tens of thousands of balls needed to help spread the sport all around the country. As soon as the warm weather hit Throggs Neck that summer, the chaise lounges and sunshades were barely out of storage and laid out in their rows on the freshly raked sand at Askov Hall before the excited Danish kids had the club's first net strung. Within a week the adults were banished to a mere scrap of their once sizable sunbathing beach, and two more nets were raised to treat the outbreak of volleyball fever that seemed to have infected every young person there.

Across the water from Throggs Neck, sitting pretty on City Island in the choicest westernmost section of Long Island Sound, the wealthier kids at the Harlem Yacht Club were equally enthused, and much better equipped. Their club's summer recreation coordinator had hired in a coach from the Bronx YMCA, and while their counterparts at Askov Hall were happily passing the summer queuing up randomly selected coed teams for friendly matches against one another, the coach in charge of the young Harlem Yacht Clubbers had split them into groups separated by sex and age, and was keeping his sharp eye on them as they performed their morning drills and afternoon scrimmages in order to identify the best male and female players for his top teams.

At the end of June, Harlem Yacht Club announced the organization of a youth volleyball tournament, open to teams formed by members of any private beach club on Long Island Sound. Scheduling the event for the last weekend in July gave the other clubs in the area precious little time to prepare to go up against them, and the prevailing opinion in the community at large was that the only players capable of mounting any real challenge against the Harlem Yacht Club teams were the athletic youths of Askov Hall, who had so spiritedly embraced the game.

With the Danish community pride now on the line, their parents hurriedly set about sucking the fun out of their beloved volleyball, and injecting some serious organization and training into it. Askov's general manager was asked to chart a schedule of practice times, and divide the players onto team rosters according to the four match categories arbitrarily set by Harlem Yacht Club: boys 12 to 15 years old, senior boys 16 to 18, and two girls teams comprised of the same age groups; although since the Askov Hall community was only large enough to supply the minimum six players needed for a team of younger girls, and there were none older than 13, not much was expected from them other than their opportunity for enjoyment of healthy competition.

The question of drilling the teams was quickly resolved when Anker, in his seemingly most generous display yet of his devotions to the Askov Hall community, volunteered his efforts as coach. None of his fellow members disputed his qualifications for a moment. His natural athleticism and knowledge of sports training were evidenced by his days as a successful professional boxer, and of all the adult members of the club, he had clearly studied the new game the most. Since the beginning of the summer, if Anker were found missing from his seat at the bar on any given afternoon, one could count on finding him on the beach, either playing right along with the kids, or—if he'd already had several drinks—observing the subtle nuances of the game as he puffed on his cigar in a chaise lounge, intently watching the children bouncing around in the sand, happily knocking the ball back and forth across the net.

Anker's approach to readying the teams quickly assured the excited Danish parents of their wisdom in selecting him as coach. His methods naturally appealed to their genetic predisposition towards hard work and order, which consisted of a strictly scheduled mix of serving and return drills, combined with an equal emphasis on strength and endurance conditioning. This latter aspect of the regimen was composed of calisthenics exercises for strength and agility, which he conducted in the low-tide surf during the hot hours of the afternoon under the shade of the wooden pier, and long, stamina-building runs in the cooler hours, when he would lead the players en masse up the still sparsely developed expanses of sandy coast that stretched to the east of the club's property.

During the evening runs, the boys and older girls suspected that their almost 40-year-old coach's own endurance was the real issue, but they kept his secret, and were even kind enough to pretend to believe him each time, when after stopping in an area of sheltering dunes not a quarter mile beyond sight of their clubhouse for group stretching, he would make excuses for the younger girls, saying their little legs could not keep up with the others, and that their time was better spent working on their ball-handling skills with him, while the other players followed his instructions to run out along the beach as far and fast as they could for half an hour before turning around to rejoin him and their little sisters.

Two weeks before the much anticipated tournament, 16-year-old Karl Andersen began to worry about his sister Elka. She had been the most excited member of the younger girls' team, but practically overnight she seemed to have lost all interest in volleyball training, and even going to Askov Hall entirely, though she would get angry with him when pressed to offer an explanation why. On the third afternoon that Elka stayed at home rather than join Karl for afternoon training, he decided to follow up on an uncomfortable hunch. After the stretching that followed the warm-up jog to the dunes, rather than follow Anker's orders to run 30 minutes down the beach, Karl dropped to the end of the pack, then carefully snuck back through the tallest hills of sand and sawgrass to see for himself what kind of ball-handling Anker was demonstrating to the five young girls that had remained nervously behind with him.

This is the first of several crucial junctures in this story where only your imagination can project what may have become of it, and the lives of its main characters, had certain members of its supporting cast played their roles differently. In the case of Karl Andersen, the boy's temperament was more intuitive than brave, though his intuition hadn't even begun to prepare him for the terrifying sight he witnessed once he peered over the top of the last hillock of sand. He lay flat on his belly for a minute, struggling with his conflicted emotions, at once both sickened and excited by what he saw. But the overriding emotion that filled Karl was fear, and he couldn't get up the guts to jump out from his hiding place behind the dune. Instead he silently retreated in the opposite direction, then ran home to wait nervously for his father's return, where he sat in stunned silence in his family's living room as the image tumbled over and over in a mind that would be forever afflicted by the memory:

Coach Allerfeldt had been standing with his back turned to him, the firmly muscled, white flesh of his bare buttocks as glaringly out of place in its nakedness as the moon when it exposes itself during the light of the day. The five girls were grouped in a semi-circle at the man's feet, each clearly intent on following the strict command that almost made Karl do the same when Anker shouted — "Keep your eyes shut tight! The one who looks at me will be very sorry!"

The girls had been made to bare themselves from their legs to their chests before dropping to the sand in front of him. They kneeled there with their legs spread apart, their shorts and underwear bunched down around their ankles, and the front of their shirts rolled up to just below their armpits. The recently cast shadows of the pubic hair showing between the wider hips of the two more developed girls seemed to wink on and off at Karl as they raised their rumps in a series of kneeling squats up and down over the backs of their heels, while the three pre-pubescent ones exposed anatomical parts that reminded Karl of two pink baby mice huddled next to each other, trying to keep from freezing to death in their cold, hairless nests as

Anker barked his commands: "Eyes shut!! Up! Down! Up! Down!..." Eventually, even the firm, only slightly puffy breast-flesh of the youngest ones were made to jiggle perceptibly as Anker increased the tempo of his shouting: "Up! Down! Up! Down! Set the ball! *Eyes closed!* Picture the net — arms up now — stretch! Get it up! Up! Down! Up! Down! Higher, higher, higher, stretch tall now! Get it up there, get it up! Get it up — up, up, *UP UP UP!!*"

Had Karl jumped out and shouted at the girls to run back to the clubhouse while the hardened little coach had his shorts dropped down around his ankles and his dick in his hand, they almost certainly would have had the head-start necessary to beat Anker back to the safety of their beach. Had they all raced back to Askov together to report what had been happening, the ruse of Anker's respectable character could have finally been exposed on the spot. His escape from the punishment that should have followed such actions would have been cut off at the quick, right there at the club where he'd tried so hard to drink enough to destroy the soul of the person he had been shaped into, from the time that his own innocence had been violated during his long-lost childhood.

If the adult Anker Allerfeldt had been stopped in his tracks there at Askov Hall, that same day in July, 1941 while Marco Frankoni still floated within the chalice of beautiful Antonina's womb, already firmly established in the lap of luxury and privilege that would shape his life and ultimately guide his path to the Buckeye to be waited upon by Anne

Allerfeldt, Anne herself would have likely not even been conceived. If she had, even our fictitious history's most flagrantly imaginative authors of all time would have had to stretch very hard to concoct the bizarre plot twist of her character's development, in which a pretty little blond girl from the Bronx grows up in a land of cock-fighting and coconut palms, spending half of her childhood desperately trying to rid herself of the tropical nightmares injected into her there, then eventually propelled by her attempts to escape them to the Buckeye Roadhouse, and the night she was to pour champagne for Marco.

***

But Karl Andersen's character was lacking the mustard needed to make him jump out from hiding and break the terrible spell of shame and silence Anker had cast upon those girls. It wasn't until that evening when Karl and Elka's father, Tor Andersen, came stomping up the Allerfeldt family's front steps did Anker discover he'd been exposed. Not one full minute after Karl finished giving the report of what he'd witnessed on the beach, his furious father began running the 15 blocks between their homes to arrive at the porch of Anker's house, pounding loudly on the heavy screen security door. Joy jumped up from their dinner to find out what was wrong, and upon seeing Tor's murderous expression behind the locked screen door, called Anker out from the dining room while she retreated to the kitchen.

Tor was one of the few men at the club Anker should have been scared of, as the hulking sheet-metal worker could have easily broken through the steel door that

Anker kept locked between them had he been absolutely certain of his rage. Joy comprehended nothing of the heated exchange between the two men as they shouted at each other in Danish, other than her husband's repeated shouts of "*Nej — Aldrig!* (No — Never!)" at the end of each of Tor's hammer-hard sentences. Tor was as impetuous as his son was cautious, and without even verifying Karl's story with his daughter, he made a beeline for Anker's door the moment the boy had finished recounting his accusation. Anker's unflinching denial of any wrongdoing cast just enough doubt into Tor's mind to second guess his right to batter the door down and beat the little man to death right then and there.

The moment after Tor turned and stormed away from their house, Anker ran through the kitchen, pushing past Joy to the basement steps, stopping the stream of his Danish mutterings to himself only for the two seconds needed to yell at her: "Go and feed your boys!" Just ten more minutes passed before Anker reappeared in the dining room, carrying a heavy sailcloth kit bag and dressed in the flannel shirt, canvas pants, and heavy boots that he hadn't worn since he'd stopped doing any of the dirty work in his plumbing business.

Anker found Joy in the dining room where she was nervously pretending to try to feed mashed up peas to little Peter as he cried in her lap, while Niels and Jack sat staring silently at their plates. With no explanation of any kind, he held his hand up to shush her and slapped a small stack of bills onto the table: "This will not last long, and I do not know when I can send more, so you must not stop working. Stay away from Askov Hall! Teach the boys not to cry, and wait to hear from me." Then with no further explanation of any kind, and without pausing for even a moment to hug or kiss his bewildered young wife, or so much as glance at his sons, Anker Allerfeldt literally ran out of his house in the opposite direction Tor had gone, towards the docks and the ships which he should have perhaps never tried to leave.

As their father ran out of their lives, the loud slap of the metal door slamming behind him shocked Niels and Jack out of their stupor, and both were soon sobbing loudly along with their baby brother at the confusion of what had just happened. Joy had taken a half dozen steps to follow Anker, but now stood frozen in shocked silence, staring at the heavy screen door left ajar in his haste to flee. The noise of her crying sons in the room next to her drowned out the hiss of its escape out that door and up into the night air, but Joy could definitely feel the deflating effect deep within her, as the first large portion of the spirit of her name fizzled from the leak she had finally sprung inside.

Joy didn't know how long she stood frozen in the middle of the floor feeling it seep away. For however many minutes Peter spent clawing at her legs, and the two older boys stood tugging her sleeves and calling for her attention, their pleas were not great enough to break through to her. Only when Tor Andersen and three other fathers from Askov Hall walked in through the still open door to stand facing her in her own living room, did she come back to consciousness.

"Breng yoor boys hupstairs und tehl yoor 'usband we'yre taking 'im foor a *drink*!" Tor's accent was thick with the effort of containing the anger behind his words, carefully chosen out of respect for the presence of her children, which his own faultless morals would not allow him to dishonor, regardless of whose sons they were, and what their father had done to his daughter. Thinking Joy hadn't understood, Tor repeated himself twice before her attention had fully returned to the moment and allowed her to reply that Anker had left. None of the men could deny the sincerity of Joy's aggrieved expression, but to assure themselves she spoke the truth, insisted on searching the house top to bottom to verify her claim that he was gone, and not simply hiding from his punishment.

Recovered from her initial shock, but still oblivious as to the offense that had so swiftly turned her husband's fellows against him, Joy trailed Tor, then each of the other men from room to room, pleading for an explanation of what had caused the trouble. Each one thinking that they were doing her and her sons a kindness, none spoke a word until they had satisfied themselves that Anker had indeed escaped. Only as they were leaving to split up into the night and search the neighborhood for him, did Tor give Joy the least hint of her husband's crime: "Tehl yoor 'usband I *weell* find hem — und be lucky you did not geev that *mahn* a daughter."

***

Future events would conspire to make a mockery of Tor Andersen's prophetic warning. The first issue lay in the big landlubber's certain expectation that Anker would be found, but it wasn't an easy thing to find a wry and wary little sailor highly motivated to remain lost back in 1941. Only after letting his trail cool for three months did Anker send a letter home to Joy. He used a favor from a Navy man returning stateside to postmark the letter from Louisiana. He enclosed no money with it, but sent his bewildered wife a photo of himself dressed in a smart linen suit, wearing a fine straw hat and smoking a large cigar in the shade of a palm tree on an unidentified tropical beach, along with a very short note in which he did not disclose his whereabouts lest it be intercepted somehow, but said only that he hoped that she and the boys were as well as he, that she must not believe any lies she might have heard about him, and that before much more time passed he would arrange for them to join him in paradise: Anker had landed in Panama.

Strengthened by the narrow escape from New York, his good fortune saw him arrive there during the midst of a major expansion of the American facilities at the Panama Canal Zone's Albrook Army Airfield. The U.S. Congress had authorized $50 million in funding for the project in 1939, and Anker's arrival just as construction was commencing put him in the right place and time to land a spot on the team of civilian engineers that was hired on by the military to assist with oversight of the project, and his pay was close to double the profits he'd been earning on his contracts back home.

Expectations were that the airfield project would be ongoing for the next several years, and Anker began plans to build a home not far from the base, move Joy and the boys down to Panama, and live the good life as a civilian on Uncle Sam's payroll in a country where 15 cents bought a man a dollar's worth of rum. Shortly after Anker wrote his letter to Joy, history would intervene. Less than a month after Marco Frankoni was born in San Francisco, the bombing of Pearl Harbor on December 7, 1941 would mark America's entry to World War II, and put major pressure on the United States to fortify its military bases all around the world. Orders were given to fast track the completion of the airfield and begin the construction of a vast new complex of barracks to accommodate the sharp increase of troops at the base.

Until March of `42, Anker put his own plans on hold and did nothing but eat, shit, and read government blueprints. On Friday of the last week that month, he hopped a military transport plane up to Fort Dix Airport in New Jersey, and arrived unannounced at his home just before midnight to sneak in through the kitchen window and check up on Joy. Without setting foot outside the house, he stayed with her 48 hours — just long enough to correct the "rumors" she'd heard about what really happened the day he ran off (*"Don't you repeat those lies to me Joy!!"* (SLAP)), and to inject his special sauce of irony into Tor Andersen's last words to her those eight months prior: "Be lucky you did not geev that *mahn* a daughter."

Confident in his psychological control over his wife, strengthened by his certainty that she would not disclose his whereabouts and blow her chance for a new life in paradise as well, Anker told Joy all about Panama and his lucrative situation there, promising that she and the boys would join him in the home he was planning to build just as soon as the war was over. Before departing in the dead of night to return to his fat paychecks and palm trees, he left her with a tidy sum of cash and his post address, at which she began writing him regularly. Two-and-a-half months of her weekly letters passed before Joy finally wrote something to her self-absorbed little husband that prompted a reply. Without question or comment on the news, he sent home two hundred and fifty dollars and a three word response: "For the baby."

Born nearly six weeks premature, and dangerously underweight, Anne Allerfeldt got pushed into the story on November 11th, 1942, exactly one year to the day after Marco Frankoni was born. While he was gleefully rubbing gobs of tiramisu birthday cake into his hair to the joy and delight of Vita Volterra the proud new Nona, and nearly three dozen other happy relatives at an extravagant party thrown for him at the Saint Francis Yacht Club, Anne was ushered into the world in Joy's bed at home, where their gallery of supporters included a tired old midwife, and a surly maid.

Report of the early birth reached Anker a little more than two weeks later. In her letter, Joy entreated him to come home and see his baby, and also told him that

Tor Andersen had enlisted in the army and shipped off to Europe as part of the troop buildups preceding the British-American invasion of North Africa. But even with the shadow of his most dangerous adversary gone, Anker's priorities remained true to himself. Eclipsing the emotionally devoid output of his previous letter to her, Anker responded to Joy's news of his prematurely born daughter's uncertain infancy, by this time sending five hundred dollars and a note that read: "More money for the girl. Let me know if she makes it."

***

Anne did make it; at least a lot further than one might have hoped. By the end of 1945 she'd cleared the risks of her shaky start on life and grown into a normal, healthy three-year-old. She had yet to reach the age when long-term memories begin coagulating in a child's mind though, so she had no reference point for the absence of any memories of her father, who saw her only twice during that time in two more equally brief surprise visits home. Unlike her brothers, who would always carry wistful memories of their early days in New York—especially those that were so blessedly free of their father's presence—little Anne made it out of the Bronx and away from the mashed up dramas of Steel-Pier, Throggs Neck, and Askov Hall with a blank canvas behind her adorable smiling eyes, all primed to soak up the brightly painted splash of her plunge into Anker's sultry tropical paradise, once his family joined him there in February of 1946.

Paradise wasn't in Panama any more though. The land-absorbing doctrine of Manifest Destiny that had so greatly increased the United States territories following the war victory against Mexico at the end of the 1840's, had grown even toothier and more subversive to the spirit of true democratic principles by the end of that century, when Spain became the last Old World power to fall to the USA's rapidly developing military might. Fifty years prior, when U.S. troops forced their next-door enemy's surrender by capturing Mexico City, clamorings by Eastern Democrats to take all of Mexico rang passionately through the halls of the U.S. Senate. It was ultimately logic such as that championed by Senator John C. Calhoun of South Carolina, that convinced those then governing the United States to stop at taking only Mexico's sparsely populated northern lands. In his speech to Congress in January of 1848, Senator Calhoun argued that: "We have never dreamt of incorporating into our Union any but the Caucasian race — the free white race. To incorporate Mexico, would be the very first instance of the kind, of incorporating an Indian race; for more than half of the Mexicans are Indians, and the other is composed chiefly of mixed tribes. I protest against such a union as that! Ours, sir, is the Government of a white race. We are anxious to force free government on all; and I see that it has been urged... that it is the mission of this country to spread civil and religious liberty over all the world, and especially over this continent. It is a great mistake."

As per that time's accepted standards of international warfare, once the United States trounced Spain in the Spanish-American war of 1898, the victor dictated the requirements of the truce. Terms of The Treaty of

Paris, which officially ended the conflict between the combatants, authorized the U.S. to ransack the former colonial superpower's remaining territorial coffers like a bear at a picnic. As its spoils of war, the U.S. opted against the full annexation of Cuba — whose revolution against Spain had been the justification for the United States to engage in the conflict in the first place. Perhaps the Cubans were seen as too riled up following their recent uprising against the Spanish to quietly submit to being traded like a joker card from Spain's busted New World hand into their northern neighbor's royally fat stack of land-grab aces. Instead, America's appetite for continued territorial expansion, and mission to "force free government on all," was sated for the time being by gobbling up from Spain's goody basket, Puerto Rico, Guam, and the Philippines, although complete and total interest in Cuba was never fully released, and to this day the oldest overseas U.S. Navy Base has been in continuous operation since 1903 in Guantanamo Bay, where in 2002, the Bush administration began operating an exclusive military prison; exclusive both in terms of its inmates' profiles, and the exclusion of the rights that would be due to them if the prison was located on U.S. soil.

Back at home on that soil in 1898, the United States was faithfully bestowing those unique charters of freedom collectively embodied within the Declaration of Independence, the Constitution, and the Bill of Rights upon all of its citizens — or to all of those who were white and male at least. With the annexation of Puerto Rico, Guam, and the Philippines, however, the U.S. would unabashedly hoist a new scepter of neoclassical imperialism to triumphantly usher in the dawning of the age of 20th century global American Democracy.

Resolving the predicament of the new land acquisitions from the defeated Spanish hinged on an unprecedented new court ruling, which was expressly designed to avoid the embarrassment of incorporating such an enormous huddled mass of non-whites into America's proud citizenry. Up to that time in history, all new territories absorbed, bargained for, or taken by the United States were acquired specifically for the purpose of becoming new states, with all of the equal rights and benefits of statehood already enjoyed by the existing ones. This time around however, a page was ripped from *The Imperialist Guide for Dummies,* which had rubbed America's Founding Fathers so wrong when Mother Britain was reading out of it 125 years earlier: each of the three countries in the USA's new 'islands-collection' were officially acquired as *colonies* rather than prospective states. In conducting its own internal review to justify the legality of the new land holdings, the U.S. Supreme Court itself ruled that full Constitutional rights did not automatically extend to all areas under American control. *Problem solved*: the United States granted itself full rights of ownership over Guam, The Philippines, and Puerto Rico; more of the world was made safe by its rapidly growing Air Force and Navy—quickly installed into expanded bases on each of the brand new colonies— and virtually overnight, fantastically unregulated new playgrounds were opened up into which droves of free white Americans quickly flocked to open textile mills and chemical plants, grow bananas, and fuck little brown girls with impunity.

But in a repeat of the mistake made by England, The United States did not read the *Imperialist Guide's* last chapter: "Recipe for Insurrection." Much to the surprise and annoyance of their new rulers, it turned out that at least some of the brown men were sore of being fucked like little girls. The Filipinos, generally speaking, were about as enamored with the idea of being America's bitches as they had been of being Spain's. Less than a year after the imperialist card-swapping following the Spanish-American War, the United States had to start killing belligerents all over again.

What would come to be called the Philippine-American War, but was referred to at the time as the Philippine Insurrection, began on February 4, 1899, when fighting broke out between the newly arrived U.S. troops, and Filipino revolutionaries still armed and organized from their struggle for independence from the Spanish. While the truth of exactly how many Filipinos were killed during the conflict is unknown, some estimates indicate that the ensuing three-year-long war that pounded them into submission and forced them to accept their fate as the biggest sub-breed of America's South-Pacific lapdogs claimed as many as a million of their people's lives.

Over the next 30-plus years, the Filipino people would have their currency minted by the U.S., English would be installed as the primary language of business and government, and a system of economic trade would be established that would result in one of the lowest standards of living on the planet—with greater than 50% of the total population living in poverty—for nearly a hundred years to come.

Within a short while, the United States wised up to the pitfalls inherent in direct, hands-on global colonialism. Rather than attempt to successfully oversee the Philippines as an officially held U.S. colony for long, the Filipino people were granted autonomy in 1916, and the promise that they would even be able to govern themselves again one day. They had to wait until 1934 for that day to come. Using the Philippines as its test-kitchen during those 18 years, the United States tinkered with the recipe until it worked out the formulaic difficulties concerning the best practice for planetary domination in the modern age. Once the right mix of controlled autonomy was cooked up, the brutal transparency of military-backed imperialism was then quickly swapped for a system of international control predicated upon the manipulation of the global economic system, and the installation of hand-picked dictators — a highly effective solution whose formula would be repeated around the world. Over the next few decades, the Philippines would see a series of nine American-managed heads of state spin in and out of the revolving door to the presidential office in Manilla's Malacañang Palace. The best and most crooked of America's Filipino puppets was eventually found in Ferdinand Marcos, a *previously convicted murderer* who was backed implicitly by the U.S. during a 20-year reign in which he bled his country of billions of dollars, and First Lady Imelda Marcos amassed one of the largest and most expensive collections of shoes ever assembled by an individual.

Marcos truly embodied the ideal U.S. friendly despot: he cut huge deals with the Rockefeller and Ford foundations, bringing full-scale chemical and industrialized agriculture to the Philippines, which, though devastating for the bulk of his country's subsistence farmers, created enormous profits for transnational corporations. Once the majority of arable land had been sapped even beyond modern agrochemical farming's ability to sustain yields, and most of the former land-holding peasants had been pushed into selling themselves into the role of sharecroppers on the land they'd once owned, revolution was again fomenting in the Filipino people. Marcos unhesitatingly responded by declaring martial law, and assassinating his political opponents. After violently crushing his people's unrest following the bursting of the chemically created agricultural bubble which decimated their economy, Marcos demonstrated an equal disregard for the country's environment, and in the last decade leading up to his eventual ouster, orchestrated the full-scale export of his nation's timber stands, sanctioning clear-cut deforestation which wiped out nearly 80% of one of the Earth's largest tropical rain-forests.

But backtrack once again to the 1940's, during the early days of the USA's manipulation of the international economy through political power-brokering and puppet-powered resource exploitation. Regardless of the installation of any figure-head rulers in its colonies, for America's global security interests at the beginning of WWII, retaining decisive ground-control in the epicenter of the South Pacific was of much greater concern than simply controlling the Philippines' populace and natural resources, so maintaining a strong military presence there was essential. The United States was not the only force jostling for position and kicking up sand in the playground as the world's superpowers wrangled for territorial position however.

In the Pacific Theater, the U.S. was bristling with embarrassment and hurt over being caught with its pants down early on the morning of December 7, 1941. The Japanese attack on Pearl Harbor was mainly a diversion tactic however, as rather than push their advantage into Hawaii, the very next day Japan's military forces initiated their first wave of full-scale invasions into the Philippines, which their generals also recognized as the true geographical pivot-point of Southeast Asian territory control. December 8, 1941 marked the beginning of a two-year struggle for command of the Philippines, that Anker Allerfeldt would pay far greater attention to than Joy's reports of his own daughter's struggle for her life up in New York.

***

From his very first years aboard the ships that carried him away from Denmark as a teen, the lore of the Philippines had been the stuff of legend whenever three or more sailors paused to swap tall tales of exotic ports, and sexual adventure. The allure of the mystical woman of the Malay race was set so deeply in his personal mythology, that Anker could practically smell the rich coconut oil and fish-stew perfume of her fabled "three o'clock pussy," whenever military intelligence reported news to the men in Panama of America's fight to hold on to Clark Air Base, the Air Force's largest crown jewel of military command outside the 48 states.

Anker's disappointment at the news that General MacArthur had retreated to Australia in the face of Japan's decisive victory in the fight to control the Philippines in May of 1942 was bitter indeed, as he imagined the treasures of her islands forever denied to all white men. With such an important piece of its military property on the line, however, the United States would stop at nothing to recapture the Philippine islands from the Japanese, and in October of 1944 mounted a campaign to retake them using battalions of ground troops numbering close to a quarter million men, supported by the largest arsenal of Navy, Air Force, and Army weaponry the U.S. had ever assembled in war.

MacArthur and his boys stormed back from Australia with a vengeance, and during the next ten months delivered a crushing blow to the Japanese forces holding the Philippines. During just the first week of battle, the Imperial Japanese Navy was so decimated as to effectively render Japan's naval power useless for the rest of the war. By the time America's re-conquest of the Philippines was complete in mid-summer of 1945, nearly a half-million Japanese troops had been killed, and Japan was clearly ready to surrender, even without the added measure of killing another 250,000 of its men, women, and children in the atomic bombings of Hiroshima and Nagasaki less than two weeks later.

If this war were a sport, Anker Allerfeldt was its most avid World Series fan. Back in Panama he anxiously tracked every step of the U.S. efforts to regain the Philippines, and even before the war with Japan was officially over in the South Pacific, not two weeks after the Americans took Clark Airbase back in January of `45, Anker had set his sights on the even more lucrative engineering contracts for the government's massive reconstruction of its largest overseas military installation. By mid-March that year, Anker concluded his business in Panama, and was on his way to the Philippines.

**

On the third night after his arrival, the Lieutenant Colonel in charge of Clark's civilian contractors took Anker to a nightclub on MacArthur Highway, not two miles from the entrance to that stronghold of American values and world order that Anker had just been hired to help rebuild. A half-dozen drinks into his first of many long nights at the *Angelwitch*, up to his eyeballs in coy little golden-skinned reminders of his volleyball girls (that he was there encouraged to do much more than just shake his prick at), Anker had an epiphany: there was a place that embraced men like him, and its name was Angeles City. He would never live back in the U.S. again.

By December of that year, the vision of the future he would carve out in his tropical Shangri-La had energized him to accomplish the work of three men. Working overtime at Clark to fund his own gated bastion of order and privilege, he devoted every other spare hour to the construction of his dream home in the middle of a two-acre garden that he walled off at an edge of the pristine jungle fifteen minutes east of Clark Air Base; a good distance from the encroaching squalor of the post-war boom engulfing Angeles City, but strategically positioned to place all of the wonderfully sordid diversions of MacArthur Highway's red-light district directly on the path of his commute between the swank new home and the entrance to the base.

With a labor pool willing to work for less than a dollar a day, and nothing in the way of construction permits or building code inspections to slow things down, in just a few short months the house was ready to start collecting memories. A low-slung beauty of understated modern design, the new five-bedroom home had cool polished cement floors, with French doors and jalousie windows in every room to circulate the afternoon breezes. The elegant, teak-furnished living room featured a view framed by expansive picture windows of the surrounding tropical garden oasis, where Anker had mango, papaya, and banana trees planted to compliment the large coconut palms already there. Off to the side of the kitchen wing, a stand-alone hut the size of a garden shed held two small sleeping rooms to house a maid, and a servant who acted as gardener, chauffeur, and handy-man, who the Allerfeldt children would learn to refer to as "House Boy."

Not surprisingly, Anker carried out all these plans, and had even made the move to the Philippines itself, without informing Joy. She puzzled over why the only two letters she received from him that year were postmarked from San Diego, rather than New Jersey, but the contents of his famously short notes shed no light on the mystery, basically stating only that paradise was almost ready.

On the second of February, 1946, Joy finally received the first detailed written communication from her husband since he had run out their front door four-and-a-half years prior. The electric thrill sparked in her by the photographs of the beautiful home that spilled from the thick envelope changed to nearly electric shock when she read his detailed instructions of the trip she and the children would have to make to get there, aboard a series of Air Force planes Anker's Lieutenant Colonel buddy had pulled strings to accommodate them on: not a single six-hour flight from New Jersey to Panama, but an incredible ordeal, crammed in amongst boisterous soldiers inside the austere cabins of three separate transport carriers to travel from New Jersey to Colorado, then to San Diego and across the Pacific, with stops in Hawaii and Guam, to finally land at Clark Air Base nearly six days later. Not yet three-and-a-half years old, Anne was the only one lucky enough to have no recollection of the nightmarish journey. She touched down in the middle of her father's tropical paradise with the same pure, unsullied memory canvas that had up until then been left so blessedly free of any impression of him.

It took a little less than a year for Anne to round the corner of early childhood development that separates pure experience from memories. It's clear from photographs of her first few years afterwards that the early ones she collected must have been full of happiness and wonder. The beautiful pictures being painted on the canvas behind the little girl's adorable eyes shine brightly through the unabashed and innocent smiles that Joy captured in those snapshots, even in black and white. But as slowly and surely as her mother would have the remaining spirit of her name drained away from her soul during her life in the Philippines, the later pictures of Anne show evidence of her long slog through the thick tropical humidity, and thicker accumulation of nightmares that ultimately took the smile from her eyes, and pushed her off the edge of the long, long downward spiral of her attempt to escape the memories of the source of the dull smoldering glow that eventually consumed the once brightly shining light behind them.

Over the years that followed, Anne struggled to bury the dark secrets of her childhood under thicker and thicker layers of denial. She put herself through the paces of normal teen development as best she could, and practiced diligently to master several useful tricks of the self-deceived in order to camouflage the pain. One exercise she picked up early, and stuck at religiously, was the morning smile. It was a ritual adopted during her beauty pageant days when she was crowned Miss Clark Air Base two years running, during her Junior and Senior years at

Wagner High School. This distinction landed her a minor supporting role in the war film "Merrill's Marauders," which was shot at Clark just before she left in 1961. The acting experience honed her ability to smile on demand, and project a warm glow up from that perfectly molded countenance of her young unblemished mask, creating the illusion that the light missing from her eyes was still being projected from within. For most of her adult life, Anne would spend 15 seconds in front of the bathroom mirror each morning, checking to make sure that smile was still perfect every day.

Back in the kitchen of the Buckeye Roadhouse on the night she drew the short straw over the other waitresses to win the opportunity to serve Marco Frankoni and his party, she didn't need a mirror to check her smile. She could feel that it was set just right as she took a deep calming breath, expelling any thoughts of the past before tugging her blouse down just a tad. Satisfied that the right amount of skin was showing below the perfectly crafted smile, she picked up the ice bucket and bottle of Dom Pérignon for his table, and strode gracefully through the swinging doors into the dining room, as self assured as any beauty queen.

***

"Fuckin' A, Marco my boy - You *killed* those cock-suckers out there!" So began the eloquent toast being raised by Hugh Lunardi to his nephew's latest and greatest win in a series of price-fixing cases he'd brought to trial in the preceding three years. Anne set the ice bucket two feet from Marco's right elbow and subtly positioned herself to give him the best view of the perfected smile framed by her lovely blonde hair, and with a suggestive turn of her wrist slowly twisted loose the little wire basket that kept the cork in place as Marco ignored her entirely, and Uncle Hugh continued: "I have to be honest with ya Marco — if I'd known for a second when I brought you on back in '66 that that old fart Abshire was gonna croak himself and give me a shoe-in to Sacramento a year later, I never woulda dragged you aboard a captainless ship. But you didn't need a mentor! All you needed were *targets*! First cosmetics, now the oil refineries; what's next Marco — the goddamn baby diapers?! Push 'em into the corner and squeeze the shit outta the motherfuckers! *Dammit* I'm proud of you!"

Maybe Anne caught a glimpse of sudden movement from the kitchen, as several of her fellow waitresses scrambled to gather around the swinging doors into the dining room to observe her performance through their round portholes. Or perhaps when Marco stood up to proudly acknowledge the boss' generous praise, something in the last words of his response triggered a crack in Anne's wall when he raised his glass to drain the last gulp of his cocktail, and promised emphatically: "There will be *no escape.*"

Whatever caused the split second break in Anne's attention, the resulting error captured Marco's more completely than any display of a waitress' creamy cleavage or lovely smile ever could have — POP-**THWACK!!**

The corks in her champagne dreams never popped like that! Only in Anne's nightmares did anything smack that hard. For another split second she thought she really might have been dreaming, as Marco dropped his highball on the floor, reeled back from the surprise blow, and slapped his cupped hand over his eye while at the top of his lungs he half screamed, half choked out: "WHORE!! ***WHORE!!!***"

But though she instinctively ducked and cringed to prepare for her recurring nightmare's coming blow, Anne suddenly knew she wasn't dreaming, because after yelling the trigger word, he didn't hit her. She needed another moment to realize with a shock that Marco wasn't in fact even yelling *at* her: he was just yelling. Sounding just like a sobbing baby mispronouncing *WHAAA! WHAAA! WHAAAA!!*—he kept yelling it—"*WHORE! WHORE! WHOOOORE!!*" as the entire restaurant stared in frozen silence. He kept at it even as Anne, herself the one with tears streaming from her eyes now, dropped the erupting bottle of the Buckeye's most expensive champagne, grabbed a fistful of ice in a white cloth napkin, and with her free hand around his waist, implored him to press the ice to his eye while she pressed herself against him, sobbing and pleading, repeating over and over again her standard words from the dream script: "I'm sorry! I'm *sorry*! I'm *so, **so** sorry*!!!"

The mountains between Kobuk and Noatak became my home. For a few years I lived as a wolf among a large pack of wolves. We would travel all over, and way up north and back to these mountains. Among these high mountains I became myself again. Somewhere in the midst of the forest I left my garb quite lifeless. That is the only meaning I can give it. My carcass was just a discarded garment that no longer was needed. I had no feeling or pity for it. Never to be worn again or never to see again, I left it there. I had no interest in what should happen to it.

from "Nathlook: Susie, My Name,"
in Lela Kiana Oman's *Eskimo Legends*

Chapter 3: **Uterine Toboggan**

I was originally named by my father. His father had been one of the earliest of us to be touched by the men who called themselves Christians. I was given the name of one of the first missionaries that came to preach to us: *Herman Valaam*. With that name, I was meant to carry the strength and will of the strange white man grandfather came to revere as intercessor between our people, and the ones who brought the new God to our land. Brother Valaam was made strong by the one God, through surviving the suffering and sickness that were the trials of His calling. Not content to control the people of His world, God, and the men who brandished His cross and their guns, drove Herman and other Christians out to carry the burden of doing His will into all the most inhospitable corners of the Earth, to find the humans who did not yet know that they were created in His image, and not one of many people living in so many wondrous physical forms upon the Earth, and in the Sky and Sea.

Before the one God, if any of our human people were made to feel the ills of an offended spirit from neglect of the rules that must be observed to keep balance, there could always be found a remedy to restore health and respect. A hunter could cut off his future catch by leaving seal's blood at his doorway. Careless acts like that disrupted the harmony between the human and the animal people, who would not give themselves to us without the ritual and respect that their life essence, known as *yua* or soul, deserved. Likewise, if a man or woman disrupted a soul's last days in our village by sewing skins, or covering the roof hole through which the departing one should pass, they could bring sickness to their own children by disrespecting the dead.

But a person's transgressions did not require their death to resolve them. Other spirits, or other mindful acts, might repair the damage and restore favor to their life's remainder. In our world, there was always time before death's final judgment to prove the failure or worth of the offender's attempt to redeem a wrong.

Once the white man came to claim our souls for the one God, all that changed. When everything is created, then controlled by a single force's will, there can be no balance. Then there can be only right or wrong, and the only reward for wrong, punishment. When the Christians came to our land, the elder *Angakkuq*, or Shaman, of that time asked them, "If we did not know about God and sin, would we go to Hell?"

"No," said the missionary, "not if you did not know."

"Then why," asked he, crying tears enough for generations to come, "did you tell us?"

***

My grandmother was one of the last of us to resist the Christians, and keep the old ways. It was her knowledge of the deepest magic of these old ways that she used to cure the sickness that nearly killed me in childhood. After hunting down my fleeing soul, and closing death's door to keep me in our world, she taught me that the weakness which allowed the fever dreams to burn me came from my father's mis-guided attempt to match me to the name-soul of the white missionary. Grandmother explained that to stray beyond the protection of our dead ancestors, was to risk falling beyond the living boundaries of our world, and that giving me the name *Ahltok* was the most important element of the cure that pulled me back from the edge of the world of death.

She told me that during the fever fight, she had looked through my eyes into the green and gold jungle, seen our cousins and their beauty, and felt the heat of the sun in that place so blessed with it, that its human people could go clothed only in their own skins. Grandmother told me that my desire to be reborn in such a place was good, but that for all people, each one of us must—before we get what we want—get what we need. When I struggled to fly from my body, Grandmother saw in the abandoned core of it, a need to be filled with the name-soul of our own people's long-dead holy man.

At the time of my return and renaming, my namesake had all but died even in the memories of the oldest of our tribe. Ahltok had been an Angakkuq as powerful as any known in our people's history. When Grandmother was only five years old, he became her teacher after identifying her as the source of powerful spirit-dreams set loose to wander our sleeping camp at night, as the forces in her were too strong to be left untrained, even at such a young age to be taken from her parents.

Most Angakkuit were simply guides or teachers to our people. By some calling from the spirits—such as a dream or near-death vision—they were identified to an elder guide, and apprenticed to teach our sacred stories. The teachings mainly told of lucky or unlucky people that were singled out by forces in the spirit-world, or the souls of the dead, because of some action or other that they carried out. These stories contained in them the rules for living, and were made to help the people do two essential things: get game, and live right.

That was all. Angakkuit did not minister to the soul of a living person, for unlike the Christians, none of us had souls that could be condemned. We had bodies that would live and then die, animated by souls that would inhabit another living, dying body over again. The Angakkuit were concerned with the length of the lives, and happiness of the human beings living them. To these ends they told stories of our people that had lived before, to teach us how to stay in balance with the spirit forces that controlled the natural world which was the source of the game animals we depended upon for food, and to live together in Love instead of Hate: which every other part of our lives depended on.

If the myths embodied in the stories of our ancestors can be called my people's religion, then the capacities of the least powerful Angakkuit among us could be likened to those of the Imam, Rabi, or Priest in familiar religions. Through years of study, they memorized hundreds of parables passed down by voice from the teacher before them. They taught the people what to do, the rules to follow, and which actions to avoid, but like so many preachers of any religion now, the bad ones only guided their followers with fear and intimidation. The worst of them even broke the most forbidden taboos they spoke against, because for them the stories were just so many empty words to be said over and over again, to maintain a position they were never truly worthy of. To the people of a community, these so-called spiritual leaders—Angakkuit in name only—were as much a bane on them as to the sons and daughters of unworthy parents; the type that force standards on their children they themselves do not uphold, and belittle the ones they should love the most with constant criticisms and threats, so that they are tricked into staying in line by expecting some new fear at every turn, instead of being taught to do good.

Other Angakkuit not only believed in and followed the wisdom passed down through the stories, but also used the clues found in them to seek out hidden sources of imbalance and unhappiness in a person, or their whole community. Even if only one person broke rules or lived wrong, grief could fall on everyone in a camp.

Illness or accidents, bad weather, or poor hunting were caused by breaking the taboos: unclean handling of game; disrespecting the dead; abusing a child; keeping meat from another hungry family when yours was fed; making a lover of another's wife or husband without permission.

When misfortune occurred following misdeeds like these, the more worthy Angakkuit proved their value to the community by journeying into the spirit-world to identify the cause of disruptions extending into our natural one. These Angakkuit possessed true powers to travel out of the human body, to communicate with non-human entities, and feel the structure of energy patterns existing beyond the natural world. The best of them, such as Grandmother, were truly healers like unto the saints. They could not only project their senses past the physical borders of the world our bodies inhabit, and detect disturbances there, but would also assert their will to correct imbalance in the lives of their people by deflecting the actions of malicious spirits, or using their healing powers to calm or cure spastic or injured spirits, whose own suffering may have been first caused by the willful or ignorant misdeeds of men or women, and were then in turn revisited on us.

But the most powerful Angakkuit would join us in human form no more than once every five or ten generations. These men or women were born, it seemed, with all the knowledge of our ways and histories. They could journey into the spirit-world, and make or break compacts there to better the lives of their tribesmen.

They could communicate with any of the animal-people in the natural world, and assume the shape of them at will. These Angakkuit were not only leaders and healers of men, they were prophets, and among this very rare breed, one was more powerful than any: if the God of Christianity sent Jesus, then the deepest rooted spirits of our planet Earth sent *Ahltok*.

Grandmother said that when Ahltok was still a young child, with no instruction from his elders, he began reciting the most esoteric narratives of the past, sifting through the complex layers of our people's oldest shared memories. With only the gods and goddesses of the spirit-world as his own teachers, he became the wisest and most powerful of our kind ever to live. As the very first part of my training as her apprentice, she made me remember the story of one very cold winter when she was only a young woman, fresh from her apprenticeship to him. It describes Ahltok's performance of the hardest task ever undertaken by one of us. It was his final act as the master Angakkuq of our race, and it cost him his human life: a thing he gave gladly out of love for his people, and love for the Earth.

***

The story tells that many years ago, when the seal and blackfish hunting should have been at its best, all of the sea's game-animals stopped giving themselves to our people. The animals had not disappeared. Their feeding grounds were as full of them as before, but when one day a wonderful hunt ended with dozens of fat seals and one young orca taken, some even by young men making first kills, the next day, not a single one would accept a harpoon, even from the most experienced and worthy hunters.

Ahltok the Man sat alone in his igloo for forty days and nights with no fire, food or water, listening to the spirit-world. During this time, the people ate every last piece of their stored food. Some died, and all were close to starving. Once Ahltok had listened enough, he rose and walked to the edge of the frozen sea-ice. He left there his fragile old person's body, lying breathless and frozen as if in death, and borrowed the shape of the largest blackfish, matriarch of the family from which the hunters had received the people's last kill more than a month before. In the form of the orca, Ahltok learned that Sedna, Mistress of the Sea and mother to all of its mammals, had been angered by a group of hunters, and forbade all of her offspring to give themselves to the people any more. None of the orca tribe knew the reason for Sedna's anger, or when she would rise again from the bottom of the ocean, where she was said to lay in bitter mourning at depths beyond the reach of blackfish breath.

Ahltok the Orca asked the pod to locate a family of sperm whales that had recently passed through the hunting grounds. The orcas had spared the life of a sperm calf who had been separated from its mother, since the seal tribe had grown in numbers that year and had been so generous with their sacrifices to the blackfish clan. Ahltok borrowed the favor owed by the sperm whale cow to the orcas, by using her body to swim to the ocean's greatest depths and take his plea to

Sedna, that she might show generosity to the human tribe once more.

Ahltok the Sperm Whale found Sedna thrashing the rocky walls of a deep sea canyon, violently berating herself for having trusted any of his human kind again. Sedna was no stranger to the treachery of humans. She had lived as a girl herself in the very first band of people to form a group larger than a single family, which came together in a time so long before Ahltok was born a person, that time itself was not then yet counted in years.

To understand the story of Sedna, it is important to know that when the first group of people came to live in the top part of the Earth, they found it very hard to get food enough for a tribe. They did not yet have the tools to fish in the rivers or ocean, and there were no mammals living in the sea yet. All they usually got to eat beyond whatever scarce berries or other vegetation they could find, were land animals too small to be anything but very stupid, or very curious: mostly rodents. When they were lucky enough to kill a caribou, or find one already dead before the wolves did, there was always a terrible squabble in the tribe, because they were all paired as one man and one woman, and each set of parents wanted the best meat for their own hungry children. It was only a short time before the lack of meat, and the constant infighting that preceded any eating of it, broke the first band of people into families that scattered themselves around the tundra.

Only one non-human person had any interest in what

might happen to the badly equipped, uncooperative humans. Raven was a roamer with a keen appetite for offal, and scoured the land in search of any share of it he could pluck from Wolf. Once the humans spread out across his territory, Raven found a new delicacy in the excrement they left behind in their constant search for a next meal: the humans' long intestines turned the combination of plant life and animal flesh that no other animal on the tundra was consuming, into a pungent treat that Raven quickly came to crave like pâté.

To get it more easily, the trickster Raven hatched a plan. Knowing that the women would be harder to fool off the scent of his real motive, he went privately to each of the men in the scattered families. Raven had seen that once the first tribe split apart, one man acting alone was never able to take another caribou. He convinced each of the men that Caribou was his enemy, having trampled his wife's nests on more than one occasion, and smashed their unhatched chicks. Raven told the men that he wanted revenge on the caribou-people, and that he would fly over the tundra to find their herds, and lead the men there to kill them. Raven foresaw that by doing this, the scattered families of humans would re-band to form hunting groups to bring down the big animals, and that to dry the meat they took for storage, they would have to gather in camps.

Now greedy Raven made his own camp next to the humans, and by feasting on the never-ending piles of shit that humans make, in a few years the ranks

ANKER FRANKONI

of his own tribe exploded on the rich and easy food source. Soon the raven-people were like a plague on Man. Their own sour droppings covered every inch of the people's camp, and the boldest of them who had learned that human feces was a dish best served warm, stopped waiting for it to even hit the ground: if a young child was not carefully guarded every time he squatted to make a bowel movement, his anus could be pecked into a bloody mess in mere seconds by the ravenous flocks.

They thought to bury their shit to keep it away from the birds, but digging a hole through the hard layers of ice over permafrost deep enough to keep it out of Raven's reach, was such slow work, that a digger had to shit again before her first hole was even half deep enough. The men directed the women to cut strips of caribou hides, and splice them together into long straps at the end of which they tied rocks. Forming a circle around the camp, the women whirled their leather ropes through the air to make a moving fence in the sky which kept the ravens out, but left no one to do the work of cutting and drying the batches of meat from the hunters' kills, which soon piled up in rotten hills next to the festering mounds of shit that was no longer being carried off by the birds.

The people eventually had to admit that they had walked into a trap, by blindly following a plan that at first seemed to hold the promise of easy living. They were about ready to disband, and wander back out over the tundra in their individual family groups to live on the meager pickings that they could collect in peace, but then Wolf came along to sell a tempting new plan to fix the broken one.

It was not Alpha Wolf who came to Man, but one of his lesser brothers, sent by the pack leader to find out what was thinning the caribou herds. Lesser Wolf's keen eye for imbalance quickly took in Man's plight with Raven, and he was about to return to Alpha Wolf with the report that the human camp was on the verge of collapse. As part of the pack, Lesser Wolf was loyal and true, but then he saw the excess meat piled up in Man's camp, and his pretty teenaged daughters dressed in animal skins, and his heart became full of cunning.

Lesser Wolf approached the men in their camp as submissively as he would have his alpha brother, and their egos were inflamed when the powerful animal with its predator's jaws bowed down to them. Lesser Wolf licked the men's moccasins to grease the way for his offer. He told the men that being a wolf, his sense of smell was too fine to let him eat human shit, but that he knew how to make a new creature that would. Lesser Wolf slyly bade the men to gather together the dozen or so orphan girls of the camp who had reached child-bearing age, and had no parents to love them or stop what would happen. He ordered that the leather traces be used to bind them one after the next in a row, each behind the other, with their faces pressed against the frozen ground all stained with raven droppings, and their haunches in the air.

Lesser Wolf told the men that he would make a new creature out of the unwanted girls, and the pups that would soon come out of them. He told them that they could call the new animal "Dog," and that it would eat their shit for them, and that they could tie them together in a line and whip them to make them run across the ice with a sled behind them so that the men would not have to carry their own burdens, and if Dog did not run fast enough, or if Dog did not move its own bowels far away from their camp, or if Man was simply angry, he could kick Dog, or hit its head with his hand or a stick, but still Dog would lick Man's moccasin to make him feel bigger; still Dog would come.

Then Lesser Wolf mounted the bound orphan girls one after another. In his own pack's hierarchy he was too low to mate, and the old leather sack that hung beneath his tail was swollen with years and years of unspent seed. Lesser Wolf unleashed wave after wave of it in a frenzy of fucking of a type too vile for any creature to inflict on a female member of his own race. The men watched Lesser Wolf go about his dirty work, seemingly powerless in their shame and fascination to stop him, or even avert their eyes, though if only one of them had been brave enough to step forward, they all would have surely been moved to raise their clubs against the beast.

One by one, Lesser Wolf used his teeth to yank the girls' animal-skin garments away from their rumps, and entered them from behind. As he battered their insides with his prickly old wolf's cock, he clawed and bit savagely at their backs and necks, and smashed their cheeks and foreheads into the ground with his pounding. The girls' screams turned to howls of pain so deep and loud, they stretched the muscles and bones of their jaws and skulls with the anguish. Smears of white raven droppings and the black soot blown across the frozen brown dirt from the people's cooking fires smudged the flesh of their scraped faces, discoloring their human complexion beyond recognition.

Into their violated wombs, Lesser Wolf pumped enough of his black-magic potion to impregnate each with a large litter of the new pups. From first to last, his thick, dark wand never stopped spewing the juice; squirting it all over each of the girls' exposed backs and legs as he pulled out of them. It burned like acid glue into their naked skin, then rolling in agony on the ground after Lesser Wolf was done with them, the hides of their clothing became stuck forever to their stinging flesh, obscuring the last human trace of the transformed bitches once they lay whimpering in the dirt, and licking their wounds.

But the strongest and most beautiful of the girls, the one that Lesser Wolf had picked as best and saved for last, vowed to fight to the death before she would let herself be fucked like a dog.

This was Sedna, and she was the only one of the orphans who had come into the tribe without parents. Her mother and father and two brothers had all died before Raven had tricked the families into reuniting for his benefit. They had been unique amongst all of the widely dispersed humans roaming the land at that time: not content with their meager diet of grasses, tundra-berries, and mice, they became the first weavers by fashioning plant fibers into a net with which to catch the small fish they had discovered sheltering against the edges of the sea-ice.

One day, after leaving young Sedna to watch them from the shelter of a rocky outcropping on a hill overlooking the ice, her parents and brothers went out to the edge of the sea to cast their net. The day was a warm one, nearing the end of winter, but a sudden wind from the south pitched a rolling bank of waves at the edge of the ice, just as all four of them heaved on the corners of the net. A piece of the thinning sheet of ice cracked off between them and the land, and within seconds the waves pulled them beyond any hope of return. From her vantage point a hundred yards off, Sedna jumped up and yelled to her family as the ocean sucked them away. Too much wind and too much distance lay between them for any chance of final words, but as they gazed bravely back at her, Sedna received the message clearly from them all: "Continue. Stay strong. Be true."

This was the first time that any humans had used their hearts and their minds instead of their mouths and hands to communicate with each other, and the outpouring of love that flowed through the message they sent to Sedna attracted the attention of ancient beings in the spirit-world, who are the original source of love. Like love, these beings are very strong, but very simple. They are spirits whose roots lay in feeling: thought and logic make up no part, and because love can never be explained—or explained away—it and the spirit sources that keep it alive, can create miracles.

Once the speck of ice that carried her family away

disappeared on the horizon, the spirits of love stayed with Sedna after she turned her back on the water and began walking. The girl had not walked far before realizing that while she could neither see nor hear any physical trace of the beings, she was not alone. Not caring if they could hear her or not, she began speaking to the spirits, asking for guidance, and in so doing Sedna became the first human to discover prayer. She asked the spirits of love to guide her to food, water, and safe shelter, and they responded in the only way they knew: with miracles. After roaming many days and nights over the tundra, the spirits completed the string of small miracles they had performed to keep her alive by guiding her to the company of her own kind in the camp that had been newly formed for the caribou hunt.

The spirits stayed close to Sedna after she joined the camp. She continued to speak to them, and tried to get others of the human tribe to do so as well. Most of the people were suspicious of her and were wary of the idea of prayer: they did not know how a girl alone could have survived on the tundra for so long, and the idea of speaking aloud to something they could neither see nor hear frightened them. A few—mainly women—understood Sedna's teachings perfectly, and began praying to the spirits of love as well.

The spirits themselves also had a lot to learn about the world of humans. They were very confused about "Anger" for instance. Anger was a spirit that Love had never encountered before coming into contact with humans. The spirits of love tried to communicate with the spirit of anger in their ancient language, but failed. Love realized that Anger was a brand new spirit: it had come to being within the community of man, and it grew more powerful day by day as the raven-people increased in numbers and harassed the humans more and more mercilessly. Love was afraid of Anger, and would sometimes hide when it got very worked up, but as soon as Anger relaxed just a little, Love would sweep it right away from the hearts and minds of all the men and women who had felt the miracle that Sedna and her guiding spirits had brought to humanity.

But on the day that Lesser Wolf raped the orphan girls, something much, much lower than dogs also came into the world of man. Unlike Anger, that could be brushed easily aside by Love, the terrible force of this new spirit rose up so cold and powerful inside the people it touched, that Love became helpless and lost: not completely destroyed, but trapped under ice.

The new spirit born that day was called Hate, and everyone involved played a part in casting the spell that brought it into existence. Lesser Wolf created a part of it from the spite he felt towards the humans for their beauty, and what he thought of himself when he defiled it. The men made another part of it by their silent acceptance of the rapes: their part seeped from their hearts through the cracks made in them from the shame they felt for wanting to see it happen, for the envy that stung them at the sight of the wolf's thick, veiny shaft, and the depth to which he sunk it into the orphans, and for the contempt they forced themselves to feel for the girls in order to allow it. Even the victims themselves created parts of the horrible new spirit. They took the anger they had learned to feel for the ravens and turned it into something uncontrollable called rage — this is what they felt for Lesser Wolf, and what they felt for the men who had sold them to him for their own selfish needs. The girls also added the last ingredient to the recipe for the bitterest brew. To spite, shame, envy, contempt, and rage, they added one more crucial element. Without it, Hate could not have been born. It was what allowed them to acquiesce to the leather harness. It was the part that let themselves be turned into subservient bitches, instead of fighting tooth and nail to the death to protect their own honor: it was self-pity.

Sedna was the only one to escape the clutches of self-pity. She threw it off with the power of her family's last message before the sea took them away: "Stay strong. Be true." Even entangled as she was in the straps that bound her at the waist and legs, she turned on Lesser Wolf with a ferocity that equaled the beast's own, punching at his underbelly, biting, and clawing at his neck and eyes.

Already close to spent from impregnating the girls before her, Lesser Wolf was unable to overpower Sedna, and snarled to the men for help. All were too repulsed to actually restrain her while the intercourse was performed, but one of the men thought to make her defenseless against the bestial attack, and stepping forward with his obsidian knife, chopped the fingers off both of Sedna's hands. This merciless display of brutality against their fellow human finally broke the spell on a few of the assembled men: one aimed a blow with his club at Lesser Wolf's side, knocking him off balance as he sprang to mount Sedna, and two others without clubs rushed in and pulled the binding straps from her. As soon as she was free, Sedna stooped towards her lost fingers, twitching at her feet on the frozen ground. Her strength and pride would let none of her sacred self be defiled, and using the thumbs still attached to the bloody stumps of her hands, swept her fingers into a pile, bent her face to the ground, and sucked them into her mouth to be kept safe.

Seeing his chance, Lesser Wolf sprang at Sedna's backside once more, but she moved too quickly for him: Sedna ducked and spun underneath his stretched-out body as he leaped over her, and using the last remaining space in her mouth that had magically expanded to take in all of her lost fingers, with one quick snap she bit Lesser Wolf's slimy penis clean off at the stump, whereupon she jumped to her feet and raced away with her squirming fingers and the wolf's wildly flopping member shut tightly up in the pouch of her cheeks, like a pelican carrying a load of fish.

With a tormented howl, Lesser Wolf raced after Sedna, who in a reverse pattern of pelican returning from ocean to land, ran as fast as she was able across the tundra in a straight line to the sea. The loss of blood and terrible pain between his legs slowed Lesser Wolf down, but the great dose of the new hate-spirit working within his blackened heart spurred him on, and he kept right on her heels in a miles-long chase. When Sedna reached the ice she did not slow or hesitate in the slightest: shocked at the death of compassion that allowed the men to watch the girls' desecration; disgusted with the shit-filled reality of the people's camp; horrified by the dark birth of Hate — she dove headlong into the churning waves. Seething with impotent madness, Lesser Wolf was compelled to his own destruction by his blind urge to punish Sedna. He leaped into the icy water after her, using all his waning strength to pursue her past any hope of resurfacing himself, as she struggled to dive as deeply as possible before the air from her final breath gave out.

But a few invisible wisps of the ancient spirits of love had not been frozen into immovable shock at the scene of the rapes, and still clung to their dear Sedna. These performed three last miraculous works after she dove into the sea. First, her lungs became swim bladders, and gills opened up at the sides of her neck to change her into an ocean-dweller. Secondly, when the last gasp of terrestrial oxygen in her was consumed, and she finally opened her mouth to discover the miracle of not drowning, the spirits worked their transformational magic on her precious fingers—and also by chance on Lesser Wolf's severed penis—changing them into the first sea mammals: Walrus and various species of seals; Beluga; Orca; Otter, and of course Sperm Whale, who was forced to pay retribution for the part he had lent to Lesser Wolf's lechery, through centuries of persecution by whalers, who hunted him down to extract the thick greasy spunk that had been thrust on the orphan girls, which he must carry forevermore in his enormous head as penance.

Before the last of the three miracles was wrought, Lesser Wolf himself received his final punishment by becoming the first meal for mighty Orca, conceived of the index finger of Sedna's right hand that would have pointed in fair judgment against him. An easy death by drowning was not for that scoundrel, and he died in bloody agony, torn asunder between the crushing jaws of the blackfish to pay for his crimes.

The rapes avenged, the last miracle unfolded as the souls of Sedna's parents and brothers, who had been transformed by merit of their work as the world's first weavers into beautiful jellyfish, were called from their wandering across the vast ocean to be reunited with the girl they had loved. They would share in their last human blessing upon her—"Continue"—after coming to rest upon the head of the new-crowned Goddess of the Sea, blessing her now immortal form with living, luminous dreadlocks of the most dazzling iridescence.

Back in the people's camp, the promise of Dog's service to them came to pass. Even before whelping their pups, the first bitches made by Lesser Wolf proved their worth to Man: they not only ate the humans' shit, and pulled or carried their burdens, but also chased Raven and other intruders away. Soon balance, in Man's physical world at least, was restored. The dog pack was allowed to increase from the original litters, and then kept in check by culling the ones that had not grown up strong, so that their numbers did not explode like the raven's had. But pups born with all white fur, missing the brown smears or black smudges that had been rubbed so violently into their great-grandmothers' skins on the day of their brutal creation, were killed at once by one of the men, their color being too stark a reminder of who they had been before the creation of their race. These killings were always done far away from camp, as expressing remorse or guilt for the creation of something so useful was considered such bad luck to every man and woman in the tribe, that an unspoken agreement came to pass that the story of Dog's savage birth was never to be spoken: it was their little secret.

Another ugly secret wedged itself between Man and Woman as a result of the damage done deep inside the men when they stood by and silently watched Lesser Wolf rape their orphans. Now when any of them felt frustration when their hunting was bad, or anger at the loss of an important tool or weapon, or weakness or self-loathing when a stronger man succeeded at a task where they had failed, they would beat their dogs in the daylight, then at night they would uncage the hateful lust of Lesser Wolf in the silent darkness of their igloos, and press their own women's faces hard into the fur hides of their sleeping mounds so they could not cry out, and fuck them fiercely from behind.

A psychosis of brutality had entered into the men when they compromised their duty to their own race by allowing Lesser Wolf to work the dark trick that created Dog, and as it dug deeper and deeper into their hearts, those most afflicted began directing the cowardly punishment not only at their women, but at their girls too. Whole families made enemies of each other when daughters hated fathers for their actions, and mothers for their silence. The resulting emotional wounds in them all would have soon destroyed the whole human race as surely as any disaster in their physical world, were it not for the actions of two men.

***

Qungagte were twin brothers each called by that. Had they been born female, they too would have been sacrificed to Lesser Wolf, as their mother had died birthing them prematurely before telling who was their father, and no man in camp would claim them as his sons. Had they mother or father to raise them, they would also have had names: they were never given names — the word Qungagte is not a name; it was what they were called from the time they were put to work. Qungagte means something like "to clean up," and if there had been more like them in the tribe, they would have been called the same. These brothers that the people called Qungagte had only themselves, the work they were made to do, and the people's ridicule. Because they were born too early, and because they were never given enough to eat, or made to feel good about themselves, they stopped growing when they were still only half as tall as the other men. When the men brought caribou back to camp, they yelled, "Qungagte, come and gut out the animal and take the meat to our women!" And the hunters would laugh at them when the dried meat was divided, and although these two had done the hardest work of butchering the kill for everyone, they said, "Together, you would have made one good man!" and they were each only given a half share.

On the day they made the deal with Lesser Wolf, when he told the men to bind the orphan girls with the leather straps, the hunters forced the two Qungagte to tie them up, because those twins were always made to do the most despicable parts of their work. The brothers were desperate to run away from the scene of the rapes as soon as they began, but the hunters restrained them, and slapped their faces when they tried to close their eyes, because if they convinced themselves that the little men were too cowardly to watch, it made it somehow easier to keep their own eyes open. Finally, once the one hunter showed enough bravery and struck at Lesser Wolf with his club, the Qungagte broke free in the confusion and showed how big they really were by rushing to untie Sedna from the straps.

Once Sedna, Lesser Wolf, and the ravens were long gone from the camp, and the evil spirit Hate started working its erosive effect on the families, the shrunken men derisively referred to as Qungagte were not filled with it like the others. Even with all the scorn and abuse they had received all their lives, they somehow did not feel self-pity, so hatred could not take root in them. What the brothers did feel, and very strongly, was remorse. Over and over they recalled the part they had played in the violation of the orphan girls, but they did not make excuses for themselves by remembering how they were forced to tie the leather harness upon them under threat of violence. Perhaps this is why self-pity did not enter them — they did not make excuses for themselves. Since the twin brothers wasted no time on self-pity, it did not take long at all for them to realize something about one of the problems of being human. This was something very, very simple then, just as it is now, although most people will live their whole lives and not learn it: if one wants remorse to go away without excuses, accepting responsibility, and taking action are the two lanes of the only path that leads to a clear heart.

What took longer for the Qungagte to realize, was how to act. Seasons passed as they searched their minds for something to do to make amends. But the orphan-girl-dogs were beyond all help, the men and women so low and withdrawn they had all but forgotten Qungagte were there to order around, and Sedna seemed to have disappeared forever. Finally one night, both of the brothers shared a dream. In it, they found the answer waiting in their hearts that had failed to enter their minds. In the dream, they travelled to the sea, and stood side by side at the furthest edge of the ice. At the ocean's edge they did the simplest, but perhaps most difficult thing any person can to begin to right a wrong. When they awoke, the answer seemed so easy, they were shocked at themselves for taking so long to come to it. They were shocked as to how the powerful hunters had buried into their collective shame for so many nights without receiving the idea, and how the women of their tribe had remained so long in silence without it.

Speaking not a word between them, the Qungagte rose and began walking towards the sea. When they arrived at the place they had both seen in their dream, those little men became the first people to use the magic words that they had received from it: words so simple, yet so powerful, we are shocked at how even today, leaders of nations can think to ignore their healing magic.

"I am sorry." Just three little words, spoken by the two smallest people. "I am sorry." With their mouths as one voice, they spoke them again. "I am sorry." They stood there with no other thought in their hearts, or words upon their lips. For many hours they let the cleansing power of the words flow out from them, over the great waters of the ocean. Neither of the brothers held any expectation of receiving anything in return. The magic simply guided them to speak the words, "I am sorry." They spoke them not to prove anything, nor to be overheard and praised by the enormous, empty sea. They spoke them unconditionally, simply to express the sincerest truth in their hearts. Therein lay the crux of the creation of real magic, without which their words would have been just four empty syllables cast by two puny figures into the vast, indifferent space of the wind and the waves. But it was magic that flew that day. It flew across the great ocean with the stamina of the albatross, grew in strength until it plunged far below the surface of the sea, and echoed through the depths until Sedna heard mankind's first true apology. Those unconditional apologies of the two Qungagte called Sedna from the depths like a giant, graceful manta ray, enticed by the Moon's loving light.

The Queen of the Sea had grown enormous in the

vastness of her new realm. There was so much to love in the beauty of the watery kingdom that her heart was filled with creation magic of its own, as powerful as that of the spirits who had first transformed her. The Great Mother's huge glowing head slowly rose out of the water at the edge of the ice, not two feet from where they stood. So sincere was their remorse, and readiness for anything Sedna would have required to expunge it, that the two brothers would not have taken a single step back, even if she were to have gobbled them down into the great maw of her barnacle-encrusted lips. But the Qungagte were just able to see the smile on Sedna's face, veiled by the long unkempt tentacles of her thick glowing locks. In that moment, the brothers realized that the simple, but very powerful act of saying "I am sorry" had presented them with the opportunity to make real reparation to Sedna, and they knew just what to do.

The tangled tresses of her living crown of jellyfish were no more knotted or slippery than the entrails of the animals the Qungagte had spent their lives cleaning, but because of her missing fingers, Sedna was not able to properly detangle them herself. They climbed bodily into the mass of her crown, and working long into the night by the light of the luminescent strands themselves, they patiently separated and smoothed each clustered curl, suffering gladly the blisters over their exposed arms and faces, as each welt raised by the venomous ringlets upon their skin helped draw out the sting of remorse from their conscience.

By the time dawn broke the following day, both

Sedna's hair and her heart were untangled by the loving service that had been bestowed on her. The twins reminded her of the human love she had shared with her own parents and brothers, and that we are all of us members of just one family. She resolved to give mankind another chance.

Sedna whistled long and high over the miles of tundra between the sea and Man's camp. Soon the remaining grandmother-dogs that first gave birth to their race, plus some of their huskiest sons appeared in response to the call. She told Qungagte that the second task required to remove the sickness from the humans' souls and sustain their future, was to restore the spirit of love. Sedna said that its expression must be shared even down to the lowest animal, and especially to Dog, who had suffered so much to come into the service of man. She commanded that all members of the dog-people be treated justly, and that especially those of all-white fur must be honored in remembrance of who they had been. Sedna told the dogs that they must still work hard, as the highest honor for all creatures is to perform the tasks for which they are best suited, but that they would henceforth receive just reward for their work by sharing in the human food of meat, and not have to only eat shit. She told Qungagte to fashion harness for the assembled team from kelp fronds, and then instructed them in the words of a new language to be spoken by Man to Dog, so that "Mush" might be used in place of the whip.

Next, Sedna called a fine young bull of the walrus-people from her ocean depths. She fondly kissed his whiskery snout, and said to him, "Sweet child of mine, your soul shall be freed to return to my sea, or take any form its essence desires, but your body shall become now a blessing of food for the tribe of man."

Brave Walrus lay down upon the ice, breathed one last great gentle breath, and let his body die. Sedna then again addressed the brothers: "You who have touched all parts of the caribou that humans have taken for food, must now teach Man to use every physical part of each animal-person from either land or sea that sacrifices its body so that your people may live. And the twin tusks of my beloved Walrus shall always serve as the sacred reminder of your humble beginnings as the two separate Qungagte who would have given up their very lives to clean up the hate and secrets that threatened to destroy mankind."

At these words from Sedna, both of the twins looked to the other for help to divine the Great Mother's meaning, but were surprised to discover that they each stood alone. Then they looked down at the two big feet firmly planted on the ice far below them, and their heart rejoiced to discover that they now stood together.

From one pair of clear, understanding eyes, the one who had been two looked at Sedna and she said, "Your work as Qungagte is done, and together, you make much more than one good man." A smile as big as the cresting waves ran across Sedna's face, and as she sank back into the ocean she said, "You have earned your name, Yuuyaraq — you are the Balanced Being, and shall return now to your people's camp and restore

Love."

Yuuyaraq then bent to one knee next to the dogs. He spoke soothingly to them to calm the pack's excitement for work performed in exchange for love, rather than the threat of the whip, and with one simple gesture he wiped away years of resentment between the dog and human people by nuzzling his face into the team leader's fury neck, and letting her lick his cheek rather than his moccasin. Then, with all the respectful actions Yuuyaraq was soon to teach the human people regarding the treatment of the dead of every species, he fastened the trailing ropes of the team's kelp harness into a hitch around the base of Walrus' twin ivory tusks, and shouting "Mush!" to the happy dogs, ran alongside them as they pulled Sedna's first offering back to camp: a clear symbol of the second chance the once-human goddess was willing to give mankind to learn how to live in balance upon Earth.

In his new body, filled with twice as much soul, intelligence, and capacity for love as any man had ever been, Yuuyaraq's capabilities expanded even beyond the conjoined powers of the two halves of his original form, and he became the three bridges interlinking the islands of humanity, nature, and the spirit-world. He was the first Shaman, the Adam that was the original seed that gave shoot to a huge family tree of Angakkuit that grew over a hundred generations, linked through roots and branches of both blood birth, and soul rebirth. With grateful Dog as his first teacher, Yuuyaraq learned how to communicate with and adopt the physical form of any animal. Through his ability for dream travel, he learned how to visit the spirit-world and perform deeds for the gods and goddesses in exchange for insight into the past, or to shed light on secrets being kept in the present.

Perhaps most importantly, Yuuyaraq was the first person to put crucial lessons about life and the world into simple words that even children can understand. He taught the first generation of Angakkuit the stories of their age, and how to put newly acquired knowledge into the same form. They in turn taught those who came after, and in that way hundreds of stories were passed down over time to explain the creation of things in the natural world, the origins of our human society, and the importance of balanced living: just like the one I have almost finished telling you.

Over the centuries following Yuuyaraq's first earthly life, the lineage of power that flowed at times through blood birth, and also through soul reincarnations and name-soul bestowal, ebbed and flowed in intensity from one Angakkuq to the next. Generations of Angakkuit would live and die with no seeming powers beyond the rote memorization of our sacred stories it was their duty to learn and repeat. Then once it seemed the magic of their line had been lost forever, suddenly from the charlatans would emerge a saint.

If a logic was at work in the midst of this mystery, it was surely a part of the spirit-world, as no man or woman could ever fathom when or where a higher power would take flesh among them. The only vaguely discernible pattern to the arrivals of our greatest Angakkuit seemed to be this: just as Yuuyaraq had at the very first, they seemed to appear in our race only at the times when humanity—whether we were aware of it or not—was most in need of their wisdom and guidance. Assuming this to be true, in hindsight, the first coming of Ahltok should have been taken as a sign of some very, very hard times to come.

***

As the legend tells it, Ahltok meditated in his ancient human body for forty days with no sustenance or warmth, then borrowed the form of a great whale to seek out Sedna the Sea Goddess in the furthest depths of her kingdom, to find out why she had withheld the animals upon whom the humans depended for their winter survival. In the huge span of time that had passed since her creation, Sedna had grown a hundredfold in the limitless expanse of her vast domain. Even in the body of the great sperm whale, Ahltok was punier in comparison than the Qungagte twins had been when they stood selflessly before her prior to being transformed into Yuuyaraq, but just as bravely, Ahltok swam as close to the thrashing goddess as he was able without being caught up in her tempest and dashed against the canyon walls. "Queen Sedna," Ahltok began. "I beg of you to tell me what Man has done to anger you so."

During the eons since her creation, the Sea-Mother had become so connected with the cycles of her sister Moon and their planet cousins, that she had developed the ability to glimpse pieces of the future. Sedna knew that Ahltok would come to her even before he did himself, and he was certainly the only person alive that she would not have at that time destroyed at once. Still, even the most benevolent of goddesses are subject to a certain amount of capriciousness, and she was not yet certain that she was prepared to help Ahltok, though he had gone to such great lengths to seek her out. "How can I speak to you, Ahltok, if I can not even see you?" Sedna had in fact so tangled her enormous mass of thick tresses again with her violent fits of sorrow and anger, that her face was completely hidden from Ahltok's view. Realizing the challenge posed by her question, as in the whale's form he was even less capable of sorting out the nappy clumps of her crown than she, Ahltok played a risky gamble beneath the sea.

Close by Sedna's canyon slept a monster of the deep well suited to the job, if only its form could be controlled for Ahltok's purpose. But Giant Squid had lived a million years, and will live a million more without a thought or care for Man or his plight. Normally Ahltok's sense for righteousness and balance would never have permitted him to occupy another being's body without invitation or fair exchange, but with his people's survival at stake, and time running out on the whale's breath, action, not etiquette, must prevail. Knowing all would be lost if he were not able to do two improbable things perfectly on his first attempt, Ahltok rushed with a great burst of speed and rammed Sperm Whale's huge blunted head into Giant Squid's side, just above his massive eye. Exactly as he had hoped, the force of impact catapulted Ahltok's yua into the vessel of the squid, while at the same time knocking the great whale unconscious, so that she would not find her body returned to her own free will and resurface immediately without him aboard.

While Sperm Whale lay in a daze upon the ocean floor, Ahltok the Giant Squid very quickly mastered the touch of his eight long rubbery tentacles. He speedily set to work at detangling Sedna's dreads to get at the root of her renewed contempt for mankind, and as he began his expert ministrations, Sedna soon relaxed and spoke openly: "I have seen a vision of a race of invader humans that shall descend upon your lands, Ahltok," she said. "Most of the men of that race have been steeped so long in the spirits of Deceit and Greed, that the only things your people can hope to receive in exchange from them are the ruin of your lands, and death of not only your bodies, but your very souls."

"An advance shadow of the evil to come lies upon you even now. In the hunt of my sea-children that I have determined shall be your people's last, the wasteful gluttony and disdain for balance that will be brought with the invaders has already entered into your hearts: the men in the kayaks who killed the final orca had already taken a walrus to please the greatest hunter, but when they saw the chance to take an even mightier blackfish, they threw its beautiful body back into the sea. Do not take my abandonment of your tribe as a curse, Ahltok: it is my one last final blessing to they who were once my ancestors, that I allow your people the honor of perishing peacefully together in starvation, before the arrival of those who will drive them to kill each other with treachery and hatred."

Ahltok's thoughts flew as fast as his flexible arms as Sedna spoke. When she finished, he said: "But Queen Sedna, your own very existence is owing to the unique human qualities of self-love, protection of honor, and persistence. Honor my people by letting us prove the power of Love: let us persist!"

"Those parts of me are long dissolved, Ahltok. My concern now is for the Earth itself. If your people are gone when the hateful race arrives to plunder my Sea, and its brother Land, and are instead greeted only by all the animal tribes which I shall turn against them, perhaps they too will perish without your people's knowledge of survival in these freezing lands, and the destruction of the sea-ice which I have foreseen will not come to pass. So no, Ahltok: the time for you to shepherd the souls of your people to the spirit-world has come. Go now, and prepare them for your journey."

But once begun, Ahltok would not leave a thing undone. In a blur of flashing tentacles he raced to complete the coiffuring of Sedna's undulating crown of glowing jellydreads. When his work to arrange her mass of hair was finished, Ahltok propelled himself directly in front of Sedna's face, where she could see her reflection in the enormous lens of the squid's giant eye. Pleased with the results of his work, Sedna heaved a sigh and then, just as fickle as any human queen, said: "Something tells me I will regret this Ahltok: but you and your people may... persist."

With as much joy as a stoic old Angakkuq in the

form of a giant squid could muster, Ahltok thanked her, then jetted quickly to Sperm Whale, whose need to resurface for air had shaken off her stupor. Ahltok wrapped Giant Squid's powerful arms around her, and pressed its beak against the side of her massive skull for the yua shift. As soon as Ahltok's life essence was transferred back into the whale, and the surly squid found itself so perfectly positioned for an attack, it decided to take revenge on the mortal enemy whose people had hunted and fed upon its tribe for so long. Giant Squid tore into the leathery flesh of Sperm Whale's head with its horny beak, intent on boring a hole into the center of her melon, and then to suck off the barrels-full of spermaceti held inside, without which her buoyancy would be denied.

Locked in a life-or-death struggle with the furious squid, Ahltok thrashed his great tail and sped along the side of the canyon walls, slamming Sperm Whale's body against the rough rocks in an attempt to break its suckery hold. Moved by her mother's love for a child, along with just a little bit of vanity, Queen Sedna shouted "STOP!" to still Ahltok's thrashing, then with a mighty wave from her arm, swept the attacking creature off the whale's head and hypnotized it with her irresistible gaze. "For the dexterous touch of your tentacles, my dear squid, you shall henceforth serve as ward of the crown." As the creature settled in to a chamber in the canyon wall near Sedna's head, the queen's parting words to Ahltok proved once more that her mood could shift as quickly as the tides when she said: "I told you your people could persist, brave

Ahltok. If you want them to eat then convince my children to lay down their lives for you again — my gifts to you are done!"

The full impact of Sedna's words became clear to Ahltok as soon as Sperm Whale surfaced at the edge of the ocean where her passenger's own body lay waiting. With a mighty cough, she blew the vapors of Ahltok's yua back into it as forcefully as if he were a Jonah, then turned tail and disappeared back below the waves. Ahltok rose unsteadily to his feet, lightheaded from his psychic exertions and the long meditative fast that his bag of bones had recently endured. He scanned the open waters from shore to horizon for any signs of life, but the ocean was as empty as if Sedna's children had never been born.

For the rest of that day and long into the night, Ahltok stood patiently and silently called to the people of the sea. He reminded Walrus of his deep connection with the Angakkuit line, and how his people were honored in the legend of the twins. He broadcast vivid pictures and sounds from his mind to the seal tribe, of the elaborate ceremonies humans performed to honor them, and he sang the wordless music they made for Beluga, so that when his dead people's souls passed from their bodies, the Angakkuit's songs would help guide them across the unfamiliar parts of Earth when they journeyed from water to the spirit-world.

Just before daybreak, a male orca in the prime of his youth surfaced near Ahltok and gazed out over the expanses of ice and tundra that began where his people's territory ended. Orca told Ahltok that he had heard his pleas to Sedna's children, but that it was a dream that beckoned him to the shore, and not the petty needs of a tribe that did not concern him. He explained that all members of the blackfish tribe would have variations of the dream from time to time, but that in him it was especially strong and often woke him up at night. In his dream, Orca runs fast across the open land. When he hunts, the blood of his kill runs rich and hot into his mouth, pure and strong and undiluted by the ocean water. When he sleeps, he is cocooned in the furry warmth of a close group of others like him: they are nestled together upon the unmoving ground, asleep in a stillness that is never felt in the constantly moving waters of the sea.

Ahltok told young Orca that his dreams stemmed from the day Sedna and all the ocean's mammals were created, when his ancestor consumed the body and soul of Lesser Wolf. Orca seemed very excited by this explanation. He told Ahltok that he believed his yua had been somehow misguided: that he knew his destiny was to be in the body of one of the wolf-people. Ahltok replied very gravely that to bring about the transformations necessary to adjust a creature's destiny always required great sacrifice. To explain with lessons from the past, he told Orca the stories of the creation of Dog, and how the Qungagte twins were recast into the form of just one man. The blackfish hinted at the shadow of cunning passed through his line via the blood of his ancestor's first meal, when he posed a far more challenging question to Ahltok then Sedna had at the bottom of the ocean: "How am I to help your people get back in the good graces of my brothers of the sea, great Ahltok, if you yourself are unwilling to perform some sacrifice for me?"

Ahltok knew he was nearing the end of his human lifetime. With his people starving to death, presented as he was with the sole chance of their survival by the only one of Sedna's children willing to speak with him, the choice was not a difficult one to make. Ahltok told Orca to assemble a delegation of all of Sedna's children, and promised that if the young blackfish was successful in convincing the various leaders of the sea-mammal tribes to allow their people to be hunted by the humans again, he would create the magic and perform the necessary sacrifice to transfer his yua to a member of the wolf-pack. Once Orca had descended below the waves to do his work, Ahltok set about preparing for his.

The direct solution to fulfill Orca's longing, and allow his yua to take the form of a wolf, would have involved a simple ceremony, in which the essential part of its physical body would be consumed by a pregnant female member of the pack. The only sacrifices required if this were to have been possible, would have been by Orca himself, and the mother wolf and one of her unborn cubs, as the first life essence already residing in its vessel would be displaced back to the spirit-world when the orca's yua entered the fetus. This straightforward approach would be impossible however: just as members of the orca tribe experienced dreams of taking the form of wolves, ever since the mysterious disappearance of Lesser Wolf, all wolf-people had an inexplicable fear of the blackfish, even though they had never known the truth of their shared histories, nor even come into contact with any, since no wolf since had ever jumped into the sea.

Of course Ahltok could have easily hypnotized any wolf into forgetting its subconscious fear of Orca and simply invited it to a seaside feast, but in the complicated alchemies concerned with cross-species yua transfers and reincarnations, unless a creature is holding the clear and conscious intention to take in the life essence of another while they are consuming the primary organ in which the yua is contained, then the soul of the one released from its meat can not be concentrated into the one who has done the eating. For these reasons, Ahltok himself was the only being capable of transporting Orca's yua from his existing form, into that of Wolf: the great Angakkuq must himself serve as both medium and sacrifice.

While Orca continued his conferences beneath the waves, Ahltok faced in the direction of the people's camp and sent a silent message across the miles to my grandmother. She was instructed to assemble a team of dogs harnessed for work, and as many of their hunters as could still survive the long walk to the edge of the sea, and to come with long-bladed knives to butcher the carcass that they would find waiting there. Then Orca reappeared at the water's edge to report that the representatives of each family of sea-mammals had agreed to restore the tradition of feeding Man with their sacrifices, provided that the human people never again dishonored the souls of any members of their tribe by disrespecting or wasting the bodies that were given to them. Orca cautioned Ahltok that the tribal leaders of each band had promised that if the taboos for the respectful treatment of their people were again broken, they would all work together to bring about the final disappearance of not just the mammals, but all the living things of the sea, and the huge bounty of its creatures of every kind, that could easily feed Man for eternity, would be made to disappear forever in less than seven generations of his race.

There was no need for Ahltok to verify Orca's claim that the other animals had given their word, or that it was true. He knew the nature of each race of creatures intimately. Wolf-people could be cunning; Orca self-centered and even manipulative; Squid, vicious. In those icy lands where Snake could not crawl, however, there were only two types of animals that were so tricky as to tell an outright lie: Raven and Man. Orca's word must therefore be truth.

"Adventurous Orca," Ahltok said. "If it is in your heart to want this change of your earthly being, you must yourself be the cause of its start. Though the desire serves your soul, the gift you will leave of your flesh is a blessing to my people, without which they will not survive. Even so, without your commitment I must let my people perish, as my duty to the Angakkuit code and to my tribe's renewed promise to all of your kin, stays my hand from killing your body to extract the yua within if this is not truly your wish: if it is, then prove it by leaving the sea forever, and leap far upon this ice to die."

As bravely and obediently as the ancestor walrus

commanded by Queen Sedna so long before, Orca rushed at the land with one final burst of liquid speed. He leaped high out of the water, then slid upon his pure white belly a great distance up onto the ice, coming to rest well past any chance of returning to the sea even if he had wanted. Ahltok, however—even in his very old and weakened state—could have used powers beyond that of physical abilities to return the great blackfish to the ocean had Orca wavered, but he did not.

Ahltok drew the razor sharp blade of his obsidian knife. He stepped close to Orca's alert, waiting eye and whispered, "Breathe.... Dream." In one long fast motion, Ahltok plunged the blade into Orca's belly just under his flipper and down the length of him to the anus, cleaving his body wide open as if along a seam where white joined black. Orca's lifeblood and guts steamed red onto the ice. Ahltok stepped back up to Orca's head, and gazing deep into his eye as the light faded he said, "Now my brave friend, together we become the journeyer."

Taking care not to tread on any of the other organs that would be the first meal to restore the strength of the starving men and dogs whom Grandmother would lead to the kill site, Ahltok carefully cut free the bladder. He pierced the tough membrane with the tip of the knife, then raised it above his head and drank down the bitter, salty urine inside. For the next hour, Ahltok knelt on the ice next to the lifeless disemboweled hulk, and cut the bladder into bite-sized chunks which would be his own last supper. He slowly chewed and swallowed each piece, one after the next, as he meditated on Orca's yua. When he had finished his stomach was near to bursting, but his heart was light, secure in the knowledge from my grandmother's message to him that her party would soon reach the great stock of meat that would save his people from starvation, and that she, his finest disciple, would see to it that every last shred of the young Orca's bodily sacrifice would be honored. Ahltok sent one more transmission to Grandmother, reminding her of the Angakkuit duty to uphold and perpetuate the wisdom of their teachings to humanity, and promising that he would appear to her in other forms as time went by. Ahltok then rose to his feet. Without a glance at its stiffening carcass, he spoke reassuringly to the young blackfish, whose yua and awareness were now inside him. Having consumed Orca's bladder—which in all mammals is the organ that serves to both filter the waters of the Earth, and house the soul—the two were ready to journey across the tundra as one, to seek out the wolf tribe.

They arrived at the wolf-people's camp many hours after nightfall to discover their beta-leaders gathered at a meeting of the Moon Circle: the wolves' equivalent of their government's congress. Their pack leader had fallen gravely ill in what should have been his heartiest years, and was not expected to survive. The representatives were locked in debate concerning the election of a new Alpha Leader, divided by two factions' support of either of two candidates, each of whom were opposed by the opposite group's concern regarding the inexperience of one, and the advanced years of the other.

Once Ahltok understood the pack's dilemma, he saw the opportunity for Orca to fulfill his wish to live as a wolf, without requiring a sacrifice of one of their people's future-born pups. The beta wolves led Ahltok to Alpha Wolf's den, where he lay dying. As many of the senior wise-wolves as could gather in the dug out chamber with him entered as well, and listened in silence for hours as Ahltok told the intricately interwoven histories of Wolf, Man, Dog, Orca, and the Creator Goddess Sedna. Ahltok then explained his duty to Orca, whose yua he carried like a mother inside him. He assured Alpha Wolf and the assembled elders that the yua of the young orca was a bold and brave essence. He told of his deal-making with the various tribes of the sea-mammals, and assured the wolves that he possessed in his core, the qualities of a great leader.

Ahltok said that the worthiest leaders are those willing to make great sacrifices, not only to better the lives of their own people, but for the combined benefit of as many races and classes as possible. He explained to Alpha Wolf that if he were willing to let his own yua go from his body immediately, without grasping on to the remaining days or weeks left to him before the illness would bring about the physical death that would release it, his form could survive to serve as the new vessel for Orca, whose indoctrination to the ways of the wolf-people would be hastened by his yua's commingling with the cellular memories contained in the tissues of Alpha Wolf's body. Ahltok cautioned Alpha Wolf that if he agreed to the plan, he must stay strong in his resolve to relinquish his body to Orca once the process was begun. He explained that Alpha Wolf's own yua would have to remain inside his weakening flesh to maintain its spark of life until Orca's entered, but once it did so, and the body held two strong souls inside it, the invigorating effect of the combined life-forces would erase all physical illness. Once healed, Alpha Wolf would feel a very strong urge to remain inside the body, as it is not the natural tendency for a being's yua to vacate its physical vessel unless it is very close to death. Ahltok warned that there are two ways in which a great nation might find itself terribly damaged by its leader: one is when a psychological imbalance occurs as a result of two naturally powerful souls vying for control of one body, and another is when an attempt is made to imbue a person with a previous generation's qualities, by transferring a name-soul to them while it is still in use by their father or grandfather, which can result in the worst kind of megalomania.

Alpha Wolf had served as a just and faithful leader to his people for many years. He was also known to be a wise Earth citizen, and kept a close watch on the caribou herds on which his people depended for survival. When hard times fell on them, he tasked the members of his tribe to live with less, produce fewer offspring, and wait to live prosperously again only once everyone joined in the balance could afford to do so. He assured Ahltok and the assembled elders of his pack that he was committed to acting selflessly for the benefit of his people and the Earth, and said he was ready to receive his instructions.

Ahltok assured Alpha Wolf that the ailing pack leader's part in what was to come would be significantly less difficult than his own. Ahltok lay down on his back upon the dirt floor of the earthen den, and spoke first to Orca's yua within his own stomach and intestines. He told him he would soon leave the darkness in which he was encased, and that when he opened his new eyes to the first sight of his terrestrial existence, he must not become distracted by the wonders of it all, in the event that he must use his spiritual strength to shove Alpha Wolf's yua in the right direction.

Ahltok's innate abilities in the ways of the Angakkuit allowed him to contain Orca's yua within his innards without its powerful force unfurling itself through his entire cellular network of flesh, so long as he remained consciously focused on the separation. He told Alpha Wolf that his essential duty to the procedure to follow, would be to meditate on inviting Orca's yua to replace his own, while eating with the greatest possible speed and dexterity the flesh in which it was trapped, as Ahltok must stay conscious while it was done to keep his body from expiring before Orca's essence was completely transferred into Alpha Wolf.

Ahltok's last instructions were to the other assembled members of the wolf tribe: he told them that once their leader's body had entirely consumed the package of his flesh containing Orca's yua, he would cause his own to exit from his human bladder, at which point he would be pleased if the elder wolves would look upon his dead body as a feast in honor of the time he had spent as a man.

Ahltok then drew once more his sharp obsidian blade, took three deep, cleansing breaths, and cut himself open from the top of his left hipbone to the base of his sternum. He continued breathing calmly, lying perfectly flat upon his back as he set the blade next to him, and then reached into his body cavity with both hands. He felt between his liver and spleen and grasped the heavy sack of his stomach, still full with more than half of Orca's bladder meat, then pulled it free of the ribcage and lay it atop his chest. Hand over hand as if pulling rope, Ahltok then extracted ten feet or more of the small intestine, until he could no longer feel any of the digested portions of his last meal in its tube. "Now Alpha Wolf, sever the line here and commence eating upwards towards me as quickly as you can," Ahltok said. As Alpha Wolf fell to eating, Ahltok kept his eyes open and maintained a pattern of slow, even breathing. He placed his hands back into the lowest section of his slit-open belly at his pelvis, covering his bladder gently with his cupped hands to calm his excited yua until he could let himself fly after feeling the last of Orca's essence leave his guts.

The meditative serenity Ahltok imposed on himself while his bowels were being consumed was suddenly shattered as Alpha Wolf turned his attention away from the half-eaten stomach, and plunged his muzzle deep into the blood-rich liver beside it. Ahltok's warning about the restoration of vitality to the sick wolf's body had been grossly understated. On top of the renewed vigor Alpha Wolf was charged with, now that the bulk of Orca's yua was inside him, he was possessed by an appetite beyond all capacities of any land dweller, and clearly intent on holding control of the powerful body he had loved for so long.

As soon as the process of the yua transfer began to go so clearly awry, a dozen of the assembled wolf-tribe elders sprang forward to take Alpha Wolf down before the creation of the raging tyrant that Ahltok had warned of could take place. With the last breath he was able to expel before his lungs were devoured, Ahltok bellowed: "STOP!" and froze the would-be assassins in their tracks. Using the last shreds of focus and determination in his rapidly fading body, Ahltok waited until he felt the final remnants of his passenger's yua slip into the ravenous wolf's gullet along with the scraps of stomach lining that had been swallowed up with his kidneys and pancreas. With his final act of strength, Ahltok then yanked free at the roots his own bladder that he had been cradling in his palms, raised his arm up to Alpha Wolf's face, and jammed it down his throat to follow Orca in.

A lifetime of travel back and forth between Earth and the ethereal, and his experience cohabiting the physical bodies of every type of animal, had prepared Ahltok well for the challenge that met him inside Alpha Wolf, but it was still no mean feat to pit his humancentric yua—inherently coded for empathy, nurturing and compassion—against the raging animalistic struggle of the two souls grappling for dominance within. The other wolves maintained a tight circle around Alpha Wolf's form, but continued to follow the order to hold off their attack while it twisted and convulsed atop the mutilated bloody mess that had been Ahltok's body. Wildly shifting patterns of black, white and gray swirled across the pelt, and sparks flew from Alpha Wolf's bristling fur as each powerful essence of the original tenant's yua, and that to whom the body had been promised, struggled to push the other out. Ahltok's yua waited carefully for the right instant to intervene between the two forces. When the perfect moment presented itself, the old Angakkuq's incredibly bright soul flashed forward, spun two straitjackets of pure energy around the raging Goliaths, and hauled the captives at the speed of light through the liquid maze of wolf's blood, bile, and piss down into the bladder. Orca's essence was pushed deep into the tissue, then the two souls of Ahltok and Alpha Wolf shot forth as one sperm-shaped bolt of lightning from the tip of the wolf's penis, and flew like a meteor beyond the confines of the earthen den up into the night. Ahltok spun like a gyroscope in the air and flung Alpha Wolf's yua 5000 light-years into the southern sky, where it became the constellation Lupus, there to spend a billion years howling its apologies to the universe for becoming so misdirected by its lust for power and dominance, at the very moment it had been presented with the ultimate opportunity to serve the greater good.

Ahltok certainly had served the greater good with the final actions of his last days on Earth. With Orca's bold new soul at the helm of the wolf leader's reinvigorated body, their tribe gained its finest Alpha; one who lived to lead their people for a great many years. The beta-wolves who stood witness to the sacrifice made by Ahltok to bring Orca's soul to the service of their people upheld their promise to honor his life on Earth by ceremoniously eating the remnants of his human body in the den that night, and through consuming his flesh a new spirit of honor and justice entered into the hearts of all of the wolf people, who became much less sly and cunning as a result.

The human tribe was rescued from the brink of starvation by the great store of meat given to them through Orca's bodily sacrifice, and balance was restored between their people and the sea-mammals: the animals served the people's need for food, and in return the humans honored and protected the animals' yuas with ceremonies and guidance when they left their bodies. Even the dog tribe's lot improved greatly as a result of the interknit events and circumstances that occurred at the end of the story: in consuming their share of Orca's organ meats waiting for them and the starving hunters when grandmother led their team to the kill site, the highly refined sense of taste and smell that had originally been possessed by Lesser Wolf, but denied to them during the ugly conception of their race, was finally bestowed by consuming the flesh of the progeny of the ancestor that had swallowed their evil father, and they never again stooped to eat human shit.

But the story of my people's tribe, and how our greatest Angakkuq performed feats beyond the powers of Man to save us from extinction once, can not be considered complete without telling of how Ahltok tried to do it again — and of how we failed to listen.

***

During his life as a man, Ahltok had been able to wear the bodies of animals. He could correct imbalances in the human mind, body, or society by carefully examining present situations, and the impact of actions that had been performed in the past. He travelled back and forth between the spirit-world and our physical one. Once the yua was permanently released from Ahltok's physical body and it decided not to seek another, it began to exist in both the spirit and earthly worlds simultaneously, just like the gods and goddesses. With no physical form to impede its further development, the force that had been in the body of Ahltok was therefore released from the constraints of time, which meant it could move through it in any direction. It could have—had it wished—existed forever in any part of the universe, even five billion years into what we call the future. Its selfless yua had not given so much to my people while existing in the form of a man, however, to give up on us so easily. Ahltok stayed close to our tribe's space and time, exploring their intersecting planes frequently, but always returning to keep teaching my grandmother, showing her visions of things yet to be.

What Queen Sedna had prophesied leagues under the sea was coming. Grandmother received a series of visions from Ahltok's yua: a new race of men would descend on us like ravens on shit. The first would come in the bellies of boats bigger than whales. Later they would actually roar down at us from the very air itself, carried like predatory spawn inside giant birds made of a thing called metal, which would drink the Earth's own blood to extract the life needed to propel their stiff screaming bodies back into the sky. In the visions, Grandmother was warned that the saddest part of what was then the future, was that most of our people would at first want what would befall us. Modern Man was on his way, and with him, the most insidious progress traps ever seen; and just like making dogs to eat our shit instead of cleaning it up ourselves, to our shame, we welcomed it all.

***

Shortly after Ahltok's yua began sharing visions with her, Grandmother urged the people to show no trace of themselves when the invaders came. They laughed and said, "Stick to guiding the yuas of our kills, and telling stories to the children; Angakkuit can't see the future." Instead of admitting she had indeed foretold the future, when the first traders came trickling in, our people called them a blessing. When seal and otter fur was swapped for steel knives and harpoons, they called those things a blessing. They were able to take and butcher more animals in less time, but the more they took, the less of each they used. With our traditional hunting tools, it took equal measures of skill, patience, attention, and the animal-people's willingness to give themselves to us to have a successful hunt. By the time the whalers came on the heels of the fur-traders, and all of our men had bartered or worked to obtain rifles, nobody knew that Mother Sedna had turned her back on us again. We were still taking her children, but they were not giving themselves to us anymore: we were murdering them with the guns.

But the blessing that first seemed best and brightest was not the steel weapons, but the new water the invaders brought. They called it a "Spirit" and it was certainly not of this world. Compared to the water we drank, this seemed like real magic. For much of the year we could only get a liquid supply of our land's water by filling seal-stomach bags with ice chips that we would have to sleep with under our furs at night to melt. The trade-water never turned to ice. A cold man could drink it and feel warm. A hungry one could drink it and forget he needed meat. In just a few short years alcohol became the primary currency of our land. Even if a hunter was down to only a handful of shells for his rifle and his children were hungry, he would give whatever pelts he had taken for a few bottles of alcohol first, before considering his children or the ammunition he needed to keep hunting.

The most terrible blessing hidden inside this well-disguised curse was that at first, all of its curses seemed like blessings. Alcohol could make a stupid man feel smart: until he became so stupid he forgot to come in out of the snow one night. It could make a stingy man generous: so generous as to give the use of his wife or daughter to another man for a few bottles of it.

After the fur-traders and the whalers came with their metal, and their rifles, and their alcohol, the most cursed blessing of all entered into not only our lands and our bodies, and our addled minds: this one invaded our spirit-world. It attacked our gods and goddesses, and sought to possess our very souls. The preachers brought it: religion.

Timing wise, the colonizers had things down to an exact science once they reached our far northern lands. Conversion through salvation is a much easier job than torture, so religion followed alcohol. That way the heathens who lived free from sin for a thousand years in balance and harmony with the Earth and the spirits before they got so drunk, were sure to have at least one demon to be saved from. In the case of my people, it became one of many. Alcoholism, forced labor, sexual slavery, disease epidemics: these were the worst of a multitude of curses first disguised as blessings upon us. By the time Grandmother was an old woman, Brother Herman—whose church would later name him a saint—had long died, but many more like him were just as eager to save us from all the sin that had piled up inside our broken souls since the arrival of their kind.

Before the outsiders came, my people believed that all beings were possessed of a yua that animated the living body, and that all things of the Earth: the sea, the sky, ice and rocks even; had an essence of spirit in them that just as much as the living things, required respect and proper treatment in recognition of their interconnected parts of the balance of life. The elemental things not possessed of life were eternal and immutable: rock would forever and always be rock in both its physical and spiritual makeup.

We thought that the yuas of the living beings were just as indestructible; just as eternal. The only difference was that each yua would experience an endless cycle of rebirth into a new living body here on Earth shortly after the death of the old. Rare exceptions existed in yuas like Ahltok's. Its mastery of the Angakkuit ways imparted the ability to cross dimensional planes at will, and the power to control itself in the spirit-world, just as on Earth. It could therefore exist permanently with no need of a physical body. That is not to say that the example of the unbodied yua that had existed physically as the human Ahltok was representative of the attainment of a higher ideal of existence. Unlike some other reincarnation beliefs, each man or woman lived within the guidelines of our traditional ideologies only to create a positive set of circumstances within the individual and communal human lives that were being lived *at that time*. Fundamentally, we perceived no greater honor in the notion of one's yua existing in the body of a human, wolf, or walrus. Since humans were not deemed superior to any other type of animal person, we therefore held no concept of improving the next time, upon whatever incarnation a living thing existed as currently.

The stories, taboos and beliefs that guided the way we lived our lives were structured entirely for the purpose of teaching our people to act in ways that would allow us to remain healthy and fulfilled, existing in peace and happiness now. Had Christianity been preached before the drunkenness, demoralization, and despair that was inflicted on us with the coming of progress and civilization, it would have been an empty message. The difference between God's religion and our beliefs was that we lived in ways that promised a good life for all of us in the present. But as our collective present became more and more miserable with each passing year, the carrot which the preachers dangled from the end of Christ's cross became increasingly enticing. Ultimately, we rejected our traditions because of the essential difference in the objective of the practice of our beliefs, versus those of Christianity. We followed our laws for a good life *now*, but we lost faith in their powers to protect us once that life had again become mired in shit. The preachers said we could follow God's laws for *salvation*... and since the main difference we could discern between what our lives had become on Earth, and what we were told of Hell was the temperature, Lord knows we wanted saving.

By the time Grandmother renamed me, most of my parents' generation had begun christening their children with the names of our oppressors: William Hensley, John Palliser, Robert Grenfell; Matthew, Mark and John. This not only dishonored our heritage, it destroyed the yuas of a great number of those of our ancestors which should have been called back to their places in our living culture through the application of their name-soul to a newborn child. Those left in the ether of limbo between life and the spirit-world which lacked a measure of the awareness and strength of purpose which Ahltok's yua possessed, could not live as pure energy, and simply dissolved.

When Grandmother said that in curing my illness she saw a need within me to be filled by the name-soul of her teacher, what she saw was our people's collective need for the love, guidance, and salvation of our own prophet. By that time nearly all the remaining members of our race knew that a man named Jesus of Nazareth gave up his own life for those who believed in him. They had forgotten all about Ahltok, who gave up his life for us whether or not we ever believed.

Receiving the name Ahltok, however, no more filled me with my predecessor's supernatural abilities, than naming a baby Jesús is guaranteed to give him the power to walk on water, multiply fishes, or heal the sick and poor. But in either case, does it ever hurt to try?

***

For the remainder of her years, Grandmother did her best to instruct me in the Angakkuit ways. The vivid pictures I retained in my mind from the fever dreams were the basis for my best, and perhaps only natural ability as an Angakkuq: storyteller. Because I could describe so clearly what I had seen outside my body in a place so unlike the world in which we all existed, learning the tales and lessons of my people that Grandmother taught to me came naturally, and for a while, even after none of the adults wanted to hear them anymore, the young people of my tribe still listened. Within a few years after Grandmother passed though, even if the children still wanted to hear the truth of what their people had been, most of them would not have even understood.

After we finished helping to pillage our seas, decimating the populations of Sedna's children, and making ourselves poor in spirit, health, and money so that the invaders could ship off the furs and oil to make themselves rich, the progress technicians turned their attentions to the Earth, and began sucking out hundreds of millions of barrels of its thick, ancient black blood every year, to feed their growing hoards of metal machines. All across my people's lands our men and women were relocated from our traditional camps and settlements into work towns. We supplied unskilled labor on the oil fields and were indoctrinated in all of the basest manners of the white culture. With little time to hunt and fish because of the new kind of work, most of our food came in cans sold in the foreign-owned trading posts where the men already exchanged most of their meager earnings for alcohol and tobacco. To alcoholism, diabetes and cancer took their places as close runners-up to the top killer of our race, replacing the smallpox and influenzas that had been the modern diseases of a few generations prior.

Schooling was not offered past ten years old in most of the towns, and since our language was not a written one, and speaking it was discouraged more and more all the time, our young people were gathered up like refugees and sent off as if to internment camps to race-segregated boarding schools as far away as Oregon and Oklahoma. When they came back from these educations, the children that had been away learning English had forgotten most of our language, and the parents with no children at home to help them struggled with the bits and pieces of the foreign tongue they had managed to pick up: the generations of our communities became like foreigners to each other.

On top of the loss of their language, most of the youth who returned to us had also lost their connection to our lands. Deacclimated by southern climates, the Arctic seas and mysteries of the tundra no longer held magic for them: they had simply become places where one might freeze. To introduce something besides alcohol to combat the problem of unrest in its upcoming generation of low-skilled, underpaid workers, the corporate-funded government that controlled our towns began building community centers in all the places where schools should have been in the first place. They were called "community centers," but were essentially gymnasiums. The people were happy to get them though, because not since the existence of our long-disappeared *Qasgit* or men's houses, did they have indoor places to gather other than bars or churches.

By that point in my life back there, the most meaningful work I was able to do as one of the last Angakkuit usually consisted of trying to help drunk men who would have otherwise frozen to death in the night, make it home to their hungry wives and children after being too long in the bars. I would sometimes also be asked to pull a child's rotten tooth with pliers if their pain grew too great before one of their parents was able to get money enough, or sober enough, for a trip to one of the very few real dentists that were sometimes fifty or a hundred miles away from our most isolated towns, even though most of those had the new community centers.

I began to roam our territories like the nomadic

hunters of our first tribes, spurred on by a dream that the centers could be places where our people might finally gather again, away from the debilitating effects of the bars' alcohol and the church's Christian agenda, and begin to mend the torn fabric of our culture. For more than a year I travelled from one town to the next, trying to make my people get to know each other again.

I could not give miracles. There was no salvation in my message. My only promise was in the stories I held in my head and wanted to share and teach, especially to our young people, simply so that they would know only one thing before the knowledge was lost forever: who we once had been. But for every person who wanted to hear the ancestral stories of their people, twenty more wanted me to clear off the gleaming, polished floors of their fancy new community centers, which were the latest "blessing" from the powers who had been with us for so long by then that they were called government, instead of invaders. I was asked to clear off so they could play: so they could play basketball.

***

Before the richness of my people's language was tarnished by disuse, we had a word—*Qivit*—that described one of the worst kinds of shame that a person could be labeled with: it meant "to quit" or give up when the going gets rough. Grandmother used to say that a mountain of reasons must fall on an honorable man to beat him with failure, but that one who *qivits* when things get too hard, lets just one thing beat him.

I let basketball beat me. Night after night I watched and waited for the youth of my broken tribe to tire of running back and forth over the flat, sterile floors of the misnamed community centers, in hopes that even a handful of them might wish to hear their histories.

I tried to convince myself that the game was good for our young people. For the individual involved, I saw some arguable benefit. Those who played could not do well if they had been drinking, so it kept many away from alcohol. Running and jumping helped keep them fit; focusing on the basket taught concentration. But I also saw in the apparently simple pastime of the exercise, another devious subjugation of my people's essential values, and the further unraveling of the tattered fabric of the communal psyche of our race.

Well before the arrival of outsiders, our people had a long tradition of games and athletic contests: Seal Hop; Four Man Carry; Kneel Jump; *Nalukataq* or Blanket Toss. These and other sports focused on honing the cooperative hunting and survival skills that ensured the success and continuity of our generations. Four Man Carry trained the strongest of our hunters in rescue and recovery, for those times when an injured tribe member could not walk back to camp. Kneel Jump training honed balance and speed to survive being caught on moving ice during spring thaw breakup. Nalukataq was the most useful of all: an air-scout could be launched thirty feet into the sky by other members of a hunting party to locate caribou herds, or pick out distant features of the landscape to navigate the huge open expanses of rolling tundra.

People from camps all over our territories would gather for great ceremonies and competition in these games. High honors were bestowed on those who mastered the skills, and the greatest awards were given not only to those with the most physical prowess, but to the ones who best demonstrated attitudes of fair play and team spirit.

Instead of community building, partnership, and the achievement of common goals, the clear result of the endless basketball games I observed was to teach the players that for each victory, another defeat must be mete out upon an equal number of their own townsfolk. For me, the game was a bitter reminder of most every other practice injected into our society by the controlling caste of invaders that had come to dominate my people: winning required losers.

The last night I spent alive in that life, I sat in silence and watched the humiliating defeat of twelve young men, badly punished on their "community center" court by an opposing team of superior players. The losers were the victors' cousins, brothers, and friends, but both the better athletes and young and old spectators alike hooted and jeered at them each time they made an error, or let another two points be scored against them. With each additional basket the stronger team grew more and more bold, intentionally drawing fouls for the sole purpose of knocking one of the weaker players to the floor, and becoming more and more aggressive and arrogant with their insults and haughty challenges. With every swish that dropped through the hoop, my spirit sunk lower and lower. Like the miserable work our men were shackled to, siphoning the Earth's blood off to fill pipelines and tanks that were constantly being drained, I watched our boys fight and sweat and struggle to fill a broken basket that was constantly made empty by the very goal of the meaningless victory.

No one even glanced my way as I stood up from my seat on the sidelines. I left my parka on the bleachers and went into the growing darkness, carrying nothing but a broken heart. I walked out into the night and paused just past the filthy outskirts of the mean little town, and waited for a moment to see if the yuas of my ancestors would reach across space and time and bid me "Continue." But in the deafness created by my qivit, I failed to hear the words in my very own memory that told the stories of our people that I had so wanted others to listen to, and I forgot one of the most important lessons of all: we do not receive, unless we ask. Then in the cold stillness as the night fell around me, I let the black crude of self-pity fill me like a drum. I let it drown the last remnants of my faith in humanity, and even my life-long dream to rebirth my yua in the lands of my Southern cousins. I determined that just like the great Ahltok before me, I would sacrifice myself to the wolf people.

Without a glance back at the lights of the town I plunged into the vastness of the tundra, towards the caribou herds and the wolves that would be tracking them. I knew that without the warmth of my parka I would not survive the freezing night, and began to call to those brothers with all the remaining force of my silent Angakkuq's voice, asking them to search me out in the darkness and accept me into their tribe, trusting that once they received my call, even if I were to die before they reached me, my guts would not freeze solid around the bladder before my essence might be joined with one of theirs.

A pack of their hunters found me just before I succumbed to the freezing night, gliding silently out of the darkness. Upwellings of both sorrow and great relief swept through me, and I spoke aloud in the language we Angakkuit had spoken to Wolf since the days of Yuuyaraq, weeping as I lamented my broken heart, and the failure that I was convinced my race had made of itself. With a sudden shock I realized that the animals which stood before me understood as little of my speech as the oldest and most isolated members of my tribe comprehended English — my tongue had become a foreign language to them.

When my knees buckled as the first two hungry carnivores dragged me down, I was still pleading; not for my life—I had given that up when I walked out of the community center—but for my soul. "Take it! Take it Brothers, and let me walk again in an honorable tribe!" But I had abandoned the bloodline Grandmother christened me with. I was no worthy sacrifice. I was a shame. Within moments the wolves had me gutted, but as soon as the stench of the organs rose from my dying carcass to meet them, the wolves turned their noses up and trotted away into the darkness: the poisoned yua swimming in the piss of my qivit-filled bladder reeked of putrefaction, and as hungry as they were, every last one of their proud race would have rather starved than risk absorbing my dishonor into their people.

But there was someone else roaming the tundra that night who relished the most repulsive effluence to ooze from a man's innards, and who sought any opportunity to play a dirty trick. Though the night was then dark as pitch, I clearly perceived the even darker etching of his shadow, as Raven swooped down to land upon me as I lay dying. Sniffing out the most revolting bit of my scrambled entrails, the black trickster snapped up my festering bladder and gulped it down, then rose heavily into the sky as my leaden yua slid down his gullet, and flew south into the night.

***

Raven had spent much time watching the new white invaders that had come to dominate the human world I had just left behind. Observing their examples, he greatly refined the techniques he had first used to fool my people, by learning to disguise the worst curses as blessings for as long as possible. He would then sate his sadistic appetite for cruel ironies by springing the truth on his victims like a sudden smack in the face, rather than a slow dawning of gradual awareness. As he carried me southward into the warming currents of my aery dream, Raven spun the dry straw of his deceit into the gold of my deepest desire, seeding the thoughts of my captured yua with the lie I was so eager to have sprouted within me: "I wish to make amends for all the times I played a hoax upon your people, Ahltok," he said. "In you I still perceive the spirit of greatness, and though your own race has become deaf to the ancient wisdom, your childhood dreams of the Southern lands were certainly a preface to your true calling. There amongst the descendants of the original Aztecs, you will find a community still hungry for your teaching, and fulfill your destiny as an unbreakable bridge between the spirit-world and all peoples of Earth. The collective soul of Man can be mended before it is too late, Ahltok! Pure hearts that retain the ancient memories of how human animals were supposed to live on this planet still beat in millions, and the cradle of this pulse is Mexico. To expunge the guilt of my own clan, and help ensure the survival of all species before Modern Man destroys us to the last, I will deliver you there, and you and your new brethren shall spread the long-forgotten truth back into the human race, once you are joined together as Juan!"

As desperate as I was to believe something good was coming, I let Raven butter me up thick, and imagined I was seeing the truth through the gaps in the mask of black feathers that was pulled over my eyes.

As he carried my essence south, Raven would now and again allow snippets of sight and sound to penetrate the mask. He carried me like a kidnapped child, trussed up and thrown in the trunk of the getaway car, stopping to give me a glimpse through the keyhole at locations well chosen along an up and down, zigzagging route, mapped out expressly to obscure the location of the hideaway. Past western Canada and through the apple orchards of central Washington he stopped and lifted the shroud for a moment: "Look," said Raven. "There are your Mexicans!" Clearing Oregon and into Sonoma County in Northern California, we paused again in the region where the wine grapes are grown: "More Mexicans," he said. "We are getting close now." Raven flew me past the San Francisco Bay, then showed me brief glimpses of the berry fields of Watsonville, and the vast bread basket of the Central Valley from Fresno to Bakersfield. In Keene, California he took the mask away longer and said "Ya estamos en Nuestra Señora Reina de La Paz, amigo; the Queen of Peace lives here, look! The gravesite of César Chávez! Soon you will be born among those praying to receive the renewed message of balance and equality; but we must take you a bit further south and into the mountains: all lasting prophecies originate in the mountains."

Raven then blindfolded my eyes tightly again and spun round and round in the arid desert currents blowing out of the Mojave over Tehachapi, then playing me like a little boy trying to pin the tail on the donkey, said: "Picture your sweet spirit catcher, Ahltok. Breathe.... Dream." Then, tiring of the miles flown to fabricate his lengthy ploy, Raven shut me off from all sight and sound again and flew fast and far to the punchline of his cruel joke.

When he next lifted the shroud, only visual messages were allowed to penetrate, and those strictly in black and white, grainy and disjointed like an early silent film. We were perched in a tall tree overlooking a wooden building and parking lot full of expensive cars. A man burst from the door of the building, tightly covering one eye with his hand. A beautiful young woman ran out close on his heels, tears streaming down her face as I watched her call out to him, her lips moving with a huge outpouring of silent emotion, as Raven kept the channel switched off to prevent me from hearing the English words: "I'm sorry Marco! I'm so, so sorry! Please, please stop; let me help you!"

Or his reply as he spun around to face her, pulled a ring of keys from his pocket, and threw it into her outstretched hand: "You want to help me? Then drive me to the fucking hospital!"

The handsome man walked briskly to the newest of the big, black Cadillacs parked below us, took his seat as the passenger in his own car, and waited impatiently as the woman fumbled to insert the key into the unfamiliar machine, and pull out of the smooth blacktop surface of the parking lot onto the pot-holed, dead-end road of their accidental short story. High up in the branches of the evergreen tree, once all was as still as a photograph again below I asked Raven: "Where are we?"

"Mexico!" he assured me.

"It doesn't feel like Mexico, Raven. Where are the mangoes?"

"Shhh! You're in Mexico, up in the mountains of Jalisco. These are the pine forests of Tapalpa, high above Lake Chapala. Here you will grow up with all of Mexico laid out below you, and know which direction to carry your message!"

Then Raven slammed the trunk lid shut on my

kidnapped yua once more, cutting off all sight, sound, and perception of time. When he let the silent, scratchy, black and white image seep back through again, night had fallen on the parking lot. It was empty save for the big, black Cadillac, now parked next to an old beat-up gray Volkswagen in the far corner. Raven lifted the shroud on my awareness too late to watch the lawyer and the waitress return to drop her off at her car, or hear his blunt request at the end of their suggestive conversation as he switched the key off, touched his bandaged eye gently and said: "Seems like the least you can do to help me get over all the frustration you've put me through tonight, sweetheart."

All I saw once the curtain was drawn back was the young man's firm rounded buttocks gleaming in the moonlight through the rear window of the car, its paint gleaming as black in the night as the feathers of the evil bird-cage from which I peered. Above his waist, the man's back was still covered in the stiff, starched collared shirt of his profession, while under him the waitress stiffly held back her tears as he pumped the dream out of her and pushed the frustration into her, pumped the dream out of her and pushed the frustration into her....

I watched the rhythmic rocking of the big sedan as Raven glided as silently as an owl out of the branches to land carefully on top of the polished roof. "This is it, Ahltok. Good luck with your mission, amigo."

"What? This doesn't seem right Raven!" I said.

"Whaddya mean not right!" the angry bird said.

"That's a tasty little piece of spirit catcher down in there you ungrateful bastard; smell it, smell it!" With that, Raven switched another channel of sensory reception open, and a rich perfume of sexual musk rushed in.

Enticing as the stewed juices of his Italian sweat and her Scandinavian pussy were, I still protested: "Something is off, Raven: I can't smell the mango!"

"Your yua has still just got fish in its nose from living all those years with those filthy Eskimos, Ahltok; these are Mexicans! Listen: he's speaking Mexican! Listen to the passion!"

Raven flipped another circuit breaker and let the sound of the man's cries rush in as he spouted a string of the favorite phrases his American-born generation had retained from their grandfathers' language: "... minchia, minchia! Prendere il cazzo, Madonna Puttana, Puttana, PUTTANAAAA!"

"He's gonna cum any second Ahltok! Now get in there before I decide to go shit your sorry yua into the sea!" With that, Raven squatted down low, lifted his tail feathers and let his own dirty-white cream spew from his ass onto the Cadillac. As the acidic shit began to eat away the clearcoat over the paint, my substanceless yua dripped directly through the roof and headliner, through the sweat now saturating the man's expensive Brooks Brothers shirt, and into the explosive force of his orgasm as he shot me deep into my seat on that uterine toboggan.

Just before my yua was stripped of all conscious awareness as the amnesic effect of the billions of cellular divisions required during reincarnation set in, my entire being constricted with foreboding as the shock of Raven's last words took hold of me, and one final thought ricocheted through my dispersing psyche: "I thought he said we were next to the *lake!!*"

Now that the slow moon's rose
on a silver trellis grows,
where arctic rivers froze, now that
the ocean is frozen in motion,
snow morning comes.
And the birds on the wing
have nothing left to sing,
blown in blue glass like a
schooner held fast on the ice.
Beside that river where I picked
the slow moon's rose,
I watched the evening wither with
a jewel at the end of my nose.
Tell-tale snails leave their trails,
running from hunters' black
blunderbuss under the sun.

Slapp Happy, *Slow Moon's Rose*
(Acnalbasac Noom)

Chapter 4: **Tight-Assed & Tongue-Tied**

My due date was Nov. 19th. In the P.M. of Nov. 17th I began having contractions of mild intensity but great regularity. Marco timed them and they were coming approximately every five minutes and lasting from 25 - 60 seconds. I had been to the doctor the previous day and discovered I was dilated about one finger and had a little thinning out. Because the contractions were so mild, however, I hesitated to call my doctor so I called my sister-in-law, who has two children (one naturally) and we concluded that it was false labor. Around Two A.M. I was awakened by contractions which were more intense, but after timing a few I concluded that they to were too irregular.

The following morning I was still having contractions. Around 10 A.M. they were coming quite regularly (about every 3 mins.) so I called the doctor and was told to come in for an examination. After examining me during a contraction Dr. Perlite concluded that I was "going to go"; despite the fact that I was still pretty thick, I was almost "two fingers." He suggested that I go to the hospital and he'd join me there later. The contractions were still so mild, however, that I balked and insisted on going to my sister-in-law's in the city to time a few "just to make sure." I did that until the contractions were about 1 min. apart and then I called Perlite again and told him the intervals of the contractions, and also that they were still extremely mild -- "I can't believe this is labor, as it's only vaguely uncomfortable." But he said to go to the hospital so I relinquished and said I would "wander down that way" to which he replied "Don't wander, go directly to the hospital."

My admission to St. Mary's was rather unusual. I wanted to be admitted to maternity and then go visit my brother-in-law who was on the fifth floor. I was told that was impossible; if I wanted to visit I would have to go up and then come back down and be put in a wheel chair and taken back up. As there was no alternative I complied.

I was finally placed in the labor room around 3 P.M. and was thoroughly prepped. I thought this would expedite things, but to my dismay it did not. The contractions were still mild and occurring rather sporadically again (every 1 - 5 mins.) At 5 P.M. Perlite checked in and was surprised that my progress had not been greater (I was still about 2 fingers). He was optimistic, however, and expected me "to go" any time. By midnight, however, the contractions had stopped almost completely. After a fitful night's sleep, I was examined by the doctor again in the morning and he declared that it was false labor and I could go home.

Back home in Sausalito I continued to have false labor until Nov. 23rd (for a total of seven days.) By then, I was feeling very discouraged; I was convinced that I would be like Marco's aunt (a doctor herself) who spent an evening in the hospital as I had and went home red-faced and big-tummied to remain for three more weeks before delivering a <u>very stubborn</u> son! While telling this story to Patty on the telephone, my water broke! This was around 10 A.M., Nov. 23rd. Patty hung up the phone and dashed over from San Fran. After a bumpy, wet ride to St. Mary's we were joined by Marco. I checked in at 10:45 & our son was born 10 1/2 hrs. later, 9:15 that evening.

Although it was a fairly long labor there was only one point during which I felt I was losing control. I was about 5 centimeters, Marco left to go to the men's room, and suddenly I had 3 successive severe contractions. I rang for the nurse, but Marco returned just as she entered and we regained control. Another period of uneasiness occurred when Dr. Perlite had me taken to X-ray. This was around 8 P.M. and he was surprised that my progress was so slow. Fortunately Marco was allowed to accompany me which allayed my fears somewhat. The X-rays revealed two things; my pelvis was smaller than usual, and the baby was a little larger than anticipated (he was expected to be 6 lbs. at most.) When this was discovered Dr.

Perlite apparently decided that the only way I was going to dilate sufficiently was to push. This was awkward as well as painful because I was still in transition and Marco and I both felt I should relax and blow when the urge to push occurred.

About 8:30 (still not fully dilated) I was taken to the delivery room. At my insistence I was not strapped to the table at all and was able to push in the manner we practiced. Dr. Perlite gave me his forearm, he and the nurses all provided loud vocal encouragement, and I raised myself and pulled and pushed (this was all done prior to complete dilation.) At about 8:50 the head crowned. There was a great deal of bustling about then and the Dr. recommended that I have a saddle block. At this point I was tired and admittedly a little frightened so I agreed. After the saddle Marco came in and the baby was delivered within 10 min.

Immediately after the anesthesia came on I was sorry, and felt like I had failed. From that point on I was no longer an active participant, but a numb being that was acted upon. I could see it, but feel nothing, as though I was witnessing something that had no relation to me, instead of one of the most important and dramatic experiences of my life. I still don't know why the doctor was so in favor of the saddle, perhaps it was because of the forceps or the extensive episiotomy. Had I known the birth was so imminent, however, I would not have agreed. Next time I'll know better and be able to participate in the entire procedure and stay brave and keep pushing, instead of praying through my tears that they don't squeeze the next baby's head too hard with those awful "tongs." The other thing I regretted was not having my glasses — if you need them, for heavens sake don't forget them!

In summation I feel the course was invaluable. I would have hated being in labor with nothing to do, no aids for relaxation or distraction, little knowledge, and no husband. Marco was a constant source of encouragement; gave me ice chips, read to me, provided lots of praise, and in general kept me relaxed and confident. Speaking of relaxation, incidentally, the exercises we practiced also helped me in the early stages of nursing—which turned out to be much, much more <u>painful</u> than I had ever imagined—and continue to help me sleep better at night, catch a needed nap during the day, etc.

***

Anne slowly folded the five pages of her writing, penned by hand on sheets torn from one of the lined yellow, legal-sized pads that were always stacked a foot high on Marco's desk. She allowed herself to drift back briefly to that sense of anticipation and resulting joy she had felt at the birth of her son a little less than a year earlier. The first several times Anne re-read her own account of the birth experience, she had cried. It was meant to be shared with the optimistic, happy couples she and Marco had met at their Lamaze class. She had ultimately missed the group's reunion, and the chance to proudly share the personal narrative that their course instructor had encouraged all the new parents to write, with those potential new friends she had imagined staying in contact with.

For at least a week leading up to it she had spoken of little else other than the party. Each morning during the half hour between 5:45 and 6:15 (when Anne diligently forced herself out of bed to join Marco for coffee before he left for the office every day), and again over the late dinners she would have laid out for his return around 7:30 each evening, Anne filled the conversation between them with excited guesses about which couples would have been lucky enough to have baby boys; which of the babies would be the most fair-skinned; how the various new mothers would have caught on to diapering and nursing tricks, and a dozen other random bits and pieces of new-mommy concerns. In return, Marco's infrequent counter-conjectures ran along sarcastic musings as to how the other new dads were enjoying the constant smell of diaper-buckets in their homes, and whether or not their wives' tits had swelled as impressively as Anne's — or grown as constantly sore; untouchable save for the suckling offspring.

Despite her outspoken excitement leading up to the day, on the morning of the Lamaze reunion Marco swigged down his last sip of coffee ten minutes earlier than usual, then before returning to the kitchen from the adjoining breakfast room, pulled his wallet from his blazer's chest-pocket. He thumbed through the thick wad of bills inside, and handed Anne a fifty. It was already after six, and late for her to join him for coffee, but she'd been awakened by Anker several times during the night, and once while attempting to nurse him back to sleep, she herself had succumbed again to slumber in the rocker next to his crib, and fallen into a particularly shocking version of the recent recurring nightmare that she had begun to think of as "the Wolves and the Blood" dreams.

With only two sips of coffee to start fueling her recovery from the hours of ruminating sleeplessness that had followed the dream, and not a word exchanged between them yet, her still-puffy eyes nevertheless lit up happily as Marco extended the cash to her; fully half the amount he doled out at the beginning of each month for her personal needs. Blotting the dream's residue from her mind, she eagerly distracted it by imagining his accompanying words:

Go downtown and treat yourself to a new outfit and get your nails done for tonight, dear. I'll try to make it home early so we can beat the Friday evening traffic over the bridge, and if the weather holds, maybe have a little extra time for a sunset walk out Muir Beach before the party starts in Mill Valley.

Her imagination's rendering of Marco's words were too weak to drown out his actual ones however. Without another glance at her, while first rinsing his empty cup at the sink, then gathering up his briefcase, keys, and glasses before walking briskly out the door, his good-morning to Anne ran like this:

"You look terrible — why don't you go back to sleep? Is that *Hippie-Birth-Day* party tonight? (No need to await her reply; he knew it was.) "Listen, my workload has shot through the roof handling the investigations the office is running on Caltex, and there's no way I'll make it home before ten tonight. I don't wanna squelch your curiosity, so you leave Anker with Nona, and take a cab over the bridge and back so you can tally up the red-headed babies and so on — Oh and, that bill is the smallest I have; get receipts from the cabbies and put the change towards your next month's spending cash."

Anne remained silent as she watched the kitchen door swing shut behind him, heard his brisk, Gucci-loafered steps walk down the hallway, then the front door close, and Marco's key lock the deadbolt from the outside. Even if Anne had had enough coffee in her by then to utter a word in response, she would have held her tongue. One more year of marriage would pass until she grew bold enough to scream at Marco, and the quick bite of rage she felt at being jilted for the Lamaze group gathering would have made a reply in any tamer form of expression impossible. Slumping back into the dinette chair, Anne expertly stifled her anger under another layer of deep-set acquiescence, accumulated like so much sedimentary rock in her over many, many years. Slowly unfolding the pages of the birth report which she had meant to rehearse for Marco before he left for work, she read it silently to herself, slow rolling tears finally dripping down her face as she reflected on her failure to resist the epidural anesthetic pushed on her by the impatient doctor so near to the culmination of Anker's delivery, and the first real hint of her gut-instinct that there would not be a "next baby" with Marco.

Though the missed party had occurred just two weeks prior—the notion of attending a Lamaze class reunion with neither husband nor baby being preposterous to Anne—she had since practically pushed the whole thing out of mind under a day in, day out schedule of mothering duties and seeing to the unpacking and settling of the new house, into which they'd moved just two weeks before the party date. Now when Anne unfolded and re-read the five yellow sheets of her writing, and *imagined* she was presenting her story to the raptly attentive group of assembled Lamaze method parents, the actress portraying herself in her mind's theater felt only pride and satisfaction, and almost no shadow of the earlier wistfulness for the lost connections with those brief peers. She knew, without even having to think the thought, that the friend-memories she kept dialogues with in her head were much tidier than the actual people would have been; people being all too apt to ask their own questions — pry at her memories. So she was happy with the solace she found in another reading of her report to the perfectly cooperative, silently attentive assemblage of immaterial acquaintances.

After a minute of this respiteful meditation, Anne forced herself back to reality, scanning the heaped up stacks of books, boxes of folders packed full of old trial briefs and depositions, and Marco's personal papers that she had still yet to organize and put away in the study of the new flat in San Francisco.

A month prior she, Marco, and baby Anker had moved from Sausalito into the city following another of Vita Volterra's famously generous offerings: after a tenant in her building gave notice, Nona had insisted that they occupy the neighboring unit in her building on Cervantes Street, in order to spare her favorite grandson the daily commute across the Golden Gate Bridge, and allow him to save money for his new family's future by living rent free in her building's largest apartment. With hardly a thought concerning the ramifications of living immediately next door to her grandmother-in-law, Anne happily moved into the sumptuous Marina District apartment, directly connected to Nona's by way of a sliding glass door next to the nursery, in the rear solarium above the back garden which both of the first-floor units shared.

Just as her brief reverie back into recently passed pleasant memories had drawn her away from the chore of organizing and filing the piles of books and papers in the study, Anne's focus was shifted again from that neglected duty by a sudden call from the rear of the flat:

"Anne? *Annie?*" The sound of the solarium door sliding shut at the rear of the house, and Nona's call out to her made Anne jump. As she hurried through the study door and down the long interior hallway past the dining room, the kitchen, and on through the master bedroom towards the adjoining nursery, she gave an angry shake of her head as she realized two things: first, that she had once more failed to immediately hear the baby's low, grinding gurgle of his wake up cry at the end of his late-afternoon nap; second, that his great-grandmother had again beaten her to the side of the crib, having heard the quavering, muted warble of Anker's constricted sobs immediately from her much closer position at the sitting room off her side of the solarium. Anne entered the nursery to find Nona already cradling him against her shoulder, softly cooing Italian nursery-rhymes to soothe Anker, while gently patting his back to stop the trembling that Nona had diagnosed during the week they first moved in as a symptom of bad dreams.

"The poor *bambino* is having nightmares again Annie. You must listen more carefully when he awakens — it is not good for a baby to lie with his mind alone and vulnerable while still under the weave of a bad dream. You must pick him up right away and draw him back to the here and now with you."

Still shaking her head, lips pursed with the effort of civil speech, Anne took Anker from Nona's arms, saying: "*Please* Vita. Please don't call me 'Annie.' My name is *Anne*. And I've asked you several times to leave Anker in his crib until I come for him. With his tongue the way it is, and the quiet... cry he makes, I don't always hear him right away from the top of the flat! Besides, Dr. Rudolf Dreikurs has concluded that immediately coddling a child when they first awaken stunts their development as independent beings. He says in his book "Children: The Challenge" that a little isolation fosters their sense of individuality."

"And bad *dreams*?!" Anne continued. "The boy isn't nearly a year old! It's inconceivable that such a young baby's mind could fabricate dreams at all; good, bad or otherwise! Why, children certainly can't start dreaming until they are at least... well, at least..."

Anne's voice trailed off, her own mind suddenly flooded by a stream of very old dream images, sporadically cut and spliced through with dark frames of silence. The blacked out segments were memories so thickly edited over two decades of censoring by her own psychological survival-mechanisms, that the scenes were no longer illuminable by her adult consciousness.

"Ridiculous!" cried Nona, yanking Anne's attention back. "The two things after food and warmth most essential to development for a young child are simply love and touch — not isolation! That Dr. Dreikurs is a fool, and the foolish parents who believe such nonsense will not only mistake their wonderful, and so brief a blessing for a *challenge*, but inflict a generation of emotional cripples upon the world!" Nona stepped closer to Anne and smoothed her hand gently down the baby's back, who immediately breathed a small sigh and relaxed to help make her point. Then she spoke again in an even, soothing tone to the young mother:

"Dreams begin in the *womb* my dear, not in the *mind*. The Father and the Mother both give a child his physical traits: color of eyes, hair... his stature and temperament. But dreams? They are transplanted in the womb *by the spirit*."

"Just think a minute," Nona went on, "How could any baby survive the shock of entering the dream of this life with no dream *already inside*, bracing his soul against the complex trick of being forced into all *this*?" With these last words, Nona stepped back, spread her fingers wide, and swept her arms out to trace a graceful, perfect circle in the air, which for a split second Anne imagined became a nearly material, luminescent sphere, expanding suddenly out into everything, stretching its soap-bubble-thin skin past the limits of perception, then silently, invisibly bursting all limits. Its sudden expansion spread out beyond the nursery-room; the flat; the city. Like a rushing tide of invisible light, it swept Anne's inner vision out to the farthest corners of the globe, splashing her mind's eye with a thousand millisecond-long glimpses of as many human struggles and triumphs, all helping to shape the ever-changing form of the web of life's human dream in that exact moment.

Flinching back from this impossible hallucination, Anne slammed her mind shut to all further consideration that the old woman had anything important to teach her, and with no concern for further civility held her baby tight to her chest, and loudly repeated her demand:

"As I've already requested, *Vita*, please do not take Anker from his crib! In fact, I would very much prefer it if you would use only the front door to this apartment for your visits — *after* knocking upon it! And you needn't worry about me not hearing my baby's cry," continued Anne. "Marco and I settled upon it last week, and have scheduled next Tuesday with Dr. Perlite to have the membrane cut. He assures me that Anker's vocal development will be absolutely normal once his tongue can move freely, and that the difficulties I've had nursing him will be eliminated as well."

Calmly standing her ground against the incensed young mother, Nona peered intently at Anne, waiting to be certain she'd said all she wanted. The old woman had either been born with, or developed very early on, the extremely rare ability to not take things personally. Still, the matriarch was unused to being told which doors of her own building she might be permitted to use, and made a mental note to make no further attempts to effect a change in the young lady's vision beyond any but the most pragmatic and worldly planes, as she said:

"Be careful, *Anne*. There is no single thing on Earth lacking purpose, and nothing in this dream of life that occurs without reason; including this baby's tongue." With these words, Nona turned and very purposefully walked back to her sitting room just the way she had come — via the solarium door.

Baby Anker's mood seemed to change as soon as Nona returned to her own apartment. His back stiffened, his legs shook with sporadic spasms for a few seconds, then he resumed the strangled, almost gagging hack of his unsettling cry. Anne's nerves crawled with frustration as she again held her son close to her chest, rocking him back and forth at a rhythm that quickened in time with his increasing angst. A lump came into her throat as she looked down at his reddening cheeks and purple-tinged tongue that seemed strapped to the floor of his mouth by a lingual frenulum so short, she had never seen the tip of it reach near the back of his lips, let alone protrude from his little mouth.

Since just after he was born, Anne had been vacillating on the decision to correct Anker's tongue-tie, first detected at the hospital just a few hours after his birth, when it became apparent that she was having difficulty nursing him. *Ankyloglossia*, as explained to her by Dr. Perlite, is a condition in which the narrow membrane that connects the tongue to the floor of the mouth—usually connected at the mid-portion—is attached much closer to the tip of the tongue, and often unusually short. The doctor said that while the abnormality would sometimes correct itself as a child's jaw and teeth developed, it was suspected of causing speech impediments if left untreated, and breast-feeding was almost always more difficult or even impossible. He urged Anne and Marco to allow him to perform a frenulectomy immediately, assuring them that the process was as simple as cutting a thread with a pair of scissors, and was such a simple, low-risk procedure that fifty years earlier, midwives had simply slit the string of skin with a sharp fingernail immediately after the birth of a tongue-tied baby.

The doctor explained all this at the side of Anne's hospital bed in her private postpartum recovery room in the maternity ward of St. Mary's Hospital during his routine examination of the baby three days after his birth. As he spoke to Marco and Anne about the simplicity of the procedure, he took a pair of latex gloves from the dispenser on the wall, then casually removed a pair of blunt-tipped scissors and a paper-wrapped sterile alcohol pad from his white lab coat pocket, and pulled a chair right up to the side of the bed. Swabbing the scissors with the towlette to disinfect them, it was his last statement—repeated verbatim from the day before—that made Anne balk:

"And taking care of this little concern while he's only a few days old," the doctor said, smiling reassuringly to Anne as he reached his left index finger and thumb towards her baby's mouth to pry his tongue up into position for the quick snip. "... means he'll have no recollection of it at all past five or ten minutes from now."

"STOP!" yelled Anne, slapping Dr. Perlite's hand away from Anker's face so loudly and abruptly she shocked everyone in the room.

"God *Damnit!*" Marco swore at Anne for making him jump. "What the hell is the matter with you? Just let him do it for Christ's sake, and get it over with!"

"NO!... No." Anne said again more calmly, her eyes fixed on the scissors in Dr. Perlite's gloved hand. "I just... I just need to think about it. The nursing really isn't that bad," she lied. "And as the doctor said, sometimes it just corrects itself, right?"

By that point in the commotion, Anker had begun his troublesome cry, his tiny body tense and shaking with the effort to drown the adults' shouting out of his ears with the weak efforts of his stifled wail.

"*Jesus* that's terrible!" Marco shouted again. "Let the doctor give the kid his fuckin' *voice* why don't you!" he said, then strode straight out the door, speaking back over his shoulder as he left, "I'm going up to check on my brother, then heading back to the office. I'll come see you at lunch tomorrow."

Following Marco's exit, Dr. Perlite made another brief, futile attempt to convince Anne to allow him to go through with the procedure, then also left the room. As soon as she was alone with her baby, Anne let herself go. Pressing her lips close in to Anker's ear, she added her own stifled sobs to his. Rocking him gently she pleaded again and again. "I'm so sorry baby, I'm so sorry, I'm so, *so* sorry."

As she begged his forgiveness, her mind ran back and forth over her raw memory of the day before: the sudden stream of blood that ran down Anker's leg as Dr. Perlite wiped clean the very same pair of blunt-edged scissors he had wanted to cut loose his tongue with; her certainty that Perlite's promise of "no recollection" was a bold-faced lie, and that the obviously extreme pain that had registered in her son's trusting eyes when the delicate foreskin of his innocent, baby penis was stretched tight, cut off, and discarded in the doctor's steel surgical tray, would surely stick somewhere in his earliest sensory memories for a very long time to come.

***

Although she and Marco had agreed, and an appointment had in fact been made, perhaps her ultimate determination to really go through with the frenulectomy was set by Anne's unwillingness to let Vita have the final word. In the nursery after the old woman's exit, Anne spoke the resolve out loud to herself and her baby once and for all: "Next Tuesday then Anker, Dr. Perlite will fix your tongue-tie, and we will finally get to hear what you really sound like."

Blocking the memory of his cut, bleeding penis out of her mind entirely, she lay him down on his back upon the changing table. As the baby tensed and struggled in anticipation of what was coming, Anne tried to distract him, and tickled Anker under his chin as she used her silly-mommy voice, smiling as she cooed: "Dat widdle tongue-tie will be gone in a snip!"

It wasn't so much that she had difficulty pronouncing *Ankyloglossia*, or that she thought Anker wouldn't understand her if she did. Rather, by always using the simple, innocuous-sounding term, "tongue-tie," she was simply better able to keep from thinking of it as a serious concern.

The other concern first identified at the hospital was something her brain adamantly refused to contemplate in anything *but* the strictest medical terms. No more than a day after he was born, it became clear that the baby's constricted attempts at discharge were not limited to the mouth end of him. Within a few hours of delivery, the nurse in charge of Anne's room determined that a mineral oil enema was required to help Anker pass the meconium that she guessed was unusually thick and sticky, so great was his effort to squeeze it out. More than 24 hours later, once Anne had finally succeeded in getting enough of her milk into Anker so that normal bowel movements should have begun, he was still pushing and straining as much as ever, the meager reward for his labored efforts limited to insubstantial strings of feces not much thicker than the worm-castings scattered on one of Marco's favorite Olympic Club putting greens after a warm spring rain.

After a series of examinations, Dr. Perlite was relieved to diagnose only a mild form of anorectal malformation in the boy. He patiently explained to the new parents that during fetal development, the bottom portion of the large intestine and the urinary tract begin forming as a lumped mass of cells, and that for several weeks during the first and second trimesters of gestation, certain processes have to take place for the rectum and anus to separate from the urinary tract and form properly. Perlite explained that in about one in every five thousand live births, the delicate balance of cell formation is upset. In extreme cases, he explained, children are born with an incomplete connection between the rectum and anus, often with the presence of a *fistula* or opening into their abdominal cavity into which stool will pass, quickly causing internal infections and the immediate need for extensive surgery.

Marco nervously cleared his throat and groaned uncomfortably at hearing this, but Anne burst into frantic tears as Dr. Perlite described this worst-case scenario. She was so mortified that the doctor immediately regretted delving so deeply into his textbook knowledge of physical birth defects, and quickly added: "But have no fear Anne! Luckily, Anker's situation involves nothing of the kind at all. His is the mildest form of abnormality described concerning health issues related to a newborn's digestive tract."

"What's causing your baby's difficult bowel movements is simply a condition known as *anal stenosis*. Essentially, a pronounced narrowing of the anal opening makes it difficult for stool to pass out easily. The good news here is that while the treatment may take several months, or even a year to do the trick, I don't think surgery is going to be required."

Marco coughed again uncomfortably and said, "And just what will the, uh... treatment consist of, Doctor?"

"Quite simple really," said Dr. Perlite. "Twice a day until a satisfactory level of permanent improvement is noted, dilatation will have to be performed using a-"

"Dil-a-tation?" interrupted Anne nervously, carefully enunciating each syllable of the unfamiliar term.

"Exactly," said Perlite, clearing his throat with a little cough of his own, then continuing his careful explanation in the most precise medical terms possible: "Treatment of stenosis involves gentle administration of anal dilatation twice daily, using a lubricated dilator to gradually stretch the anus until it reaches normal-"

"HA!" A single short, sharp, shot of staccato laughter burst from Marco's lips as the doctor's delicately presented explanation suddenly gelled in his head in its simplest form. "So basically what you're saying, Doctor, is that the kid has a tight ass, and that a couple times a day she..." Marco jerked his thumb at

Anne "...is gonna have to poke him with a baby-sized dildo until he loosens up. Have I got that right?"

Dr. Perlite glanced at Marco's amused expression, then down at the floor for a second before taking a deep breath and looking back up at him, then said: "In the *basest* of terms Mr. Frankoni, yes."

Then turning away from the father, he spoke only to Anne as he continued: "Although my best guess right now is that the baby's... opening is so narrow, that fitting even the smallest diameter *dilator* may take some time, and you may need to use your little finger initially — being careful to always use a sterile glove, and keep the nail trimmed very short obviously."

"HA!" Another of Marco's pops of laughter punctuated the end of the doctor's speech to Anne. "Looks like you've got this in the bag Anne. I'll see you tomorrow." Marco said, and walked out of the room and down the hallway, shaking his head and chuckling to himself.

***

Back in the nursery a little more than nine months after coming home from the hospital, Anker's stenosis had still not loosened sufficiently to allow Anne to insert anything larger than her pinkie into his rectum, although she diligently did so twice daily as prescribed. Each time, it was necessary for her to block out the crass reference Marco had made regarding the "baby-sized dildo," along with other much more deeply balled up memories within her, in order to avoid a panic attack of nerves while performing the process.

Like a robotic nurse, she silently focused all of her attention on the clinical nature of her duty: with her left forearm over Anker's chest, Anne pinned him down on the changing-table while he twisted his head from side to side, futilely thrashing his legs in the air in a vain attempt to kick her away. Careful to keep her face out of his reach, she bent to pluck a surgical glove from the box on the shelf under the foam-padded surface on which he lay. She released Anker for a moment, quickly pulled the glove onto her right hand, and before he was able to roll onto his stomach, pinned him again with her left elbow and the flat of her biceps planted across his chest and navel. With the thumb of her gloved hand she popped open a canister of Vaseline, and twisted her little finger down into the jelly until it was well coated all around. Still pressing firmly down with her upper arm and elbow, Anne wrapped the fingers of her left hand under his right knee, and like a giantess wrestling a dwarf, scissored her son's legs apart and rolled his hips up into the air, his weight pressing down on his little shoulder blades as he vainly tried to make a loud, angry noise with the tongue that was stuck almost as firmly to the floor of his mouth, as he was to the table.

Averting her eyes from his, Anne gently coated the rim of Anker's tightly puckered anus with a film of the petroleum jelly, then slowly eased the tip of her finger into it just past the first knuckle. She paused for a moment, took a few shallow breaths as she blocked out a rising swell of unwanted thoughts, and waited until she felt the clamp of the tight pink ring of muscle loosen just enough to push the second knuckle through. Attempting to bolster the fragile top-layer of conscious thoughts in her mind with a padding of benign words, she muttered a string of phrases from the hospital out loud: "Anal Stenosis; Therapeutic Dilatation; Anorectal Malformation.... Stenosis... *Anal Stenosis!*"

Too late! Was it the stress of the move? Or did the exchange with Nona regarding the inheritance of dreams unnerve her? Whatever the cause, Anne's careful focus suddenly crumbled as deep cracks split open in her thought-layers. In horror she realized that rather than holding her finger gently inside her struggling baby's bottom to let the stretch take effect, she had begun unwittingly reaming it as a sulfured blast of suppressed images bubbled up through the rift in her subconscious. Simultaneous with this shock of realization, in terms much baser than Marco's comments on the subject had ever been, ugly words erupted from her pursed lips and she shouted aloud her mind's inescapable interpretation of the act: "*Finger-fucking* my baby's ASS!!"

"Ohhhh NO! No, no, no, no!" Anne shuddered back to reality, her heart pounding uncontrollably as the full impact of her words hit home. "It's OK! It's OK Anker, let go now—come on baby, please, *please*—it's OK!" The child's tiny asshole had clamped down tighter than ever in defense against her poking. Closing her eyes for a moment to compose herself, the flashing image of the mouth of a small tropical sea lamprey that had once attached itself to Anne's leg while swimming on Mactan Island as a young girl, slithered unbidden through her head as she pulled her hand back firmly to extract her pinkie from the equally tenacious grasp of Anker's spasming sphincter.

Anne's terror tripled once she pulled her finger free. With the recent distractions of the move, and daily focus on settling into the new flat, she had overlooked her usual attention to her own self-care routine, and allowed the nails of her normally impeccably manicured hands to grow too long. "Jesus! Ohhh shit... Christ— SHIT!" Anne gasped, examining the mustard-brown and bright red smeared nail protruding from the ragged flap of the glove's torn open tip.

Anker's face turned nearly purple as Anne watched him squirm with hurt and strain. Pushing hard, a wormy strip of poop oozed out of him onto the small white fitted sheet atop the changing table, the taffy-like ribbon of crimson-flecked excrement followed by a tablespoon or more of straight blood that quickly streamed out of him to form a dark stain on the sheet six inches across.

"Oh God! Ohhh no-no-no! Oh my God, Oh SHIT!!" Anne nearly beat her breast in her sudden panic, but instead yanked the ruined glove from her hand and actually smacked herself once briskly on the side of the face. Then, quickly drawing on her deepest reserves of perfectly fermented denial, she instinctively did the thing she was best practiced at — took control of her emotions.

Though her still-shaky hands were slower to cooperate, Anne flew into action with a singular purpose. Left hand grasping both ankles, she lifted Anker's legs and torso up high, leaving only his shoulders and head still resting on the table. She quickly pulled the elasticized corners of the fitted sheet from the foot of the changing table mat, used a clean section of it to wipe the blood and poo from his inner thighs, buttocks and lower back, then rolled it up under his hips to keep the soiled parts from smearing him again.

All the while she worked, Anne kept up a steady stream of talk in the calmest voice she could muster: "Everything's fine. You're OK Anker, you're OK. Don't cry—don't cry sweetie—you're fine." She grabbed a clean cloth diaper from the shelf below and slipped it under him, then with a spontaneous flash of questionable ingenuity, Anne pulled the front of her house dress up, squatted slightly as she pushed her hand down the front of her panties, and tugged loose the still clean Stayfree pad she had placed there earlier that morning in the event of spotting during the tail end of her period. Placing the sanitary napkin inside the diaper, she carefully positioned the thick absorbent pad between the center of her baby's butt-cheeks. She then wrapped the diaper quite a bit tighter around his legs and waist than usual, tucked it up carefully, and affixed large safety-pins with little plastic teddy-bear heads on either side.

Anne scooped her hands under Anker's shoulders and lifted him up to her face. "See Baby? Everything is fine: You're OK... you're OK..." She repeated the words as she shifted Anker gently to her side. Cocking her hip out as far as possible, she settled him gently there, tentatively placing his legs around her waist and balancing him with her arm wrapped up around the small of his back to avoid putting pressure on his behind. Using her free hand, Anne pulled the top corners of the sheet free, rolled the rest of it up, and used the wad of ruined cloth to wipe away the last traces of blood that had seeped through it onto the leak-proof cover of the thin foam changing table mattress.

After a close second look at the surface to ensure that all traces of the mess had been wiped up, Anne looked into Anker's face and forced a careful smile at him. In a perfect display of one of the greatest mysteries of childhood behavior patterns, Anker responded by wrapping his arms around her neck, and even though his cheeks were still wet with tears, smiled for a moment right back, then squeezed himself close to her and buried his face in her long blonde hair; a touching example of the incredible pattern repeated by a million children around the world each day, as they instinctually respond with unconditional love and forgiveness, even towards those who may have hurt them most deeply.

But as darkness follows light, a detestable example of repeated adult behavior patterns was hinted at in Anne's next unrehearsed line. A few fat tears of relief suddenly trickled down her own cheeks when he smiled at her, and with just as little conscious thought to the words that spilled out behind them, she hugged him tightly to her breast and whispered: "Oh thank goodness, Anker — See? You're OK. Everything's fine... you'll be just fine... *It's our little secret.*"

***

Secrets, however, kept themselves with much difficulty around Vita Volterra, who unbeknownst to Anne, had been standing in the shadows behind the solarium door peering intently through the nursery window since Anne's tense expletives had tugged her up from her sitting room chair once more. A witness to every detail of the gut-wrenching scene, Nona nevertheless made no move to interfere with either the young mother's struggle with the helpless child in her hands, or that with the ghosts she could see in Anne's head. Standing perfectly motionless for a full minute after Anne carried Anker out of the nursery, through the master bedroom and out the door leading to the top of the apartment, the old woman finally nodded a brief reminder to herself that there is nothing in life that occurs without reason. Equally true for Nona was the theory that trying to delve deeper into the mystery of "*Why*" is always the best practice, and with that, she silently turned and walked back through her sitting room and on into her own hallway, towards the kitchen and its back pantry steps leading to the garden, where she would gather up a carefully selected batch of snails for a freshly prepared bed of cornmeal.

On her side of the building, Anne's long-established practice of concealment and denial was a near mirror opposite. Upon leaving the bedroom, she moved as quickly up the hallway as possible without jarring Anker against her hip. Entering the kitchen, she pulled the garbage can out from under the sink, removed the newspaper that Marco had tossed there that morning, and dropped the rolled up bloodied sheet into it. She then stuffed the paper forcefully back down on top, burying it as far out of sight as the ghosts she'd pressed as firmly out of mind, having chased them back through the hole in her heart, then blocked their escape from the beating vessel with layered patches of powerful unspoken word-spells—*College Graduate—Lawyer's Wife—Mother*—drowning them until they were once again pulverized against the rock-hard deposits which lined its inner chambers, by the incessant crashing waves of her unaccountably brave blood.

With the evidence disposed of, Anne calmed her pace and carried Anker slowly into the dimly lit study once more, feeling the kind of relief one normally receives after hours of constant stress or worry finally pass, though less than 15 minutes had gone by since Nona had called out to her from the nursery. She cleared a stack of files from the tobacco-brown leather upholstered easy chair and lowered herself into it. Unbuttoning the top of her dress, she slipped a smooth, round breast from her bra and coaxed the nipple into Anker's mouth. After a series of false-starts and adjustments, she got him properly latched on to her and suckling as well as he was able to without the normal use of his tongue.

A baby with free movement of his tongue will naturally use it to cup the mother's nipple up against the front and mid portions of the mouth's upper palate, allowing him to suckle while opening his mouth wide enough to seal his lips around the areola of the breast, positioning her much more sensitive nipple past his lips and bony gums. Anker and other babies born with pronounced ankyloglossia, are unable to raise their tongues up off the floor of the mouth to clamp the nipple against the roof. The only way for these babies to nurse is to pucker their lips into a much more narrowly opened hole, squeezing the mother's teat between the gums, and directly focusing the sucking action much more acutely onto the nipple, rather than the less sensitive areola of her breast. Since most children develop their first teeth between four and seven months of age, kids with untreated tongue-tie are almost never nursed for long, and miss out on additional months, or even years of the profound physical and emotional benefits of breast-feeding. Anker's physical development, however, was markedly different from the charted norms in two notable respects: just before he was eight months old he began pulling himself up on the furniture to take his first shaky steps, but at almost ten months, had not even cut his first tooth.

As soon as Anne was satisfied that Anker had latched on to her constantly sore nipple as best he could, and hardly a trickle of her milk was leaking out around his lips' tenuous grip on it, she closed her eyes, sank back in the comfortable overstuffed chair, and began the deep breathing relaxation exercises she had learned in the Lamaze classes, in half-time measures to the gentle rocking of her cradled arms. Only a few short minutes passed before the painful numbness of the overworked nipple began to spread up over Anne's shoulder, then down her spine to her sacrum, then even lower, her own anus now contracting tightly against a searing cold that seemed as intent on penetrating into the core of her, as she had been while ministering to Anker's stenosis.

Anne's head drooped so deeply that her chin came to rest on her chest under the influence of her slow, steady breaths. Though she had acted as both hypnotist and subject, once under, she was unable to snap herself back out of a paralysis so complete, she was powerless to move anything but her eyes. These she opened, expecting only to see Anker's face, and the dark brown leather-wrapped arms of the chair.

The sleep paralysis was suddenly nothing to the petrifying shock of horror that gripped her: when Anne opened her eyes, she discovered that the chair and room in which she'd sat down upon it had vanished, and that they were floating precariously down a wide wintry river. She sat cross-legged, slumped motionless over the baby in her lap as they both moved along rapidly with the current, stranded atop the center of an insubstantial sheet of broken ice which listed dangerously with the erratic ripples of the river's run. Anne's body itself was frozen as solid as the ice, and she remained unable to move in the slightest anything but her eyes. Rolling them as hard and far around in their sockets as she was able in an attempt to take in as much of her surroundings as possible in the extremely narrow field of vision afforded from her immobile, slumped over sitting position on the ice raft, Anne could see nothing through the curtain of hair that hung down all around her face but fast flowing, freezing gray water on her right side. On her left, she was just able to detect the river shore; a barren line of rocks and boulders, occasionally broken by a washed up drift-wood log, or even entire uprooted tree, all thickly dusted with snow.

Anne couldn't see more than two or three yards beyond the edge of the ice sheet before her eyebrows blocked her downstream view, and so had no warning of the whitewater bubbling just ahead. Sliding like a soapstone statuette across the polished surface of an upset coffee table when the chunk of ice first plunged forward into the rapids, Anne and Anker were nearly pitched headlong into the swirling whitewater before the counterswell of the next swirling eddy surging up from the boulders below tipped its aft end back. A jarring crunch shuddered across the careening ice sheet as a hunk many times the size of their meager raft slammed into it from the right side, its irresistible force shoving them several feet further to the left. One horrifying moment later, the barge of ice that had battered them slammed into the thick trunk of a partially submerged tree. Great spear-head shaped pieces of it broke off and rotated fast through the current, pushing Anne and her baby closer and closer to the side. The surging ice floe chunks nearly capsized them once again, then butted the edge of their badly fractured ice craft hard up against the frozen riverbank.

Once they'd run aground, every shred of Anne's will strained to leap to the safety of the shore, but she remained as petrified as the snow-covered rocks strewn up and down its length, still only able to shift her eyes in their sockets despite her most desperate attempts at movement. Fixing her attention on the baby in her lap, she saw that Anker was wholly unfazed by it all. Seemingly oblivious to the freezing spray of water splashing all around them as the rushing river caught against the lip of their beached sheet of ice, he lay in her arms more relaxed and at ease than she had ever seen him. Peering intently into his eyes, Anne watched with fascination as the hazel sheen imparted to Anker's irises by the blending of Marco's deep-brown eyes, and Anne's blue, seemed to lighten until they took on an amber-yellow hue unlike any she had ever seen painted on the windows to a human soul.

Anne then felt the grip of all physical sensation slip from her, and the biting cold of her icy seat faded into a nearly imperceptible numbness. The paralysis weighing down her rock hard limbs melted away, though she continued to sit as stock-still as before, her rapt attention now completely entranced by Anker's preternatural gaze, fixed hungrily on her as he continued nursing in her lap. Forcing her attention beyond the glow of his mesmerizing orbs, Anne marked with fascination how deeply her breast was drawn into his greedy mouth. His entire face and jaw seemed to have somehow lengthened, and the wide open, hard-sucking lips stretched well past the dark areola as nearly half of her squishy breast meat disappeared down his mouth.

Anne sighed in a near ecstasy of relief as her swollen tit was drained of the warm, nourishing milk.

A moment later, ecstasy turned to intrigue, then bewilderment, as she watched in fascination as her baby's mouth curled up in a toothy grin. Still dazzling her with those brightly glowing, inhuman yellow eyes, the now definitely shape-shifting child let the empty breast slip from his mouth. He reached for the next tit with a pair of grotesquely misshapen hands, the nails protruding from each of his fat, stubby fingers all black and thickly rounded, curving like crescent moons into sharply pointed tips. With these, Anker swiped at the thin fabric of Anne's soaking wet housedress, ripping a gash in the cotton through which fell a second helping of plump, ripe milkmelon. Parting long, loose lips again, the boy stretched a fat pink tongue six inches past the end of his mouth and wetly lapped at the full round jug of creamy flesh.

A dimly remembered slice of childhood fairy tale floated up into Anne's mind, then out her mouth as she said aloud, "But Anker — What a big tongue you have!" Too surprised to consciously register that both her eyes and mouth had been freed of the paralysis that still gripped the rest of her body, a shrill scream nevertheless escaped her lips as the full impact of the child's nearly complete transformation suddenly dawned on her.

The creature that she had been cradling in her lap only a few moments before had grown to five, then ten times the size of a human baby. It opened its mouth wide, exposing rows of sharp canine teeth dripping with milk, then savagely clamped down on Anne's breast, sending a blasting wave of pain through her whole body as the keen fangs deeply punctured the tender sphere of flesh. The beast that had been her baby set all four of its drastically deformed limbs against the surface of the ice. A deep, ravening growl rose from its chest as he bit down even harder. Claws scrabbling against the slick deck of the ice raft, the monster then yanked and toppled Anne off onto the rocky shore, where she screamed again in pain and terror as it fiercely shook her in the steel-trap of its toothy maw. Anne peered across the top of the rough snow-covered rocks of the riverbank, and perceived the opening of a dark lair at the base of a jumbled pile of logs and boulders some 15 feet from the water's edge. Towards this hole the still mutating wolf-son began roughly jerking her over the rocks and snow.

As the creature pulled Anne closer and closer to its pit, the last vestige of its human form was fast disappearing. The bony stub at the base of its spine lengthened into a long naked whip, then from the tip of the suddenly sprouted tail running back towards its haunches, a thick, grayish-black fur began to cover its smooth caucasian skin. The jarring of her bones over the rough rocks shook the paralysis from Anne's limbs, and she began flailing and clawing at the beast's back and sides, desperately ripping great tufts of thick, oily hair from its skin in an attempt to prevent the cloaking of this remaining trace of its humanity.

The monster's efforts only quickened under her attack. Anker straddled the mother with all four of his enormous hairy paws, tightened his bite on her badly bleeding tit, and continued dragging her even faster towards the den. Once hidden in the half-light of the dirty cave below the tree trunks and boulders, the ferocious babe commenced to feed. Anne's shrill scream was choked short as a thick clot of bile rose up from her sickened stomach when the teeth ripped into her chest for a hungry bite of the breast meat. In silent fury now, she raked her fingernails faster and faster, harder and harder, against the ribcage of the vile thing. Though the fur flew thickly through the air as Anne scraped large bald patches across the creature's sides and shoulders with her violent scratching, the exposed hide below was now nothing at all like the living skin of either human or animal, but rather a thick, tanned, weather-toughened leather.

For several seconds right before Anne blacked out, she saw the distinct mold of human features morph over the creature's wolven shape once more. Anker's snout drew back from the gaping hole in her chest, and his jaws shrank back to human proportions. All perspective on time and space orientation were skewed on several other planes, however. The impression that her son had pulled his head away from her body to look into her eyes seemed turned entirely upside down, and instead it was Anne's sensation of floating up above his head that put her out of his reach. Nor was this to be confused for some pre-death, spiritual experience: Anne was not looking back down at her body as the creature continued to maul her — this was her entire form, all psychic and physical parts, minus the ripped out flesh of her breast, intact and levitating. As she peered down at Anker's rehumanized features, Anne was not surprised—indeed she was past all surprise—

to recognize her son's face in the man that now stood erect, looking up into the sky from below.

It *was* Anker. A very acute examination of him was impossible, as the rays of daylight filtering into the den—indeed even the hole in the earth below the rocks and logs; the riverbank; the very river itself—were all gone, but yes, the person was very definitely her son, and she knew him in both her head and her heart. But physically, this Anker was as unknown to her as the wolf-son. This was a man, or something very close to it at least. A young man; mid to late 20's, with dark chestnut-colored hair and a face that looked as if it could wear a kind smile. He stood motionless, almost without breath upon the soft ground of a forest floor. The beastly amber glow in them had disappeared, but his gaze was no less disturbing as he stared intently into the sky with eyes colored starkly black and white. Any color at all was completely obscured by the man's enormous pupils, stretched beyond all normal limits, as if opened wide by some ancient, powerful drug, or the supreme shock of witnessing something far beyond the realm of wonder. The last conscious thought that flitted through Anne's mind concerning the mannish version of her son that stood transfixed below her, was the awareness that he stared directly at the space in which she floated with the huge, jet-black pupils, but as if through an invisible gas, without seeing even a ghost of her shadow.

No sooner had Anne formed that thought in her mind, Anker appeared to see her very clearly indeed. Shock and awe registered suddenly in his face as the extraordinary eyes locked directly onto hers. He reached out to her and opened his mouth to speak, but instead of words, a black gush of what must have been a throatful of blood from his feeding on her spewed from between the disguised monster's lips. Even so, the mother instinct overrode all other emotion in Anne as Anker turned to run. Notwithstanding the unfamiliar guise of the young man, Anne's drive was to protect and console the spirit of her child. The moment he ran from her, Anne cried out: "It's OK Baby — Wait!"

She flew after him. As soon as her hand clutched his shoulder, the transformation from man to monster snapped back into play with full and immediate effect: with a quick flash of its powerful jaws, her instantly rebeastiated child flipped her out of the air back onto the ground beneath its crushing paws, and fell to devouring along with the great chunks of flesh he bit from her chest, the blind care and trust that had so heedlessly burst forth from her.

Just before the last convulsions of her death throes, Anne screamed at the monster: "Don't you know you'll kill me, Anker?? You'll kill me! Anker! You'll KILL me!!"

One last dim spark of recognition flitted across the lenses of the creature's jaundiced eyes, as for a moment it stopped and stared at Anne, globules of crimson-stained fat from the mammary tissue dripping into the mutilated chest cavity. It extended its long tongue once again and lapped gently at her impossible wounds, then baring its fangs, with the force of a bullet it punched its muzzle in all the way through her ribs for the killing bite, rupturing the heart and sending a hot stream of blood coursing down her chest, belly and thighs as the blackness took her away.

***

"Anne? Anne... *ANNE!*" Marco had come home slightly earlier than usual. Entering the silent apartment, he walked first to the kitchen, annoyed to find that his pots were cold. Still carrying his jacket and briefcase, he traced his steps back up the hallway and pushed open the study door with his foot to find his wife and son both asleep in the dark. Shrouded by the long blonde hair cascading down from Anne's head into her lap, Marco could just make out by the light cast into the room from the hall, the figure of the child sleeping fitfully there. The boy lay sporadically twitching his head back and forth, and opening and closing the little mouth framed by lips pursed and shining with a sticky coating of the last sips of the milk he'd sucked from his sleeping mother, her dress soaked through all the way down to her waist with the leakage.

Marco's heart skipped a beat for one split second after turning his attention to Anne. She sat so deeply hunched over and motionless that for a moment the word "dead" flashed through his mind. She was certainly dead to the world, and for the brief interval after Marco pulled the chain to light the room by the floor lamp standing next to the easy chair, she remained absolutely unresponsive as he first began calling her name. Finally she muttered a few muffled sounds from behind the curtain of blonde locks; the merest traces of the words she was shouting in her head, deep below the icy hold of the dream-paralysis.

Though still asleep, enough of Anne finally broke through to resurface in the present that her head flopped back up against the chair cushion. Before she opened her eyes though, Marco watched uncomfortably as every muscle and tendon in Anne's forearms and hands stood out with extreme strain and pressure, as her fingers clenched the arms of the leather upholstered chair with all her might. Marco jumped in shock when Anne's eyes suddenly snapped open and she screamed aloud: "YOU'LL KILL ME!!"

"Fuckin' God *Damnit!*" The oath burst from Marco's lips with the jolt of adrenaline her violent awakening had shot into his bloodstream. "What the *Hell* is the matter with you??" Marco yelled.

The shouts of his parents shocked baby Anker out of his uneasy sleep, and he immediately set up the loudest din his handicapped tongue could muster, assailing their ears with a high-pitched wailing growl. The noise spooked Anne tremendously. With a freakish whimper she shrank back into the chair as if to get as far away from the baby as possible, crossing her arms tightly over her chest as if to ward off an evil force.

Very concerned now, Marco dropped his briefcase and jacket on the rug and was about to put his hands on Anne to try and calm her, but then he noticed the arms of his favorite reading chair, the smooth patina of its supple leather upholstery badly marred by the scraping of her nails.

"Jesus H. Fuckin' Christ on a Popsicle Stick! What

the *Hell*?! Can you tell me just what in God's name is going on with you?"

"Actually; you know what? I don't wanna know! Go to the front closet, get the bottle of fuckin' neatsfoot oil I use on my golf bag, and rub these goddamned marks off my chair right now!"

After delivering his instructions, Marco bent down and picked Anker up from her lap, then walked out into the hallway towards the kitchen. With a sudden jolt of paranoia, Anne leapt up from the chair and hurried to do as she'd been told, wondering how much time she might have before the "secret" was discovered. Moving as fast as she could without arousing his suspicions, she scurried to the front hallway closet for the leather conditioner. She passed him in the hallway on the way back into the study as Marco exited the kitchen with his crying son in one arm, his free hand clutching a tumbler of ice cubes headed for the spacious living room overlooking Cervantes Street.

With a frenzied application of elbow grease and neatsfoot oil, Anne rubbed out the ugly marks on the chair's arms as best she could, then hurried into the living room. Opposite the ornate marble mantel of the fireplace upon which his second Camel burned in a fancy glass ashtray, Marco stood at the built-in bar cabinet pouring himself another three fingers of whisky when she walked in. His unpracticed attempts at soothing his crying son—breathing alcohol and tobacco fumes into his face as he bobbled Anker in the crook of his arm—were not producing the intended effect, and he was relieved to give him back to Anne as soon as she appeared.

Marco glanced with disdain at his wife's disheveled hair and milk-stained dress as he passed the baby off. "Why don't you go get yourself cleaned up. Bring the boy over to Nona and we'll go get dinner at the restaurant, since there doesn't seem to be any around here tonight. And you'd better change him first: whatever you're doing to his butt finally seems to be working; I feel a nice sized lump down there."

Anne looked coldly at Marco, wondering to herself why she should have worried for a second that he might even peek into his baby's diaper, let alone think of ever changing one. Returning his disdainful look she said simply: "Go by yourself," and walked on down the hall.

***

The following Tuesday evening Marco remained in the apartment for all of five minutes before leaving to go eat by himself at the restaurant again, even though Anne was hurrying to get dinner on the table when he arrived home.

To Anne's great relief, by that morning all traces of the blood she had detected in Anker's stool during the three days following her frightfully botched *dilatation* of the baby's anus had disappeared, for true to her word to Nona, she kept the morning appointment at Dr. Perlite's office to have his frenulum cut. As it turned out, Anne's concern that the wound she had inflicted inside Anker might have been discovered was unnecessary, as when the doctor entered the examination room he said:

"We're going to keep this real easy today, Anne. The quicker we get Anker out of here, the quicker he'll forget all about it, so I'll check progress on the stenosis at your next appointment." He put on a pair of surgical gloves, and picked up the already sterilized scissors from the steel tray on the counter.

"Ready?" asked Dr. Perlite, checking in with Anne to quickly ascertain that he was not at risk for another of her sudden slaps. With a silent nod, Anne held her breath and tightly shut her eyes as the doctor pinched Anker's tongue firmly between his thumb and forefinger, carefully slipped the blunt-edged scissors around the stubby membrane under it, and with one quick *snip* ...set in motion a chain of events that led almost as quickly to his parents' divorce, as the surprise of Anker's conception had to their marriage.

***

With her eyes still shut tight in the doctor's office, one of the most disturbing of Anne's unrepressed memories from childhood in the Philippines suddenly burst into her head a second after the barely audible *snip* of the doctor's scissors:

Anne was nine years old when Joy brought her and the family maid to the market stalls in Angeles City to buy a suckling pig for their annual Easter *lechón* party. Because of her disappointment with the quality of the previous year's meat, the maid insisted that it must be very fresh and healthy, and in her mind the only way to be sure of this was to examine it "on the hoof," as she said. A plump, handsome example was carefully selected from a crowded pen full of live animals at the back end of the market, and after the traditionally expected haggling was done, the pig vendor hopped into the enclosure with a short length of rope, quickly threw a loop around its neck, and tied it up firmly against the side of the pen rail.

By the early 1950's, most American kids only ate meat bought from butcher shops and grocery stores, and the young ones often had no concept of the farm-to-table realities that put food on their family dining tables. Growing up in the much less sterilized and commercialized environment of the third-world tropics, Anne was in no way confused about where meat came from, and was certainly clear on the purpose of the shopping trip that day. Nevertheless, something pulled at the strings of compassion inherent in all little girls as she watched the pig seller raise the shining blade of the killing knife above the animal's adorable pink head, poised to stick it hard between the base of the skull and the neck for a quick clean death.

"STOP!" Anne yelled just before the moment that the blade came down, surprising the man and throwing his well-practiced hand off the mark. The edge of the blade glanced forward across the skull, cleaving a bloody gash down the side of its head and across the eye-ball and tender snout, splitting it open like a beggar child's cleft palette as the piglet opened its mouth and *Screeeeeeamed!*

On the morning Dr. Perlite cut her baby's tongue loose, that fat little pig's excruciating scream of agony was finally dislodged from its position in Anne's memory as the loudest and shrillest sound she ever heard come from a living creature. Her eyes popped open at the intensity of Anker's first full-blown shriek, and it was all she could do to keep herself from clapping her hands over her ears and letting him slip from her lap onto the tile floor below the exam table. Perlite was lucky enough to avoid jabbing the scissors into the side of his own head when he stuck his index fingers in his ears to drown out the boy's howl. Throwing out a quick laugh to mask his own surprise at the results, he had to raise his voice almost to a yell to be sure Anne heard him.

"Wow! That did the trick, eh? Go on and get him home Anne. Don't stop at reception on the way out — Nancy will drop the bill in the mail. Swab diluted peroxide on the cut after each nursing for the next few days, and call us right away if you see infection. Oh, and better tell Dad to start saving for music lessons Anne: sounds like you and Marco have an opera singer on your hands!"

When Marco returned home at dinner time that first evening, his son's formidable new vocal ability was *not* music to his ears. The doctor's promise that Anker would forget the experience of having the delicate membrane cut loose after a few minutes, seemed as false as Anne suspected the one about his circumcision had been, and all day long he fussed and complained with the loud new cry. The one huge relief for Anne was that Anker's ability to nurse had changed just as dramatically as the tone and volume of his voice, and she was thrilled to discover that he instinctively modified his sucking action on her from the first, taking her entire nipple deep into his mouth well past the hard bony gums that had made her so sore for so long. Each time he nursed however, the cut under his tongue would reopen within a few minutes of starting, and before he'd gotten nearly enough in him, would spit out a thick pink froth of milk, blood, and drool with a howl. No matter how close he was to falling asleep, once the blood flowed thickly enough to make the milk unswallowable, Anker's own loud angry yell would snap him back from the brink of it, thus preventing him from napping all day, and making for a very cranky boy. Anne, consequently, had achieved nothing beyond preparing dinner, and was rushing to complete even this when her husband appeared in the kitchen after twelve exhausting hours at the office.

Marco stood motionless in the doorway, staring in disbelief at what seemed to him like a scene from Lewis Carroll's kitchen. A saucepot over a burner obviously set too high was dropping splashes of a phlegmy ooze all over the stovetop as the thick bubbles in Anne's lumpy gravy popped out all over its surface. Her attempts to stir this periodically while rummaging through the dirty plates, utensils and glasses in the dishwasher that had not been run, in an attempt to find two matching sets of each to wash by hand, had her skipping from one side of the kitchen to the other. A pan of misshapen dumplings were congealing on the counter next to the sink amidst a jumble of dirty bowls, mixing spoons, and the remains of a spilled bag of flour; traces of which could be seen wiped across

Anne's left ear and cheek, and down the shoulder of her dress. In the sink itself, balanced delicately upon a small pile of more dirty dishes, was a roasting pan in which an overdone chicken seemed to have been pulled apart by hand into serving-sized chunks, rather than carved with a knife.

None of the noise that should have been audible from Anne's frenzied efforts with the gravy and the dishes could be detected in the slightest over the terrible cacophony happening on the kitchen floor. To keep Anker distracted and allow her the use of both hands while preparing the meal, Anne had opened the low cupboard in the corner where cookie sheets, bread pans and muffin tins were kept so that he might amuse himself. Clearly past all amusement, Anker was kicking his legs out on the floor in front of him, scooting around angrily amidst an assortment of clanking bakeware on the slippery pajama-bottomed butt that was still only a little less sore than the newly freed tongue. He held in one hand a cupcake tray, and in the other a bundt cake pan. These he beat together spastically like the two crashing brass symbols of a mechanical circus-monkey doll with its spring wound too tight, as he screamed and screamed and *screamed* louder than any child Marco had ever heard in his life. Anne glanced up from her gravy pot and shouted, "Dinner will be on the table in five minutes, Marco." Then dipping the same finger into the gravy twice to be sure of the taste, completed the mad scene for him when she shook her head and said, "Needs more pepper!" At this, Marco—wanting nothing to do with such a tea-party—turned around and calmly walked back up the hall and out the front door without a word.

By the time he telephoned from the restaurant just after nine o'clock that night, Anne had thrown away all traces of the spurned meal, cleaned up the kitchen, finished crying, and finally gotten the exhausted Anker asleep in his crib. She assured Marco that it was safe to come home, and was already in bed herself by the time she heard him walk down the hallway, undress in their walk-in closet, brush his teeth, and climb under the covers next to her. Minutes of silence passed in the dark between them, each waiting to reply to what neither of them knew how to begin. It was Marco who finally caved to the inevitability of their plight, speaking volumes on the fractured love between them with just two little words: "Goodnight Anne," he said, and rolled over and fell asleep.

Nearly two whole hours passed before they were both jolted awake. The near demonic scream that ripped the still fabric of the night was so loud, that the doctor's comparison to an opera singer in describing Anker's unbridled new voice talent proved a just analogy; provided only that one imagined the child in the role of Mephistopheles. Up until that night, Marco had slept soundly until the chime of his 5:00 AM alarm-bell each morning. Only Anne, who had conditioned her ears to hear Anker's low-volume mewling when he woke up for a diaper-change or nursing at night, was ever disturbed from sleep, and then usually only once or twice before morning. By the time the sun rose on the dark bags under their blood-shot eyes on that first morning after Anker's tongue obstruction was cut, however, their son had woken them up five times in as many hours with his hellish cry, and any chance there might have been for the young couple to repair the bad feelings left by their total lack of communication the night before, was lost forever in the frazzled haze of sleep deprivation that gripped them both.

After the third night of this crazy-making sleeplessness, Marco laid down some new rules: Anne would no longer allow the baby to nap during the day, and would observe a strict 7:00 PM bedtime for Anker, so that his son would be sleeping by the time Marco returned home, which he now started doing at eight o'clock or later, so that Anne would have time after the baby went down to prepare his dinner properly. None of it mattered. For five or six hours past seven o'clock, the exhausted child slept like a rock from being kept up all day. Inevitably, some time after midnight— sometimes even past one or two in the morning, but never later—the high-pitched, terrified shrieking would rip through the silent house for the first of an average half dozen times throughout the night.

A week into the pattern, after phoning his sympathetic aunt, who was director of psychiatric services on the fifth floor of St. Mary's Hospital, Marco came home with a bottle of a hundred Valium pills. It took just two nights to find the perfect recipe — three pills swallowed down with a half-tumbler of scotch or bourbon put Marco into an all night sleep that could have survived a college marching band competition, never mind the opera. Problem solved, he urged Anne to take a couple herself and join him in the sleep of the dead. For Marco, Anne's vehement refusal to try even half of one of the harmless sedative pills, was just one more of the perplexing mysteries of the young woman he'd married five months before the birth of their son, and another reminder of just how little he really knew her.

Night after night Anne lay next to her unconscious husband, sometimes snatching an hour-long catnap between Anker's outbursts, other times just staring into the dark, doing her best to stay focused on the puzzle of what might have caused such a complete and abrupt disruption in his sleep patterns, in order to blot out much more unpleasant topics that always threatened to invade the nocturnal meanderings of her sleep-deprived brain. Anne's best guess was that the double dose of discomfort from the frenulectomy and the dilatation therapy had combined to produce a physical reason for Anker's hourly night fits, and she stopped stretching his anus for several weeks, even long after the severed membrane under his tongue had clearly healed. The impenetrable truth, however, was that the root cause of the terror that manifested itself in the child's screams was hardly physical. Nor was it psychosomatic, as it technically had nothing to do with baby Anker's *mind*. Rather, his was a problem of spirit; or to be even more precise — *Spirits*.

***

When Nona told Anne that an unborn child's dreams begin when they are transplanted in the womb by the spirit, she split into terms with which Anne was familiar, the conjoined mystery that is a fusion of two parts that can never be wholly described using the words *spirit* and *dream*; though no two more accurate ones exist in any language. What she did not explain is that each part is consubstantial with the other; that neither one can exist apart from the second. An apt comparison can be found in the way that Christian theology seeks to explain the greater mystery of all that "God" is by teaching the Holy Trinity: a force composed of portions of a whole entity that are distinct, but can never exist apart, as the one substance must by its very nature cease to exist if any of its elements are eliminated.

What Nona could not explain, was the knowledge beyond even her intuition of the endless variations of extraphysical manifestations of this force, which if one had to label in a similar fashion by choosing a single sound in language just as woefully unable to describe all the wonders that "God" is, "Soul" would by default be the logical choice.

Dr. Perlite, with his decades-long knowledge of the flesh, had done a good job explaining the anomalies that occur during early cellular formation in roughly one in every five thousand live births. An elder healer of an entirely different sort—of the type whose practices transcend the corporeal in ways that the likes of pragmatically educated men such as Perlite could never fathom—might have explained that the problem evidencing itself in Anker's night-screams was the result of a phenomenon occurring in about the same percentage of all fertilized ova. In these very rare cases, for reasons nearly as varied as the number of instances that occur, sparks of a unique soul will ignite themselves within a developing human fetus that has already been lit by another.

When this occurs, one of three things normally follows. Most often, the dominant soul simply extinguishes the weaker one. Nearly as often, two equally matched and aggressive souls will smother each other out, resulting in the stillbirth or miscarriage of the flesh. Much less often, two souls well practiced in the magic of love will merge into one entity: the rare human beings that are animated by these powerful essences have always been the cause of the most positive evolutionary advances of our race.

An extremely uncommon fourth alternative plays out in less than one percent of these already rare cases. When this happens, both souls remain separate and viable after the birth of the infant host. Most people born with a set of these dual, independent souls suffer from severe mental disorders from infancy until death. Many commit suicide. The luckiest recipient hosts of dual independent souls are able to move through life and society almost identically to people with only one, usually because the older, wiser soul will choose to place itself in remission when the host person is still in very early childhood, well before the time that speech development begins. These souls may remain silent for an individual's lifetime, or assert influence over the host in one way or another several times in a year, or once in three decades. The perceived effect of such visitations upon the affected person can range in intensity from a feeling of mild déjà vu, to a visitation from God, or demonic possession.

***

Not long after conception, the rapidly dividing slivers of tissue that would become Anker Frankoni was possessed of a powerful new soul. Composed of the same ancient material that created the solar systems of our universe, it was a self-actualized manifestation of strong, fresh spiritual energy, catalyzed by a perfectly balanced, clean dose of dream essence. This soul was also imbued with a finely tuned synchronicity between it and the pulses of the terrestrial and heavenly worlds. It detected these vibrations—from the beating of Anne's heart all the way to the revolution of the planets— and reacted intuitively to their signals; witness its influence on its host's and mother's physical bodies, delaying Anker's birthday until the 23rd of November in order to align with Sagittarius, and avoid the grave complications of spending a human life on earth as the Scorpio issue of two intensely mis-matched Scorpios.

As perceptive as the new soul was, even it could not detect the presence of one that had lodged before it in the multiplying microscopic cells just seconds after conception. This was a very old soul, almost prehistoric, having come through generation after generation of human hosts, and none truly part of the modern age. But it was a soul misguided by its own faltering perceptions. It was driven to enter the vessel seeded in Anne by a confused sense of desire that was planted in it by the dying passion of its former host. This passion overwhelmed all the spiritual knowledge it had accumulated through so many cycles of existence. This was a soul willing to risk all of its distilled wisdom for one desperate shot at a dream. It was a resilient soul however; a patient soul. Aware almost immediately that fatal navigational errors had resulted in a crash quite far from its mapped landing, it sank itself, like a vampire going into the earth before dawn, into the deepest recesses of the pin-head sized clump of cells growing within Anne, where it might patiently remain frozen in silence to wait out that short human lifespan for its next chance.

So it was that the new soul destined to animate the body of Anker perceived the vessel as unoccupied. To sense the presence of the old one withdrawn so deeply, would have been like detecting flecks of crystal locked below the surface of a granite rock, simply by examining its dull gray, weatherworn surface with the naked eye.

Anker probably would have lived out his entire life as much aware of the dormant hidden soul, as a man who never develops appendicitis is affected by his appendix. But even ancient vampires may awaken from millennia of stony slumber if their tombs are invaded too deeply. As frozen as the soul was in the darkest secret chambers of baby Anker, it was still not buried far enough beyond the reach of the host's cellular synapses to be unaffected by the waves of pain that penetrated the child's body from the three tenderest parts of him. In addition to the abrasive signals of the invading physical pain, a veritable riptide of psychic energy spilled regularly from the dreams of wolves and blood that gushed from Anne's psyche at night, beckoning to the old soul's primitive instincts like the call of Cthulhu.

On the night of the frenulectomy, the awakening of Ahltok within the baby Anker finally came on with a sudden violent rage, like that of a captured wild beast finding itself behind bars once the dart gun's sedation wears off. In its habitat, the beast is majestic to behold; a thing of powerful beauty that moves through its territory with the sure presence of instinct and purpose. Caged where it knows it does not belong, a wild thing's graceful ease turns to panic, its repertoire of fluent movements and natural behaviors quickly reduces to endless pacing and manic repetitions of the same deranged cry or snarl.

The beast that paces the cage of baby Anker's head is the trapped wild essence of the awakened Ahltok, made even more terrifying to the boy because he is trapped in the cage with it, and it is inside of him. Night after endless night the child screams himself awake over and over again as the horror congeals. Only the physical components—lungs, mouth, tongue, and the ear-splitting shrieks that burst from them—belong to Anker: the nightmare is Ahltok's alone.

The unbroken walls which surround it are whiter than any snow remembered from the last place it held a human form. Words do not exist in this empty cell. Color does not exist in this empty cell. Love does not exist in this empty cell. Ahltok can not take solid form, but the mist or static that it is will not disperse or fade — Ahltok is both trapped in and made of nothingness. Nothing exists but confusion. Nothing exists but loss. Nothing exists but the question, but the question is as forgotten as the language that could ask it, even though the urge to scream it is there! And it screams it! Hour after hour, night after night, Ahltok is screaming; Anker is screaming. Neither they, Anne nor Nona can guess at the meaning.

Screams of unknown loss from the depths of the lungs. Screams missing words from the loosened tongue. Only the screams themselves know what speech would take shape on each, were the screamer's brain and mouth able to produce the words:

"Where the hell are my Mexicans!?!"

"This is a very bad book you're
writing," I said to myself.
"I know," I said.
"You're afraid you'll kill yourself the
way your mother did," I said.
"I know," I said.

Kurt Vonnegut, *Breakfast of Champions*

Chapter 5: **Mom's Bomb**

WHAT am I doing here? It's the same question I've asked myself for three of the past four mornings this week, and too many of the mornings over a greater number of recently past weeks than I can recall right now. Being careful to keep my balance on the stool, I shift my weight so I can straighten my leg to pull the phone from my pocket and check the time: it's a Thursday morning, 9:15 AM in the middle of April, 2005. *Closing in on a year now,* I think. I pick the burning butt of my American Spirit from the edge of the ashtray at my elbow, and take a deep drag. I aim a thick gray cloud of tobacco smoke up at the black vinyl-upholstered drop ceiling above the bar, and watch it fill the recessed lowball cocktail-glass light fixtures that are such a cool element of the kitschy decor at JJ's; briefly blurring the crisp outline of the small red lightbulbs in my glowing crimson fog.

I reach for another sip of my breakfast. As I drink, I try to remember where I'd read the quote about

Irish Coffee... something about it being the perfect nourishment, since it contains all four essential food groups: alcohol, caffeine, sugar, and fat. "Well thish is diet-food," I grin and mutter out loud to myself after swallowing a hot, bitter gulp of the straight Bushmills and black coffee. Diet or not, I'm on my third double-shot round. With a little start I realize I've become lubricated enough to begin talking to myself. I clamp my lips shut tight and grab the edge of the bar, then lean steeply to cock my opposite hip enough to pull the phone from my pocket again — 9:17.

I got nowhere to go, I think as I stare at the clock on the two-inch screen of the same Motorola flip-phone I've had since just before my oldest daughter was born in 1999. As I wait for a new minute to appear, another deep drag from my cigarette sets off a rumbly reminder of my morning schedule down in my guts: "Exshept to take'a crap," I slur aloud, then snap my mouth shut again and shoot a glance down to the far end of the bar to see if Jack, the seventy-something-year-old owner who usually bartends the morning shift, or the silent grim-faced couple he is mixing Bloody Marys for, have heard me. I assure myself they did not, and with the help of the brass boot-rail which runs along the base of the bar between me and the two other morning drinkers, I climb carefully from my stool and head to the men's room.

I like the men's room at JJ's. A Fifties-era, all the way to the floor style urinal is tucked between the wall of the single sit-down stall, and a small porcelain sink so old that it sports separate faucets for the hot and cold water. The floor space between the stall and the sink is tight, but I can spread my feet just wide enough to step sufficiently close to the big open catchment of the old urinal to achieve the proper downward sloping angle to avoid backsplash, while keeping the end of my dick within an inch or two of the back surface. I have to stand that close to make sure the sidewalls contain the twin streams of piss that splash like the forked tongue of a spitting serpent from the two openings at the head of my penis.

The thick stainless steel ring that is more or less permanently affixed through them, prevents either the original or secondary hole, a half inch further down the underside of the shaft below my urethral orifice, from squirting out a clean, directable stream, so unless I'm going outside in the bushes, or slow-dancing with one of these beautiful tall old urinals, I have to sit down like a woman to pee in a toilet to prevent spraying piss all over my pants, shoes, and the floor.

One of the unanticipated side-effects of the Prince Albert piercing I'd received close to a year prior, was that I finally really do understand why women get annoyed when men neglect to raise the toilet seat before peeing. It's especially annoying for me now, given how often I need to sit on public men's room toilets these days.

Sometimes I'm sure it's the constant stimulation of the metal ring hanging from the end of my penis. Other times I wonder if the vasectomy operation I got not long after the piercing has anything to do with it. When my thoughts occasionally sink deeper, and I catch myself wondering if there might be a connection between the new increased frequency of my urine output, and the blood I've been occasionally noticing in the toilet after a bowel movement; I... quickly think of something else.

I'm not in here to piss though. I latch the stall door behind me and tear a length of toilet paper from the roll, which I fold to double twice. I then bend over carefully to wipe the toilet seat without losing my balance. It's only force of habit that makes me wipe the seat at JJ's, as the entire restroom is always impeccably clean. *It's either a testament to Jack's pride of ownership*, I think, "or 'is cushmers know he'serious 'bout tha' sign!" I say aloud to the empty bathroom.

I'm getting into the rhythm, carefully tracing a third or fourth revolution around the dry seat, when another rumble nearer to my asshole makes me stand up quickly. I realize suddenly a loose one is coming, and toss the folded paper into the waste basket. I quickly pull two more strips of paper from the roll, each three squares long, then lay them one after the next, side by side in the bowl, completely covering the surface of the water. I repeat this with another two pieces of paper, laying these perpendicularly over the first layer. Doing this makes me think of an old friend from the year I made my first go at college. I haven't seen him for almost sixteen years. In the past five we've swapped one Christmas card and spoken twice on the phone. Don't matter. I'll never forget him: I think of Spencer maybe one out of every four or five times I take a shit. For the hundredth time I wonder if he planned it that way; inject a subtle idea into a person's head that is tied to a regular private habit, and make them remember you forever?

Lost in the distraction of my tangent, I nearly miss heeding my bowels' last insistent call to action. An urgent pressure at my rectum makes me straighten up fast from my reflections on the toilet bowl, and whirl around quickly as I fumble with my belt and zipper. The abrupt movement makes my head spin, and I lose my balance and stumble forward against the tiled wall facing the toilet. Luckily, the cramped layout of JJ's men's room is several feet short of being ADA compliant in every direction: with only about three feet between the toilet and the wall, I can't fall over far enough to end up on the floor. I still manage to knock myself pretty hard against the wall though, because my synapses aren't firing fast enough to raise my arms to brace for the impact. At least I manage to turn my head in time, so my chest, cheek and ear thud heavily against the vertical tiled surface, rather than slamming my nose and teeth directly against it.

I'm racing now to unfasten my belt in time and can't afford to steal the seconds it would take to push myself away from the wall before my pants are down. I keep fighting with the buckle as the side of my face remains pressed against the cold tiles, my nose two inches from the corner of the neatly framed sign that I figure Jack fastened to the wall sometime in the last 20 to 40 years. It reads:

Please help me keep your drinks affordable by treating everything in this room with respect. ~Jack Jensen

Just in the nick of time I get my belt, button, and zipper undone and let my pants fall down around my ankles. Counting much more on luck than coordination, I shove myself away from the wall, take one backward shuffling hop on the way down, and manage to plop my butt directly over the center of the toilet seat at the exact instant that the hot stream of nearly liquid shit spews out of me. Notwithstanding the sudden force of the explosive ejection of my watery crap, I can feel that my rump and legs have stayed dry: Spencer's little trick has worked again. "Grassy-ass Amigo!" I chuckle aloud, blurting out my thanks to the old friend twenty-seven hundred miles away, who I never talk to or see, but won't ever forget.

Now my mood takes a sudden sharp, sour swing as I glance back up at Jack's sign. I've read it dozens of times before this morning. Previously, the only response it ever provoked in me was polite attention to the request. But today, perhaps the combination of the nervous adrenaline shot into my system by the fear of shitting my pants, and the surfeit of caffeine, nicotine and whisky coursing through me, has turned my blood into an organic equivalent of acetone, lithium, hydrochloric acid and ammonia soup. Instead of angry white chunks of meth crystalizing in the matrix, red hot rocks of rage bubble up in me, fumigating my head with dark, seething clouds of bitter resentment as I blurt out: "Reeeespect! Fuckin' Respect?... RESPECT!?"

I spit the last iteration of the word out with such force, I slap my hand over my mouth, suddenly aware that someone out in the bar will hear me yelling at myself in the crapper if I'm not careful. I purse my lips tightly to keep my angry ruminations on 'Respect' inside my head: *How is it,* I think, *that a parade of drunk strangers can be counted on to treat something you're meant to SHIT into, with more respect than people who were part of most of my life treated ME??*

I start swinging the wrecking ball of this self-pitiable thought around in my head, and with no aim or order begin crashing it chaotically against the thick walls of the haphazard mental constructs I've been piling up day after day in there, one brick at a time, mortared into place with a thick paste of hatred, regret and sorrow, turned muddy by gallons of alcohol, then dried to a hard black cement by the chill winds of my own guilt.

How Could You do This to Me? Upon the foundation of those seven words, repeated a thousand times to myself in less than a year, I've built the most fortified of these misconstructed monuments to my clinging grief.

SMASH! SMASH! I swing the wrecking ball wildly at its highest ramparts... with no perceivable effect. Slumping forward I place my elbows on my knees, rest my eyes in the palms of my hands and slowly shake my head back and forth, building up momentum in the arc of the two-ton ball that hangs from the hardened steel cable attached to the bottom of my brainstem. I crane my head far to the side to swing it with all possible force against a big patch of ugly lettering I myself have scrawled on the wall's rough bricks: *Two weeks to the day after the birth of your third sweet grandkid!*

CRASH! I slam the wrecking ball in my head against the graffitied brick surface in my mind's eye, at the same instant that my skull bangs against the unblemished painted wooden wall of the toilet stall. The impact knocks my elbows off my knees and my head pitches forward, but I don't open my eyes. Covering both with my left hand now, I clutch the side of my head with my right and keep waving it back and forth, taking aim at the next patch of writing I can clearly read on the thickest section of the built-up bricks: *One fucking NIGHT before my wife's goddamned BIRTHDAY!?*

Just before the fast-flying iron ball smashes into it, the writing disappears in a flash, as quickly as a wet sponge swipes words from a chalkboard. In its place, an image of my mother's face suddenly materializes. No time to pull the crane boom back! It crunches into her forehead and I sit bolt-upright at the shocking clarity of the vision, then slump back immediately against the toilet and harshly groan aloud, "Cunnnnnnt!"

An acidic lump of bile comes up in my mouth as the horrible insult I've uttered at the ghost of my mother takes shape in my ear. It's not the coffee and liquor in my stomach, but shame and disappointment squeezed directly from the center of my chest, that presses into the back of my throat to choke me. "Oh God," I moan. "God *damnit*, Mom."

My eyes are fixed now on the bathroom's tile wall, staring directly at Jack's neatly framed request for respect, but the looming walls of the twisted bricked-up fortresses in my head fill my vision almost as solidly. Biting dust from the impact of the wrecking ball showers down in slow motion, stinging my eyes as the already dim light in the windowless toilet stall seems to dull. I clamp my eyes shut hard against the growing burn, locking whatever might have tried to wash some of the pain away tightly behind the lids; and I'm at the controls of the wrecking ball crane again.

Piled near the seemingly indestructible bulwarks built atop the thick reinforced slab foundation of "*How Could You,*" the ugliest and most skewed of my monstrous cranial constructions rises from the center of a mess of scattered bricks. The latest of the fortifications I've been building up against my perception of the mistreatments meted out to me, its precariously leaning walls look like the work of a blind man. My visibly shoddy workmanship belies the structure's strength however, as the joints of its bricks are filled to overflowing with the strongest concentration of my sticky alcoholic mortar, all stacked atop the heaviest foundation of all: *Why Didn't You?*

Facing the splattered accusations I've painted all over the walls of the empty *"How Could You"* castle, is nothing compared to the horror of battling the ghosts of alternate realities that creep down from the battlements atop the *"Why Didn't You"* tower. The saddest ones start the attack first — *Why didn't you tell us how bad it had gotten? Why didn't you let me help you? Why didn't you just stop taking the pills??* I squeeze my eyes shut even tighter to stop anything wet coming out, swing the demolition crane's boom into play, and pulverize the three sorrowful *"Why Didn't You"* ghosts into a greasy stain upon the uneven brick surface with one lucky blow of my wrecking ball.

The next wave of ghosts to appear are made of much sturdier stuff than sorrow and remorse. These are molded from a huge scoop of resentment, peppered with more than just a little greed, then hardened in the smoke of my still smoldering sense of entitlement — *Why didn't you divorce him five years ago? Why didn't you rewrite the trust to protect what you wanted me and my children to have? Why didn't you take care of ME??*

These and a dozen more ghoulish entries from the bitter list of *"Why Didn't Yous"* that I thrust daily at the specter of my dead mother, pour down onto the tower walls and begin crawling towards the most susceptible soft spots of my brain. Desperate to keep them at bay, I toss and swing my head wildly about to keep the wrecking ball in motion, slamming it again and again against the wraiths as they slither down the side of the brick tower, like I'm playing a giant crazy vertical game of Whac-A-Mole in some psycho circus.

To my amazement, my mental wrecking ball finds the tower's keystone with a direct hit! The structure sways, then topples into a pile of broken excuses at my feet. But before any relief sets in, the dust clears around the broken castle walls to expose the worst of what was kept inside. A jagged faultline in the very center of the rocky floor has cracked the seal on the locked dungeon below, and a sickening shudder grips my empty guts as I watch the flagstones shift and crumble as the demonized apparition I had trapped there rises into view: I've released the Stepfucker once again.

He clambers up from the deepest recesses of the black pit in which I've tried over and over to bury his memory, and advances towards me, arms outstretched. Crimson streaks run down his forearms from pools of blood in his palms that I can't see: only the hairy knuckles of the backs of his hands are visible; three fingers curled down, and each of the two middle ones raised in furious accusation directly at me.

At first I recoil as I'd nearly always done, pushing my back up hard against the toilet tank as I shrink from him. But then one of the chunks of chemical rage bubbling in my blood flares hot: "Nowhere to hide now, Sam!" I shout, and rear up unsteadily off the toilet seat. I raise my arm high and step forward to smash my fist into his face this time; unlike when I'd finally been pushed far enough, two days before Christmas last year, and stood on his front porch punching the door he had fearfully slammed in my face until my knuckles bled, as I yelled at the top of my lungs for all of his neighbors to hear: "My Christmas wish for you this year *and every year to come*, is that you die an early, lonely, violent death! Just like the one you helped arrange for my mother!!"

Too eager for violence, I lunge forward without a pause, trip on the pants bunched around my ankles, and fall right through the vivid hallucination of the man who had been my mother's third husband. This time, my already outstretched hand stops me before my face meets the wall. I keep it planted firmly on the tiles for support as I stand shakily for a minute, waiting for my head to stop spinning, and the last shadow of Sam's hard-lined face to fade from view.

Now my head clears and I can focus once more, and my eyes lock onto Jack's sign again. I take a deep breath and allow the essential words from his message to fill me. I roll them rhythmically through my head in time with my breathing, which they help me to calm as I repeat them silently like a meditation: *treat everything in this room with respect... treat everything in this room with respect... treat everything — with respect.*

Another minute passes before I stop cycling the mantra to ponder aloud: "Does that include me?" Before I can answer, I direct the question even further into myself by asking: "What about my memories?"

As if responding to an open invitation, a flood of them pour into the cramped restroom stall and swirl in and out of my thoughts. I latch briefly onto as many of the beautiful ones as I can as they fly all around me. The first I pause to savor is that of meeting my lovely wife Gia for the first time. It happened in another little dive-bar called "Dick's Place," one rainy winter's night nearly seven years prior, in the isolated coastal town of Mendocino, California. That time, an entirely different kind of thirst beckoned me to duck in for a drink; one to be quenched by raising a glass to celebrate the beauty of life, adventure, and the grand possibilities of my youth, long before the deep-set pain

I'm trying to drink into remission again this morning had done anything more than hint at its coming.

Not quite 27-years-old, I'd managed to beat back the disappointments of a long string of failed temporary relationships, one divorce, and two soul-sucking visits to the same abortion clinic with different women, enough to somehow still believe very strongly in the idea of True Love, and soul-mate connection. I couldn't have dreamed that I might find mine at a place called "Dick's," in the stunning 22-year-old beauty who would first become the only woman I'd ever taken home from a bar, and very quickly thereafter, my wife.

A broad grin lights up my face as visions of the three incredible results of that chance encounter with Gia make an appearance: our six-year-old daughter, Piera, her little brother Ariosto, and the baby sister, Vita; all three named to celebrate the Italian roots Gia and I share, and Vita to honor the memory of my great-grandmother — an inspiration that Gia readily agreed to when I proposed it following a vivid dream I had of Nonna, the very first night after our daughter was born last summer, just two... just two weeks before... before Anne...

"DAMN YOU PEOPLE!" I raise my voice too high again, then drop it nearly to a whisper as I whine: "Why can't you just leave me in peace?"

But these irrepressible haunts consume an unfair share of my sober attention, and an even greater measure of my drunken reflections. They crowd out this morning's fresh memories of kissing Vita and Gia goodbye, and the words I spoke to paste yet another little lie over the big one I've secreted between us: "I'm gonna head to the gym for a couple hours after I drop the kids at school Honey." Then they wipe out the happy smiles on Piera and Ari's faces as I watch them skip again down the walkway to join the other lucky children at Santa Cruz Montessori... and I'm stuck in this empty bathroom stall, naked from the waist down, leaning drunkenly against the cold tile wall, forced to reckon with the stale dregs of the two ghosts in my head; one still living, and the other very much dead.

They drag me back across a span of nearly twenty years, to the day I first met Sam: a thing from which I might have derived good. But that was a day very badly planned for new beginnings, and at this stage in my life I can see by now that things are largely shaped by how they start, and not by how we try to fix them.

***

"There's someone here for you to meet," Anne said without looking at me. They were the first words either of us had spoken during the silent two-hour car ride from Robert Luis Stevenson School in Pebble Beach, to the driveway of the fancy home in Atherton; hers as a result of the divorce settlement from her second marriage.

She switched the ignition off and put her hand back on the steering wheel as I groaned: "Aww God, Mom! Today? Why can't you just let me be by myself today?" It was the beginning of what should have been the sixth week of my sophomore year as a boarding student at Stevenson, but my weekend trip had changed all that: after the Judiciary Committee's decision on my expulsion that Monday morning, Anne had been notified by the Dean of Students that I would need to be removed from campus within twenty-four hours.

I assumed she'd found another therapist to try, and that this one made house-calls: "C'mon, Mom! Just give me a day or two to get past this, OK? I promise I'll talk to anyone you want later this week — why did you have to bring someone over here *today?*"

"I didn't *bring him over*, Anker. He's been... he's been here since you left for school."

"Uh... I'm lost Mom — What?"

"He's the man I've been seeing Anker, *OK?* He's been living here until we—"

"*What??* The 'man I've been seeing' Oh! And he's *living* here? When the hell were you planning to inform me of this, might I ask?" From the time I hit puberty, I looked quite a bit older than my age. A year at the pretentious boarding school had gotten me talking that way too.

"STOP IT!!" Anne yelled: "*Yes!* The man I've been seeing, Anker, alright!? YOU don't get—" She checked herself abruptly and tightened her lips as fiercely as her grip on the wheel. Seconds of frozen silence filled the car, then I glanced sideways at her, and for just a moment I wondered if I was having a flash-back of the visions from Saturday night; could a person have a flash-back from their very first dose? I knew so little about the incredible world I'd just sacrificed my Stevenson School education to take a glimpse into...

"Impossible," I barely whispered, but a faintly visible aura of pulsing light seemed to radiate from my mother as she sat with her eyes closed and took control of her breath. I watched the glow fade from a heated red, to a gentle blue, as she relaxed her fingers on the steering wheel. The next instant, I knew for sure I was still tripping.

As I stared at her profile in the driver's seat, a ripple—like ghost-station static wavering across an old TV screen—passed directly through her, and showed me a shadow of the skull beneath her flesh. I watched her perform the familiar ritual I'd seen so many times before without the benefit of psychedelic clarity, and marveled at the realization that much more than I ever knew was at work underneath my mother's skin during her carefully controlled periods of emotional metamorphosis. As she steadied her breath, and replaced the tense grimace on her face with the perfectly set smile that she could always pass off as genuine to anyone but me, my momentary gift of X-ray vision clearly showed the skeletal outline of a toothy wolf's jaw, just before her even breathing forced it back to human form. Then with her eyes still closed, she said in a voice barely louder than my whisper: "Impossible? Should it really be impossible for me to be happy?"

Anne appeared completely normal again once she turned to look at me. Perfectly composed, she placed her hands in her lap and spoke in an even, soothing tone: "I know this is a lot to absorb Anker, and I probably should have written to tell you the news."

"Or just *told* me! You could have just told me on the phone any of the, what; five or six times I called you since school started?"

"I'm sorry Anker." She said gently. "This just didn't seem like the kind of news to give you over the phone."

"How you might have given me the news isn't the point, Mom! You got a new boyfriend, OK, what else is new — but he's living here for more than a month, and you don't think I deserve to know that?" I knew I was scraping dangerously at her carefully applied coating of self-control, but I was too pissed off to care, and yelled angrily at her: "This is my house too!"

"Alright, *Anker!*" She spit my name out through a wide crack in the control-layer, like it was something that tasted like shit. Only very rarely did Anne speak my name that way — like something she hated. The force with which she hurled it at me in the car that morning sent me flying back to my memory of the year before, at the end of the summer between eighth grade and boarding school, the night she made such a bad job of trying to give me the "sex talk" that she had put off for too long.

That was the summer before I turned fifteen; the summer I took my last vacation with Anne; the third and final time I would visit the Philippines and see the dying grandfather whose name I shared. It was also the summer I lost my virginity.

Over a span of many years after my parents' divorce, I watched my mother claw her way up from working as a cash-strapped waitress, to an underpaid school teacher, then to a frustrated salesperson working for a technology division of the Exxon Corporation in the late 70's, and finally into a career as an extremely successful commercial real estate broker, during the Silicon Valley construction boom of the 80's and 90's. By the time I was fourteen, she had gotten used to giving herself the things she had lived without for so many years.

The extravagant five-week vacation she booked that summer started with a lavish three-day layover at the Halekulani hotel on Waikiki beach before heading to the Philippines. We then spent ten days with her parents in the home she'd grown up in; a part of the trip that neither of us spoke a word about once we began our whirlwind adventure through three cities in Japan, a weekend in Hong Kong, and ten final days in China. There, we walked the Great Wall together, visited Beijing's Forbidden City, and saw the Terracotta Army in Xi'an.

On the afternoon I'd been sent to the market in Angeles City with my grandparents' "House Boy" in the Philippines, I'd refused his invitation to visit "the fucking girls." ("You sure Anker? Your uncles always so happy after making good time with the fucking girls — I know *best* fucking girls!")

Instead, my first time would be with an adventurous 17-year-old French Canadian girl from Quebec, on a 4th-floor balcony of the Xi'an Hotel, after getting drunk with her at the rooftop bar while Anne slept in our hotel room after an exhausting all-day tour of the Terracotta Warriors.

It was well past midnight by the time I finally staggered down the right hallway and found the number on the door that matched my room-key. Perhaps I might have kept my secret, but I couldn't get the key in the hotel room door for about six minutes. And my mom was sitting straight up in bed with her arms crossed when the lock finally tumbled.

"Where the *Hell* have you been!" I was late, drunk, just pumped, 'till that last split second—that last mind-blowing thrust—before I pulled out fast and bust; into my hand; into the air; into the night. Into nothing. After spilling my seed with the willing girl, I spilled too many of the beans to the angry woman.

She shot out of bed and stomped straight over to where I stood unsteadily just inside the door: "Let me smell your breath!" Anne shouted.

Too late, too drunk, and too confused to make up stories, I just broke down and cried, and Anne fell silent as I told her all about the missing condom, and the lies I'd told the girl about my age to get into her pants.

I remember that Anne finally put her arm around me, tucked me into the bed next to hers with my clothes still on, and just before I either passed out or fell asleep, she switched off the light, bent over in the dark to put her hand on my shoulder and whispered: "First times can be much worse."

The next morning the silence between us was as thick as the pain in my head, and once I'd made it even more sore by processing all my feelings about the night before, the main thought that stuck with me was that I would never again allow myself to cry in front of Anne.

We made it home to Atherton, and through most of the rest of that summer before she spoke of it again. It was late one Thursday or Friday evening, after I'd spent another long day enjoying the big empty house all to myself: first a swim and a hot-tub before a late breakfast, then a few hours playing Space Invaders, Dig Dug, and Jungle Hunt on the Atari. In the middle of the afternoon I rode my bike from our cul-de-sac through the quiet streets of Atherton and Menlo Park to buy myself a roast-beef sandwich from Draeger's Market, and a half-pound of Jelly Bellys at the Candy Depot on Santa Cruz Avenue. In those sleepy days before the Internet, a kid could ride his bike right up and down the middle of the sidewalks in that town, and across El Camino Real without even stopping to look both ways.

Back at home I hung out and ate my lunch by the pool, then pushed back the giant sliding glass wall that created a ten foot wide entry between the living room and the outside, and wandered in and out as I ate the whole big bag of candy, and played favorite tracks from my record collection on the expensive stereo system tucked behind magnetically latched hinged panels in the living room, that were hidden in a twelve-foot high checkerboard wall of richly polished walnut and maple. The top-of-the-line Polk Audio equipment had belonged to the man whose house it had been when Anne and I moved in just before they were married in `79. The stereo system was one of several of his possessions that he had not removed during the brief separation that led up to their divorce, and once Anne owned title to the house, she flat out refused to allow him to enter it again, or send him any of the things he had left behind. He backed down without an argument, either because as the sole heir of a substantial fortune from a Houston oil family he could easily afford to replace it, or he had simply learned quickly during his brief three-year marriage to my mother, that she was not someone to keep fighting with.

It was close to nine o'clock that night—though earlier than I expected her back—when Anne returned home after a long day of meetings all around San Jose and Santa Clara, followed by a two-hour business dinner entertaining one of Silicon Valley's big real estate developers with another of the young hot-shot female agents from her office. I was in my room by then, playing music on my cheap Zenith record player while going through my LPs to decide which ones to bring to boarding school. I'd just tabled the A-side of Duran Duran's *Seven and the Ragged Tiger*, and was singing aloud to "New Moon on Monday" (*Breaking away with the beast of both worlds, a smile that you can't disguise. Every minute I keep finding clues that you leave behind. Save me from these reminders; as if I'd forget tonight...*)

I was surely the teenaged poster-boy for the pinnacle of 80's pop-music embarrassments, as I danced around singing along with Simon Le Bon, but in the privacy of my own room, with my eyes shut tight and the music cranked up, the packed arena of my adoring fans ate it up, and pumped their fists for more. I took a deep breath while I spun around on the hardwood floor in my socks, and was facing the door when I opened my eyes to belt out the chorus into my microphone-thumb, and came face to face with a very unappreciative audience of one. I choked hard to stop the next line from bursting past my lips, and my face flushed red when I saw Anne standing silently at the open doorway, looking down her nose at my performance; like all she wanted in that moment was to be saved from these reminders.

Without a word, Anne walked briskly past me to the record player, filling the air of my room with her sense of annoyance and the smell of white wine, and dragged the needle across the face of my record to stop the music. I didn't think she was drunk, but Anne seemed to be steadying herself somehow during the several seconds she stood with her back to me before turning around. When she did, I saw that she held a white paper bag printed with "Preuss Pharmacy" on it. "Aw gee, Mom"—I said as soon as I spotted it, eager to skirt any talk of my embarrassing song and dance number—"I was right across the street from Preuss when I rode my bike up to Santa Cruz Avenue this afternoon. I could have gotten that for you."

"Take a seat, Anker," she said, pointing to my bed with her free hand.

Up to even just a year or two earlier, whenever Anne told me to "take a seat," the phrase seemed odd coming from her. The directive always struck me as such a terse, masculine phrase; something a man—a father—should be saying, though mine never had.

I imagined mothers better suited to the use of more feminine sounding openers, things like "we need to talk," and, "I'm worried about you." But Anne was a firm believer in gender equality on every level. She took that phrase and made it hers; owned it fair and square. By that time in my life, I'd received her curt, no bullshit delivery of them enough times so that those three words had become my Pavlovian response trigger to go on high-alert. "Take a seat" could only mean one of three things: a lecture; a punishment; or an interrogation.

That time, it was to be a lecture: "I didn't buy these today, Anker, they've been in the trunk of my car for weeks. I've been meaning to have this conversation with you since we got back from the trip."

I took a quick glance at the paper bag again, uncomfortably suspicious of where this was headed, but made myself look faintly confused and replied: "OK; conversation about what?"

"About the girl from Canada!" She started getting flustered right off the bat: "About you having sex, Anker!"

My relaxed facade cracked then too: "Mom, we talked about it! Remember?"

"No, you talked about it! I just listened to you talk... and cry; don't *you* remember!?"

The look on my face must have given away just how much I did. "Oh, Jesus! I'm sorry, Anker. I really didn't want to screw this up." She placed the bag on my desk, pulled the chair out, and turned it around to sit facing me.

"OK, listen Anker," she started again smoothly, then suddenly slapped her hands down hard on her knees and stood up to look out the window into the yard. Anne mumbled something under her breath, then quickly turned to face me again, snatched the bag back off the desk and shook it as she said angrily: "Your father should be doing this goddamnit! I asked him to! I told him what happened with you in China, and told him to talk to you, you know. Did he? Did he say anything at all when you went to visit him last weekend?"

For a second my dad's words from that weekend flashed through my head. About every other weekend since I'd turned 12, when they decided I was old enough to ride alone and spare either of them the drive, Anne would put me on the Friday afternoon commuter train from Menlo Park to San Francisco, where Marco would pick me up at the 4th Street Caltrain station after leaving his downtown office. Usually he would drive straight out Townsend Street to Pier 40, then follow the curve of the bay up the Embarcadero, and all the way beyond Fort Mason before turning to climb the steep grade up Fillmore Street to his home in Pacific Heights overlooking the eastern edge of the Presidio, and the distant views of the Palace of Fine Arts and the St. Francis Yacht Club far below. Sometimes if he was in a hurry, Marco would skip the scenic route and the half hour or so of silent time it ate up between us, and drive straight up 3rd Street, take a left on California, and head directly to his neighborhood.

When I threw my backpack into the trunk and got in his car that evening, Marco took Townsend in the opposite direction from the bay all the way to 7th Street, then up across Market into the heart of the Tenderloin district. That was before any of the cleanup and gentrification of that area, and the sidewalks of the Tenderloin were full of suggestively clad streetwalkers, and homeless alcoholics. He drove through some of the worst of it in silence for a while, then started picking out some of the most obvious specimens: "Check out that tall glass of water," he pointed at a woman in bright pink hot-pants and stiletto heels. Then another one: "Whoa! There's a hot tomato!" And finally: "Jesus, Anker — check out the tits on that one!"

Each time I looked, but didn't say a word, totally confused about the bizarre tour we were on, or what it was he expected me to say as he shot the occasional glance at me after drawing my attention to another of the hookers. Marco fell silent again as he drove up and down a few more blocks, and had just passed the Mitchell Brothers theatre on O'Farrell Street and was about to take a right onto Polk when he said: "Your mother told me you fucked some Canadian girl when the two of you were in China."

I didn't respond to that either, and we both sat in silence as he continued along Polk Street, away from the prostitutes and derelicts of the Tenderloin, up through the main artery of one of San Francisco's biggest gay scenes. He drove past California street, then stopped to wait for the light to turn green at the corner of Polk and Washington so he could drive the last dozen blocks that would take us back to Pacific Heights, and worlds away from the parade of biker caps, mustaches and leather pants outside my window. He didn't use his finger to point on Polk Street, but kept both hands on the steering wheel and just jutted his chin to call my attention to the group of men standing underneath a bar sign that read "The White Swallow."

"Christ. Look at those fuckin' faggots over there." Marco shifted his eyes to me once more, and I just looked down at my shoes as the light turned green.

He drove a few blocks before speaking again: "Your mother said you cried; that you cried after having sex with that girl."

I kept looking down at my shoes, but finally broke my silence and said: "No Dad. I didn't cry after having sex with her. I cried in the hotel room... after Mom yelled at me."

"You don't have a problem with girls then?"

"No."

"Good."

We drove on in silence, then just a few blocks from his house, my father said more words to me in a row than I think he ever had: "Sex is confusing, Anker. If you don't get it figured out in the next few years, I'll take you to the Mustang Ranch in Nevada when you turn 18, and you'll learn everything you need to know in about twenty minutes. Stay away from the kinda shit we saw on the streets down there though, OK? Once a woman's selling herself on the street, all you can get from that is a disease. And about this conversation — don't tell your mother."

"No Dad — I won't."

And I didn't: not even when Anne pulled the box of condoms from the bag on the night she ruined my Duran Duran show, and held it up like a piece of evidence and asked me again: "Did your dad say anything at all to you about using condoms, Anker?"

"No, Mom" (and that was the truth — Marco's version of the "sex talk" hadn't once mentioned condoms).

"Typical. Leave it up to me then!" Anne said, and sat down in front of me in the desk chair, placing the box of condoms in her lap.

"I don't want to go into a lot of detail about that night in China again, Anker," Anne continued. "Suffice it to say that, aside from the drinking—which you better *damned* well not do at boarding school— the thing that concerns me most is the fact that you had sex without using a condom."

"OK, I know Mom."

"You know?! You don't know! If you knew, then you would have known how important it is!"

She locked her eyes on mine and held her gaze firmly for a moment to prove how serious she was, then tried to speak calmly as she continued: "Anker, I know there are a lot of changes happening in you right now — a lot of changes. I know you're eager to experience as much as you can, but don't be in a hurry for this! Being a teenager is complicated enough, Anker. Think how complicated things would suddenly be if you got someone pregnant!"

"OK, Mom!" I leaned forward and grabbed the condoms from her lap and threw them into the pile of things next to my desk that I would pack for school, "I won't get anyone pregnant, OK? I got it!"

"Got it?? GOT IT?!" She jumped up from the seat and snatched the box from the floor and whipped around to shake it in my face, all composure completely gone. "Don't you be goddamned flippant with me, *Anker!*" A distinct change in the way she spoke my name had begun: "No, you don't GET IT, *Anker!* You don't have a goddamned clue! Until you get someone pregnant and have to face the reality of what to do about it, knowing that no matter what you choose your lives are changed forever, you don't fucking GET IT!"

If Anne wanted to scare the shit out of me, she was doing a beautiful job, but I grit my teeth on the promise I'd made to never again let her see me cry, and pushed as much of the anger back at her as I could muster, and yelled: "Why are you talking to me this way?!"

"Because I gave up a huge part of my life to let you have yours, and I'm not going to just shut up and watch you throw away all the chances you still have for a *happy* future!"

Something about the stress Anne placed on the word "Happy" pulled me back from my defensive position, and let me ignore the sting of her first remark. I know there was no conscious thought behind it, and have no idea which part of me the intuition came from to slip the next question in through the widening rupture in her emotional state, or what in the world made me address her as I did, not as "Mom," but with the name I'd last heard spoken—no, yelled—like a plea by my Grandfather, when I was awakened a few hours before dawn by the sounds of their living room conversation the night before we left the Philippines: a muffled stream of fast, angry sounding exchanges, pockmarked by broken sobs, then his last line spoken loudly enough for me to hear: "Please Annie! *Please*, I beg of you — don't let me die with this on my head!" Then the slamming of a door and silence, just after she yelled even louder: "It's too late! *Thirty* years too late, *Dad!*"

It almost didn't feel like me talking as my mother stood fuming in the center of my room, angrily clutching the box of condoms that had become such an odd prop in the rapidly careening conversation, and I looked straight into her eyes and with a voice so deep it surprised me, I calmly asked: "Why are you so angry, Annie?"

Anne's face turned ashen as the echo of her father's

name for her flew from my lips and ricocheted silently between us. The question sunk itself like a fathoming rod way down into the nearly overflowing pool of her past secrets, and displaced two thin trickles of tears that ran down her cheeks.

She only got a few steady words out before the trickle became a stream: "Why am I angry? Because it's not just about pregnancy." She looked at the box in her hand and clutched it harder, clenched her jaw tightly for a moment and then yelled as the tears started to flow: "It's about disease! Not the kind they teach about in health class, or that you read about in the news, Anker! *Real* diseases, that happen to *real* people!"

Anne suddenly became aware that she was crying, and her anger flared up fast again as she looked down at her chest and saw the dark spots all over the front of her expensive silk blouse. She swiped the tears from her face with the palm of her empty hand, and furiously shook the moisture from it like she was flinging away something that had gotten her dirty, and screamed: "You really wanna know why I'm so angry, Anker?? Because I HAVE HERPES, OK?! I have a disease! I got it when I was very young, and I will *never* be rid of it, or the memory of the bastard who gave it to me, *ANKER!*"

She hurled my name at me like a curse, then crushed the thin cardboard box in her fist and threw it directly at the center of my chest, where it burst apart and spilled the strips of Trojans into my lap as she said: "Just wear a fucking rubber, *Anker*." And that was the end of Mom's "sex talk."

But I wasn't done yet. I let the broken box of rubbers fall to the floor as I stood up from the bed and demanded: "Why do you say my name like that? You say it like you hate me! Why did you name me *Anker* if it's something you hate?"

I wonder sometimes about how things might have changed between us—or for her—if the upwelling of Anne's secrets had spilled over just a bit more in that moment; if the emotional catharsis that had pushed all of those painfully honest words out of her had squeezed just a little harder, and made her spit out something close to the truth, something like: "I thought I could take my father's power away, by stealing his name."

But I didn't really have an inkling of the knowledge that might have made me suspect a truth like that then, and she had already closed the cracks up tight; no more truth would come out that night. She narrowed her eyes and took a step away from me, as if she feared I would try to catch her, and said: "It's tradition to name sons after their grandfather."

"Then why couldn't I have been named after my other grandfather! Why couldn't I have been *Francis!*"

"*Francis* Frankoni? Are you serious? Have you ever really *listened* to those names? Francis Frankoni? Vita Volterra? *Lodovico* Lunardi??" Anne scoffed at me, folded her arms tightly across her chest, then punched each of her last words out for emphasis as she said: "Those people all sound like they're picking fucking pecks of pickled peppers, *Anker!*"

She slammed the door and walked down the long

hallway to her room, leaving me alone to contemplate the broken box of condoms on the floor, and the mystery of my name. More than a year would pass before either of us said a word to pretend the conversation had ever even happened.

***

On the morning I was expelled from Stevenson, after pulling into the driveway of the Atherton house, and receiving Anne's news of the live-in boyfriend she hadn't wanted to tell me about on the phone, I quickly discovered that there were more surprises in store.

"I'm going in to let him know we're here. Bring the suitcase with your clothes inside and unload the rest of your things into the garage before you come in."

"The garage? Why?! Don't I still have my bedroom?"

Anne put her hands back on the steering wheel and gripped it tightly once, and looked away from me out the window as she said: "We closed escrow on a home in San Jose last week, Anker. It doesn't make sense to unpack your things: this house will go on the market when we move at the end of the month."

"WHAT?!"

"We didn't want to start things off between us in a home with bad memories in it, we—"

"What the HELL, Mom?! You do all this without telling me a thing? *This is my house too!!*"

"NO!" Anne yelled as she whipped around to face

me: "It *was* your house! You were supposed to be at the expensive boarding school I sent you to for the next three years, and then go to college! But you fucked that up good didn't you? *Didn't you!?* So NO! This is not your house, *Anker*, and this is NOT your day to give ME any shit! YOU are the one who's in a heap of fucking trouble right now! Do you have any clue how much Stevenson was costing me? Fourteen THOUSAND dollars a year, Anker, and not a penny from your father! Know how much of that I'll get back since they kicked you out?? ZERO!" She pinched her thumb and forefinger together to make the symbol for nothing, and shook it at me as she screamed "ZERO! ZERO! ZERO, *ANKER!* ZER—O!!"

I was suddenly seconds away from breaking my promise—no more tears in front of my mom—so I held them back fiercely with the only emotion guaranteed to keep them from flowing; more anger: "ALRIGHT! I *fucking* get it, alright? I'M ZERO! I fucked up! I fucked up and there's not a single thing I can do to make it right!"

"But what about what you're doing, Mom?! I don't have any bad memories in this house! You're willing to sell this beautiful home and move to San Jose because of some random new *boyfriend* from the past six weeks?? What happens when it doesn't work out? What happens six months from now when he turns out—"

"HUSBAND!" She blurted out loud; no other single word could have shut me up so completely as that. She then repeated it gently, as if attempting to soothe me with it: "*Husband*, Anker."

"Husband?" I said softly, looking down at my shoes and letting my shoulders slump in defeat.

"Yes, Anker. We're going to be married just before Thanksgiving. Do you see now why I didn't want to tell you this on the phone?"

"Married... Married again?" My shoulders slumped even further: "Who is this guy, Mom?"

"He's — well... He's a news reporter at Channel 5 in San Jose. He just moved up here from Southern California at the end of the summer."

"How did you meet him?"

"I saw an interview the station did when he joined their lineup. He's really a good guy, Anker!"

"So you saw him on TV? Yeah, but, how did you *meet* him?"

"Actually, I invited him out to lunch. After I saw the piece on him I sent him a card at the station and invited him out to lunch. I told him I thought his morals were laudable, and—"

"Laudable? What does that even *mean?*"

"It means worthy, Anker! It means *admirable* — a man who knows what's right and does it! He left a full-time weekday anchorman position at one of the biggest stations in L.A. for the weekend spot here, and a big pay-cut just so he could live near his son. Anker, he's going to be good for you, I know it!"

My slumping shoulders were going to pull my head right into my lap. I put my elbows on my knees, and rested my eye sockets in the palms of my hands to keep it up, and said quietly: "So I get a step-brother out of the bargain too then."

"You'll like him Anker, you'll really like him! He's a few years younger than you, but Niran is a really good kid, he—"

"Near-on? *Near-on?* What's Near-on?"

"His name is 'Nir*an*' Anker! His mother is from Thailand and very traditional. She—"

"What's *his* name??" I snapped, cutting Anne off and jerking my head back up to look at her.

"Who?"

"Him! Your new boyfriend; fiancé; husband—whatever! My new STEP-DAD! What's his *name?*"

"Sam. His name is Sam, Anker."

"Sam... Sam, Sam! Sam *what?*"

Anne looked away from me through the windshield again and said softly "Salt. His name is Sam Salt."

She kept looking straight ahead, but I'm sure Anne felt the contempt flash from my eyes and burn into the side of her face, and I knew I intentionally wanted to hurt her when I slowly said in a low, mean voice: "Who's picking fucking pickled peppers now, *Annie?*"

The color ran right out of her cheeks. A single tear appeared at the corner of her right eye and slowly trickled down her face, and the whispered voice cracked like a little girl's as she said: "Don't fuck this up for me." Then she bowed her head towards her lap as I had done, but kept her hands fastened firmly on the wheel, all the color drained from them now too from the force of her grip, and she said again in a low growl this time: "Don't fuck this up for me."

For years afterwards, every time I replayed the scene of what happened next, I tried to convince myself that I really was having an LSD flashback from the trip I had taken three days before. But I know now that isn't the truth; there was no hallucination; no dim outline of the otherworldly wolf-skull. It was real. It was inside of her, and it was its invisible rage that flared to ignite the red aura which radiated suddenly from her head and chest again, and hottest all around the claws that she tore from the steering wheel as she lunged towards me, grabbed the front of my shirt and yanked my face to within six inches of hers and screamed: "DON'T FUCK THIS UP FOR ME!"

She pushed me hard back over to my side of the car; no apology; no way to contain her anger now once I'd uncapped that flood of it: "Get your goddamned things into the garage, Anker! Then wash and vacuum the car, and come inside to meet Sam — It's time to clean up your act! And you better clean up your *fucking* language too if you know what's good for you: Sam doesn't like a dirty mouth!"

I did as I was told, unpacked and cleaned the car, then walked inside with my suitcase. I placed it in the hallway next to the door of the room that had been mine—not yet daring to look inside to see if my things were still in it—and went to the kitchen, where I found Anne making sandwiches.

"Sam's out on the patio waiting to meet you." She said without looking up from her work. Apparently there was to be no official introduction to this man my mother thought would be so good for me; and for her.

I walked through the living room and out to the patio through the open glass wall to the sound of classical music being played through the stereo system I had come to think of as mine; Anne never used it. I stopped short before approaching him, shocked by the sight of the man sitting at the table near my pool reading a newspaper, while puffing on a thick cigar. The chiseled lines of his face, stubborn slightly cleft chin, and strict military-style haircut sent a disarming wave of recollection through me I was unable to place. He turned to look at me as I approached him slowly, and I noticed the faint scar just below his eye next to his nose, that ran down to disappear in the frown-line of his face. It would be several months before I learned that the scar was the result of an attack by a knife-wielding Viet Cong rebel, just before Sam broke his neck during a pre-dawn raid on his platoon's camp in Vietnam. It would be several years before I found out that Sam had served three tours of duty in the Vietnam War, the first beginning just after he turned 17-years-old, when a military program was in effect that granted early release to some minors in juvenile detention centers, if they volunteered for active military duty.

After finding something that he was really good at, Sam enlisted again as a soldier, then moved up the ranks quickly to become one of the Army's youngest First Lieutenants. Sam spent a little more than five years fighting in Vietnam, and didn't come home until he was almost 23, after the night of the raid on the platoon he was leader of wiped out all but 26 of the 118 young men whose lives were in his command, and left him scarred for life.

But it wasn't the scar that made the connection for me as I walked past the pool towards him on the day of our first meeting: it was the eyes. They were the same cold, crafty blue eyes, radiating the same thinly shrouded hint of malice that glared from the photographs of my grandfather as a young man, that I'd last seen in his living room in the Philippines.

I extended my hand as I approached him: "Hi. You... um... you must be Sam."

There was to be no handshake: "Take a seat, Anker. I've heard a lot about you. If there was ever a day that felt like the first day of the rest of your life, kid, I bet that's today. Now listen up as I tell you what's going to be required of you, if you wish to maintain a place in this new arrangement."

***

But the beginning of Anne and Sam's life together hardly ever crossed my mind. Nor did the memory of the end of my brief place stuck in the middle of it, only seven months after the move from Atherton, just a few weeks before I would have completed my sophomore year at James Lick Public High School with a string of solid Cs and Ds.

It was a Thursday afternoon when I walked home from the bus stop near the top of Alum Rock Avenue to the new house on Country Club Drive, way up in the foothills where all the homes in the area had such beautiful views of downtown San Jose, that none of the stigma of the "East Side" reached up to touch them. My mother's car was in the garage, so I had no clue she had returned early from work when I walked through the front door, wishing it was Friday so Sam would be at the station, already preparing for his weekend newscast. They were both sitting on the living room couch facing the entryway, and called me to join them the moment I shut the door. The interrogation started without me even being told to take a seat; it was to be that brief and to the point: everything had been decided.

Anne began it: "What is *that*, Anker?" She was pointing to a tiny zip-lock bag half full of marijuana on the coffee table: the remainder of a dime-bag I had finally been able to buy in the hallways of my school more than two months earlier, once word finally got around that I—the old-looking sophomore who showed up out of the blue nearly two months into the school year—wasn't really a narc.

I shifted my eyes uneasily from the little baggy to both of their faces, and remained silent until Anne spoke again: "I'm asking you, Anker, what *is* that? Or do you have to smell it to be sure, or *smoke* some!"

"It's... it's pot. It's pot, mom," I said quietly.

"Yes. It's pot. And now, will you please tell me where this pot came from?"

I knew exactly where it had come from: the very bottom of a box of comic books at the far end of the shelf in the top of my closet.

"My room," I said.

Now it was Sam's turn: "So you admit this is pot, and understand that I found it in your room. You know what conclusion we draw from this, don't you? You keeping pot in your room must lead us to believe that you have been smoking pot. Not part of our deal, was it Anker?"

"No."

"Where have you been smoking pot? At school?"

Saying that trying to make my days at James Lick more enjoyable by getting high would have been a waste of good pot, seemed like the wrong thing to say, and I remained silent.

Anne broke her silence by jumping up from the couch and grabbing the measly dime bag, pointing it at me, and yelling: "Have you been smoking pot at school, *Anker?!*"

"No! No! Not at school, I swear!"

"Then where?" Sam asked.

"Just a tiny bit. Just every once in a while." I skirted the "where" issue, worried that if I admitted that all the pot smoking had occurred during the Friday afternoons when Anne was still out making real estate deals, and Sam was preparing for his weekend at Channel 5, I would be made to accompany him to the station, and lose the one day of the week I had to be by myself on the only day when the house was empty, and I could play my own music on what didn't feel like "my" stereo any longer.

My mother had sat back down on the couch next to him, and remained silent as Sam gave me the next part: "Let's forget it Anker, because you know what? Where you've been smoking this dope just doesn't even matter. The fact is that smoking it—any of it, anywhere, even once—is a direct violation of the instructions I gave you on the day you were kicked out of Stevenson: No drinking, and no drugs while you live in this house. Period. The fact that you made that promise to me, and have been unable to keep it, forces your mother and I to only one possible conclusion: your willpower over this is faulty; you have lost control over your addiction to drugs."

"Drug addiction? It's just a little pot!"

"You smoking 'just a little pot' wasn't the deal, kid! And it may be just pot now, but if you can't control even that, you're on a sure path to ruin."

"Ruin or *death!*" Anne shouted then: "You want to end up like your cousin Glen?! Decapitated on the side of a highway, so much goddamned angel dust in his system that he probably didn't even feel his fucking *head* come off?? Do you, *Anker?!*"

"No! Jesus, Mom! It's just a little *pot!*"

"And once again, Anker," Sam said, "that argument is exactly what has forced your mother and I to make this decision: your inability to resist even 'just a little pot' means that you have no control over your drug addiction." Sam looked at Anne. She met his eyes, placed her hand on top of his, nodded almost imperceptibly, then looked down into her lap as he continued.

"I spent the morning making phone calls, and have found a place where you can get help with this, while there's still time to correct the tail-spin you're in."

"WHAT?!"

"We will both be driving you up to Millbrae tomorrow morning. You'll be entering the adolescent drug-treatment center at the Mills-Peninsula Hospital. It's the most highly regarded program in the area. Most kids come back out of there totally changed after a month, ready to get back into a successful life and maintain it drug-free with the skills and awareness they gain by completing the 12-steps of the Narcotics Anonymous system." Sam used his best announcer's voice as he spoke the words he'd been told on the phone by the intake counselor at Mills-Peninsula earlier that day, and then used to convince Anne that it was the only solution to the problem.

But as I said, the beginning of Anne's marriage to Sam, my experience living with them at the start of it, and even dealing with their influence over my life for nearly two decades afterwards, occupies just a sliver of space inside my head. All these memories seem to flash through it in the space of only five seconds, as I'm leaning drunkenly against the tiled wall in JJ's bathroom with my pants down around my ankles. The one I'm left with, the one that now consumes hours of every waking day, is the gnawing memory of the very end of it. Not the last years or months; not the last week. It's the last moment of the day that Anne terminated her marriage to Sam, and the mind-numbing mishmash of images that roll incessantly through my head as I try to imagine the look on my mother's face, the instant before she brought it to an irreversible end.

***

The 17-year marriage between Anne and Sam ended abruptly one Saturday afternoon when she told him she was going to the movies. Instead, she pulled into the back parking lot at the high school a mile from the home in Sonoma County they had purchased less then five months before, and already had listed for sale again by then. After parking, Anne locked the car doors, placed two notes on the passenger seat, fired one bullet through the floor between her feet, then shot herself in the heart with the remaining shell that was chambered in his .38 caliber Colt revolver: the same pistol that Sam promised me had been removed from his sock drawer, disassembled, then hidden at the bottom of a box of his old camping gear stored in their garage months prior, the very day after her latest psychiatrist had warned us of the possible side-effects of the combined medications he had prescribed.

"Fugging piece a shit." I mumble. "You deshpic'ble pile a fucking filth." As the constant grinding wheel of the primary memory begins its endless rotations through my head once more, Sam slips himself right up into the six-inch gap between me and the restroom wall, his ghost totally eclipsing my view of Jack's sign again with a form made all the more solid since its spirit emanates from a still living, breathing man.

"You goddamned killer... murderer! That fucking gun was never anywhere but where my mom could find it — wasn't it! You just bided your time, didn't you, you fucking maggot! Filling her mind with fear, uncertainty, and doubt — pullin'er to the freakin' edge!

"'I don't think that doctor is experienced enough to help you Anne'... 'let's try upping the dose a little tonight and see if you can't get some sleep'... 'if you can't take the wind up here let's sell the house and move down into town; the wind's never gonna stop Anne! The wind's never gonna stop—it's never gonna stop—it's never gonna—'

"FUCK YOU SAM! You as good as pulled the trigger yourself you *motherfugger!*"

I'm well past the stage of any conscious thought about the volume of my voice here in JJ's shitter now, and I keep hurling my curses at the spirit of the man that looms so solidly in front of my face that I can almost feel flesh as I grab Sam by the neck, slam his head into the tile wall, push my knee up against his crotch and say: "You know how I'd do it to *you?* Cut you. Cut you, you bastard! Not outside, like that ugly fuckin' scar on your shitty face. Nah, man — I'd cut your fuckin' insides up! I'd cut your shitty guts up into ribbons, then watch you bleed to death without even a goddamned drop of your cheap blood hitting the ground!"

I squeeze his neck harder, shove his head back viciously against the tiles again and slam my knee twice more into his groin, relishing this upwelling of too-long unexpressed fury, finally pouring out from me onto the man guilty of my mother's death! I'm about to lay the final shocker on him, by blurting out the gory details of how I'd dispose of his body, when I'm suddenly distracted by a warm, ticklish trickle of liquid slowly creeping down the inside of the leg I'm standing on. I don't even release Sam's throat, or lower my knee away from his balls, but just drop my free hand down and wrap it around the back of my leg to wipe the tickle away without a moment's thought.

As soon as my fingers hit the sticky drip, I remember exactly where I am and what I've been doing: shooting a stream of diarrhea into the toilet; and I just jumped up off of it without wiping my butt. *That's OK,* I think, *now I'll have something to smear on Sam's ugly face!* But as I raise my hand to wipe it on him, I'm the one slapped with the surprise: "Oh — *shit.*" But even the runniest shit is still brown — my hand is stained bright red.

The shock of it makes me lower my other foot to the floor, almost tripping as I do on the pant-leg that turned itself inside out around my shoe as I kneed

Sam in the balls. I barely notice as the thick ghostly presence of the part of Sam I was abusing in the men's room exhales sharply once I also release my grip on its neck, and disappears back into the clouds of my memory, leaving me alone to ponder the crimson blot upon my palm.

In my current state, not a single shred of logical thought regarding the physical cause for the bleeding interferes with my clear, almost immediate understanding of the deeper meaning of this. No second-guessing; nothing to suppress; no denying what to make of this message: *There's blood on my hands too.*

As I stare at the blood, my hand swells and becomes a screen upon which images from the slideshow of my mother's face are projected. They start flipping slowly, then faster and faster, dozens of possibilities flashing maddeningly across the surface of my palm, as I try once again to decide which one to believe in; what did her face *look* like when she pointed Sam's gun at the center of her chest, took one last breath, and pulled the trigger? Was it anguish? Resolve? Despair? Relief? ...*Peace?*

"Why did this have to get so fucking *real* for you, Mom?!" It's just like old times again: I'm sitting in the passenger seat of the car with her, arguing. Only she's the one in the hot-seat now. "You were going to be fine! You just had to make it through one last move! We were all here to *help* you!"

But I know now that isn't the truth. I didn't help Anne, and with the muzzle of the gun still pressed against her heart, she turns to face me, and gently asks: "Are you afraid I'll kill myself, Anker?"

But she doesn't give me a chance! Before I can even open my mouth to shout "YES!" she pulls the trigger; she pulls the trigger, and in an instant it's over. And now she will never hear me, no matter how many times, or how loudly I say it: "I *fucking* get it, alright? WRONG ANSWER! I fucked up! I fucked up and there's not a single thing I can do to make it right!"

How could I have been so stupid? How could *anyone* be so stupid! The answer was, is, and always will be, "YES!"

I share this with you now: I share it because—as I promised at the start—this is my love letter to you. Ten thousand people may read this book, and never need to know this. I pray a million people read it, and not a single one of you are ever asked the question. But just in case, make note of this thing that I have learned — There is one question, and as far as I know it may be the only question, that you must *always* answer YES to: "Are you afraid I'll kill myself?"

Make any reply to that question other than "*Yes,*" and it may haunt you for life. I didn't say "*Yes*" — I said "*No.*" On the afternoon I last saw Anne alive, I sat at the table across from her in the kitchen crowded with half-packed moving boxes, as she told me: "I *can't* do it Anker. I just can't deal with all of this *stuff* — I can't make this move!"

"Yes you can! Mom, it's almost done! You're practically there already: there's only one more room to do after the kitchen; the movers come on Tuesday; the new house in Glen Ellen is all ready — it's beautiful!"

"It's a rental. It's a *rental*, Anker."

"Who cares? It's beautiful! And you and Sam are already starting to look in Sonoma, right? That's going to be a great town for you. You can walk all around the big square, the restaurants there are the best in the county, and you already have your friends Bob and Judy there."

"You don't understand, Anker! I've owned my own homes for the past *thirty* years! I haven't been a renter since you and I lived in Strawberry before we moved out to San Rafael, and that's when you were *five!*"

"Mom, who cares? Look, you closed escrow on the ridge house ten days ago right? Did the new owner move in yet?"

"No." She pursed her lips hard and looked down at the table: "It's still empty."

"But it's a done deal, right? Money in the bank?"

"You know damn well it is! You know we did everything we could do to reverse the sale!"

"It's *OK*, Mom. I know you had a lot of mixed feelings about selling that house, but you spent four years up there, and the same story every year; loved it in the spring and summer, but in the winter, that cold fog blew up out of Bodega and hit the ridge and you were miserable! It's all we ever heard about, Mom! You were right to sell that place; the wind wasn't ever gonna stop."

"Anyway, it was just a house. And how much did you clear after the remodeling costs, two hundred and fifty thousand?"

"Closer to three."

"Alright! Close to three hundred thousand. And now you have this house that you paid seven twenty-five for five months ago, listed for nine hundred thousand — and you know you'll get it! You told me yourself the homes have been selling for over asking price in this neighborhood all of a sudden. So you're looking at close to a half-million cash positive to you from selling two houses in the same year? And you said you were retired from real estate!"

I leaned forward to reach across the table and put my hand on hers, but as soon as I started to, the end of my dick got pinched in the fold of my jeans, and I drew back quickly without touching her, and squirmed in my seat trying to reposition it and stop the throbbing pain.

The head of my penis was smeared with vaseline, then taped up in gauze, as the bleeding hadn't stopped from the hole through which the new Prince Albert ring was inserted. It was the second piece of jewelry I'd had put into my penis with a needle, the first being a frenum post done many years earlier.

The frenulum piercing involves clamping the loose skin of the penile shaft, just below the cleft of its head where the rim of the corona meets at the underside, then using a hollow surgical needle to remove a plug of the skin; essentially slicing a round hole through it as opposed to puncturing it. When the needle is run through the flesh, watching it—and feeling it—is akin to the insertion of the arms of a miniature cross.

I had that done at the end of my short first marriage to the 36-year-old I married when I was 23. I think I did it as a symbolic gesture; showed myself I had really taken my dick back from her, and nobody could tell me what to do or don't do with it. Also, I was spending a lot of time at a clothing-optional hot springs resort in Lake County called Harbin. Perhaps I did it to distinguish myself at the pools: instead of just another average height, average weight, average length white guy with a couple of tattoos, maybe I thought the occasional flash of the stainless steel barbell peeking from the underside of my penis as I stepped in and out of the mineral baths, or lounged on the sun-bathing decks with all the other naked people, set me apart from the crowd; made me look like I knew that you're not hardcore unless you live hardcore.

Any reflections on the reasoning behind my decision to have a needle stuck right through the middle of my dick-skin didn't come until quite a while later: at the time, I just went the hell ahead and did it.

I don't think I ever really had the chance to ask myself exactly why I got the Prince Albert; everything changed so fast before it had even stopped bleeding, that I didn't know any more why I was doing anything, or what was really in control of my behavior.

Even before Vita was born two weeks before Anne's death, well ahead of any conversations with Gia about it, I was already starting to think very seriously about a vasectomy operation after the third child. Perhaps then, I saw dangling a big metal ring off the end of my cock as a kind of retirement badge. For years I swam the churning waters of serial-monogamy, promiscuity and worse. I had made it through one very badly matched marriage quickly, relatively unscarred, and without fathering children (one of the trips to the abortion clinic). Now the relationship-game years were behind me, and I had three healthy kids, and a sexy young wife who I loved to fuck. Didn't I have it made? Well done, Soldier! Decorate yourself!

So maybe that's what it was: me awarding myself a medal... maybe in some odd way, the stainless-steel ring through the end of my penis was my granite trophy arch; my Chippendale dining table. Even without anyone else knowing about it or seeing it, it told me that I, Anker Frankoni, had truly arrived. It wasn't a place I'd come to by earning dollars, but by the love I shared with the woman who I'd had my three children with. It was a symbol of the fact that I was truly satisfied with the way my life had become settled: happy to have three children with Gia, and that I knew without a doubt that I would never want others with another woman; because I knew absolutely that there could be no Prince Albert ring without the vasectomy. So really, It was my final step towards cementing in my head the monogamous promise I had made to Gia once we discovered she was first pregnant with Piera. Not that I had once broken it, but until then, I had yet to rule out completely the idea that I wouldn't ever seek out new sex partners in the future.

It was a promise made wholeheartedly, but with an "until some uncertain possible ending in the indefinite future" clause attached to it in my mind.

And so really, I had made the final decision that I would get the vasectomy operation already, before I walked into Staircase Tattoo and Body Piercing nine or ten days after Vita was born, because I knew from a sad accident with a condom that broke on the frenum jewelry during the time between my divorce from the first wife and meeting Gia, that after I had two pieces of metal on the end of my penis, the probability of condom failure during sex would just be too high to count on them as reliable birth control. So the ring was to be the constant reminder of my conscious decision that I was happy to save my naked cock for just one beautiful woman's ass and pussy for the rest of my sexually active days... because I certainly wasn't going to go outside my marriage for some random fuck, knowing there could be no high level of certainty that the condom wouldn't break: it didn't matter that I wouldn't be able to get anyone pregnant; I could catch a disease... my mother had taught me that.

On the other hand, might not this quest for deeper meaning, this lament for my cock, sore and crucified, simply be the purposeless mental ruminations of a man with too much time on his hands? More than likely, it's a lot simpler than these complex justifications I try to piece together: like many men, I'm just in love with my own penis, and thought it might be nice to buy it some jewelry.

If that is the case then, could it be perhaps that the

most tragic irony in Anne's story, is that her life was destroyed—from beginning to end—because of a few men's obsession with their cocks; even as one of them might have made a difference just before it was too late?

Because I believe Anne had already written, or at least started writing the notes that she placed on the passenger seat of the car before shooting herself, by the time I sat down at the kitchen table and spoke with her for the last time. When I flinched back from the sudden pain at the end of my penis instead of holding my mother's hand, I think now that she must have interpreted the grimace on my face for something else. Otherwise, was it really apropos of nothing that at that moment she looked me in the face and asked: "Are you afraid I'll kill myself, Anker?" She just didn't communicate like that: something always had to prod her to open up.

And I sat squirming uncomfortably in the chair across from her, and all I was thinking about was my dick—which means of course I wasn't thinking at all—and said: "No!! My God Mom, why even say that?? You're going to be *fine*. You and Sam will finish the packing this weekend, the movers come on Tuesday, and on Wednesday I'll come back up with Gia and the kids, and while Sam and I get the big things unpacked you can just take it easy and enjoy them. You won't believe how much Vita has changed since you saw her at the hospital. She's going to be so pretty! We named her after Nonna, but I think she got her looks from you, Mom... she's going to be so pretty."

"OK, Anker."

"OK? You know what you have to do then, Mom?"

"Yeah, Anker," she looked down at the table again and said quietly: "I know what I have to do."

"OK, Mom. I gotta get going then. It's a long drive to Santa Cruz, and I know Gia wants me back to help with the kids." I stood up carefully then, walked around to her side of the table and put my hand on her shoulder, but I didn't bend over to hug her, too worried that I might pinch my dick in the crotch of my jeans again.

She looked up at me one more time — right into my eyes, and said simply: "Goodbye, Anker."

"I'll see you *Wednesday*, Mom. Everything's going to work out just fine."

The woman who had already decided not to be Anne Allerfeldt anymore was staring quietly at the table again, as I turned around without another word and slowly walked out of the kitchen, through the living room, and out the front door. I left her sitting by herself like that; the woman who bore me, the woman who loved me, raised me, and supported me. The woman who fought so hard with me, fighting the best fight she knew how, just to help me find my way to something she never really had, the thing that was taken away from her from the very beginning: a *happy* future. I just left her sitting there.

I lowered myself gently into the seat of my car and stuck my hand down my pants to reposition my sore cock as best I could for the long drive, then just before I turned the key in the ignition, I remembered that I'd forgotten to tell my mom the good news. On the day I left work at the start of my two-week paid paternity leave just before Vita was born, I had been called into the CFO's office.

"Anker, congratulations again on the expanding family. We'll miss you in the coming weeks, but keep all your attention where it needs to be: don't think of anything but your wife and kids."

"I won't, Bob. Thanks."

"There is actually one other thing I want you to think about while you're out, Anker."

It wasn't Bob's voice, but one coming from the speaker on the phone on his desk.

"Jim's on the line from the Philadelphia office, Anker," Bob said. "He has a question for you."

Jim was President of the software company I'd landed a spot with not even a year earlier, when I'd been hired into their expanding telesales team. I'd spoken with Jim only once before, through the same speaker-phone on Bob's desk three months after my arrival, when I was asked if I would like to work as the assistant to the Sales Manager, a veteran of computer industry sales with a career dating all the way back to a position with IBM in the 70's. Bernie had great old-school pluck and character, but not much in the way of current technology skills. Within three months of my promotion, I had all 35 of our in-house sales and client support team members, plus nearly 20 outside sales reps dialed into the faithful use of an online database I designed to replace the lead-sheets Bernie was still sending out by Fax every morning, and the dozens of spreadsheets locked in his computer, where prospects from trade shows and magazine ads were sent to suffocate and die.

"Anker," Jim said through the speaker-phone, "We've had a development this week here in Philadelphia: Courtney has put her notice in."

"Oh? I'm sorry to hear that; I hope it's for the best." I wasn't sorry to hear that: Courtney was the persnickety little Cornell MBA grad who was our company's Director of Marketing. Once I started working under Bernie, and began to have regular contact with her, the vibe became quickly apparent: I was beneath her.

"Before I tell you what I'm thinking, Anker, I want you to know that I never would have considered this when you came in as a new hire last year; your lack of a college degree would have simply precluded it. I've been in this business long enough to learn something though; the important thing is what a man does, not what a piece of paper says about what he might be able to do. What you've done to add to our success as a company since you've been here is evidence enough for me: how would you like to take on the role of Director of Marketing?"

"I'm flattered Jim. Thank you for saying that: would I have to relocate to Philly? I'd definitely have to talk it over with my wife if so."

"I don't see a reason for that, Anker. We were thinking you would take the office next to Bernie's — you'll still need to keep supporting him to some extent of course. You would report on your daily activities to Bob, and teleconference with me each week."

"Absolutely."

"Absolutely? That's it, no other questions?"

"No, Sir! I'm your man. Thank you so much for this opportunity."

"Well! So the part about your base-pay increase from fifty-two thousand to, shall we say, sixty-seven? That makes no difference to you? Because I don't mind saving the cash!"

"That makes a huge difference, Sir: *Thank* you."

"Alright, Anker, this is the kind of enthusiasm that convinces me one-hundred percent that this was the right move. Now go take care of your wife! I know you have a lot on your mind, so once you're back in two weeks, we'll talk about your piece of the manager's level profit share, and you can convince me that the terrible loss of your negotiation skills was just a temporary symptom of new baby jitters!"

Remembering this conversation, I took my hand off the key, and was about to get out of the car and walk back up the driveway. I imagined just poking my head in the front door and yelling proudly: "Oh, and Mom! Guess whose favorite college drop-out got promoted to Director of Marketing at MaxTour Systems?" But another angry twinge from the end of my penis made me wince. I sucked my breath in quick, and muttered: "I'll save it for Wednesday," and stayed seated.

"And that woulda been... hmm, lessee... 42? Wednesdays ago?" I say from where I'm seated now, as I realize I'm sitting back down on the toilet in JJ's again, staring at the blood on my hand, and I think I've been in here too long.

I reach across my lap to pull a fresh strip of toilet paper from the roll with my clean hand and try to wipe it off, but most of it has already dried. I wipe the paper up the inside of my leg, then grab some more and wipe my ass. I stand up, just a little unsteadily, then pull my pants and underwear up, using just the tips of my thumb and forefinger of the bloodied hand to avoid marking my pants, then fasten my belt and flush the toilet. I unlatch the stall door, move to the sink, then stand staring at it for a while trying to decide: do I want to freeze my hands, or burn them? Eventually I turn both the separate hot and cold water faucets on, and move my hands back and forth between both streams just fast enough to do neither, but not so quickly that I splash water around Jack's bathroom. Once my hands are clean I walk back into the stall, and using several brown paper towels that I've dampened at the sink, carefully wipe up the droplets of blood on the floor next to the wall, and swipe down the toilet seat properly. Then I take a glance back up at Jack's sign and say: "Hope that's respectful enough for you my friend: time for another affordable drink!"

***

When I re-enter the bar I discover It's completely empty save for Jack, who is reading the newspaper behind the counter next to his cash register. I walk back over to my stool and glance down before I climb on to be sure my briefcase is still safely wedged between the boot-rail and the bar on the floor next to it, then take my seat. Jack hasn't cleared my space or poured my drink out, In fact he placed a coaster over the top of my coffee mug, emptied my ashtray, and arranged my pack of American Spirits next to it by placing the lighter on top; very welcoming.

I pull a fresh cigarette from the pack and light it up, grateful for Jack's intelligent refusal to enforce the statewide smoking ban that California passed years prior. When I asked him about it shortly after becoming a regular at his place, Jack said: "Smoking in bars is like motor oil in a car; they don't run right if you take it out. I'm better off paying a couple fines every year than losing half my customers."

I look up after lighting my smoke, and find that Jack is looking at me. I'm not sure if he's scratching his head, or gesturing to make some kind of subtle double-meaning out of his question, but he kind of taps two fingers near his temple as he asks: "Everything OK back there, Anker?"

"Huh? Oh! Uhh, yeah, yeah, Jack — Thanks. I was, um, just a little uh, bound up, you know; took a little while to work it out."

"OK. Good," Jack says, then goes back to his

newspaper.

After a few drags off my cigarette, I remove the coaster from the top of my mug, raise it to my lips for a sip, then grimace and spit it back into the cup: it's nearly ice cold.

I feel my brow furl slightly in response to this puzzle, then slowly lean to the side of my bar-stool, straighten my leg out, and pull the phone from my pocket to check the time — 10:22.

I sense more than see that Jack is looking over the top of his newspaper at me again as I sit staring at the phone, trying to somehow fix the math to convince myself that I wasn't just in that bathroom for over an hour.

"Get cold? Want me to warm that up for you?" Jack asks.

"Jesus... yeah," I sigh, as I snap the phone shut and shove it back into my pocket: "Warm it up and spice it up, Jack: I need a little booster shot."

Jack puts his newspaper down by the cash register, walks down to the end of the bar and returns with the coffee pot, and fills my mug to the top with all coffee. I don't say anything about the missing shot, in fact, rather than complain, I think: *he's probably right.*

After taking a few sips of my properly warmed coffee, that now only stings slightly from the dregs of the Bushmills left from the drink I let get cold, I ask Jack: "What happened to that couple? They looked like the more-than-one-round type to me."

Jack lets a moment pass, turns a page of the newspaper, and without looking up replies: "They left a little bit ago. Woman looked like she thought the place was haunted or something."

I don't get the meaning behind Jack's remark, but I don't ask him to explain. I figure if it's important, he'll elaborate. I keep smoking and taking small sips of the coffee, happy to be just sitting there in silence in the empty room with this bartender who makes me feel so comfortable. I realize how rarely I've come across people like him, then contemplate the concept for a few minutes as I finish my cigarette: Is it an individual trait, or a chemistry between two people, two personalities? Though he must be close to 40 years older, Jack reminds me a lot of my old friend Spencer. Spencer and I could sit for hours in one of our dorm-rooms when I knew him in college, maybe take a bong hit or two, drink a beer, and not say six sentences between us; just sit in perfectly comfortable silence. Every once in a while though, something truly profound, or completely unexpected would come out of him, like the time we were sitting around my room after another Chicken a la King night at the cafeteria.

"Anker," he said.

"Yeah, Spence?"

"You know those times, when you're standing over the can about to take a shit, and you just know it's gonna come out real fast and loose?"

"Do I? How often do they feed us that fuckin' Chicken a la Sting?"

"Yup. Well here's what you do: take a few sheets of toilet paper and lay them flat out over the water. Crisscross another layer over that; the trick is complete coverage over the surface of the water, with the edges all around lapping up an inch or two above it on the sides of the bowl, you follow?"

"I think so."

"Then when you shit, the stream will pierce the center of the paper layer, which acts like a membrane over the surface of the water, preventing splashback up onto your ass and legs."

"Hmmm. Thanks, Spencer: I'll try that."

"Sure," Spencer said, then got up and walked out the door without another word. That was the way he operated: except for the rare occasions I spoke with him on the phone, I never once heard him say "Hello" or "Goodbye." He was simply there or not, no explanation necessary. That's how I feel with Jack right now, sitting in his empty bar, no explanation necessary.

I finish my coffee along with another cigarette, let a few more minutes pass sitting silently near Jack, then climb down from my bar-stool much more easily; my head is starting to clear. I retrieve my briefcase from behind the boot-rail and move to one of the cocktail tables at the rear of the bar, and take a seat in one of the wooden armchairs there. I open the briefcase, pull out the almost brand new MacBook in it, then slide the briefcase to the side.

Only a few months have gone by since the last round of real bad fighting with Sam Salt ended. When the dust settled, I was left with more cash in the bank than I think even 20 really good years at MaxTour would have allowed me to save, but lost the ownership of the 12-unit apartment building in Menlo Park that had been the main investment into which Anne poured her savings from 20 years in real estate. The apartment building was the sole asset she placed into a separate property trust, which stipulated that the income from it would be split evenly between Sam and me until his death, then pass to me or my heirs as sole property.

Not quite two weeks before her suicide, just a day or two after Vita was born, Anne took one last proactive step towards settling her affairs. Unbeknownst to Sam, she sold shares in a Schwab investment account that had been listed as part of their community property trust. The money was theirs in name only; she had earned every penny of it.

A couple years into their marriage, Sam left Channel 5, frustrated with the writing on the wall that told him he was never going to move up to the weekday anchor position there. Anne set him up with a video production business, so he could make corporate videos for the booming technology companies sprouting up all over Silicon Valley. He worked six years at that before the first break-even point was met, and the two of them finally decided it was better if he stayed home... cooking... gardening; riding his Harley: Man-Wife stuff.

Anne used the almost seven-hundred thousand in cash from the Schwab shares to pay off the mortgage on the apartments, leaving them totally free and clear, owned outright by the trust. After Anne was dead, and the house she couldn't pack her things up in one last time was sold, Sam was worth somewhere in the neighborhood of $2.4 million all told, not counting any claim to the apartments.

In response to the Christmas-Wish Curse I had yelled so passionately at Sam's front door when things really started coming to a head between us, I received a letter from his lawyer on December 27th of the year Anne died, informing me that a lawsuit would be filed to recover the full amount of the money Anne had used to pay off the apartment's mortgage: now that she was dead, the money that she had taken from their community listed account was deemed Sam's rightful property. As an alternative, the letter informed me, Sam's offer to buy my interest in the apartments outright for a sum amounting to approximately sixty-five percent of their market value was enclosed; would I sign the offer, or see them in court?

Anne would have seen them in court. Marco suggested that I hit them quickly with a wrongful death countersuit. Maybe it was the extra day I spent in her at the beginning: Sagittarius people are lovers, not fighters. I went the hell ahead and signed the offer.

I had already lost my job at MaxTour Systems well before that. After taking two weeks of paid bereavement leave back to back with the paternity time, I spent five weeks in the new office next to Bernie's before having one last speaker-phone chat with Jim. He was sorry, he said, and assured me he knew that the original decision was a good one, but I no longer seemed like the same guy he had made the offer to.

Once my liquidated inheritance was in the bank, a chorus of voices from everyone close to me—older cousins; my mother-in-law; an uncle in France; even Bernie, who I stayed in touch with for a while after leaving MaxTour—all urged me to sock the money away in CD accounts where I couldn't tempt myself with it for a year, and do nothing: don't look for a job, don't think about long-term investments, don't buy a house, just... recover.

I scraped a little more than just our rent and projected basic living expenses off the top before putting the bulk of it out of harm's way: I switched out the `87 Volvo sedan Gia and I had been sharing for three years for a nice, low-miles `99 wagon — still a Volvo of course; sensible. I let her pick out new sheets and towels for the house, and even a brand-new couch. And I didn't go Ikea cheap on her either! The beautiful leather sectional she fell in love with at Scandinavian Designs was completely out of place in our little rented Santa Cruz bungalow, but I knew we wouldn't be renters forever; not now. And besides, what was four-thousand dollars and change to get her something that seemed to make her that happy for no particular reason, at a time when she could just enjoy it? Her birthday after all... well... I didn't even want to think about Gia's birthday: not yet. And I knew I couldn't just go cold-turkey from working

50, sometimes 60 hours a week to nothing, just watch the days go by. So for myself, I splurged on a new MacBook, not even knowing what I would do with it.

And I still don't know what the hell I'm doing with it: "Write... jus' write!" I mutter. I'm staring at no more than five or six sentences on the screen. It's not quite eleven in the morning on a Thursday. My beautiful first daughter and son are safe at one of the best schools in Santa Cruz, getting ready for happy futures. My still almost brand-new baby daughter is at home with my lovely wife, less than eight blocks away from where I'm sitting — I could be sitting with them right now.

Instead, I've been drinking long enough this morning so that I'm already starting to feel hung over, and I'm still sitting in a dark bar with a silent old man, staring at the screen of this computer again, about to wipe away another shitty attempt at a first paragraph. "Some recovery," I sigh, then hit delete to clear the screen.

I lean forward, place my elbows on the glass-topped table, and rest my forehead on my outstretched fingers, my eyes focusing in and out of the blank screen. "You wrote a thousand pages of crap to sell the shit you were hawkin' for the past seven years," I say softly at the table, "and now one fuckin' letter? Can't even write one lousy letter?"

Because that's all I'm trying to write — just a letter to Anne. Even though she'll never get it now, I think that if I can just write it; write it, read it, then tear it up or burn it, maybe I can understand some of this, maybe I really can "recover." I try again.

Dear Mom,

I was a happier person than you! I had a hard start, but damn you I was making it! I know you thought I'd never have a "pot to piss in" as you said, but you didn't even stick around long enough to find out that I'd finally gotten a real job, with a good company! And I know you didn't like Gia, but her goddamned BIRTHDAY?! What the fuck! 'Dear Daughter-in-law, happy fuckin' birthday you little cunt, BANG!—

"Shit... Shit!" I grit my teeth, select all, and hit delete to clear the page. Start again.

Dear Mom,

What did Sam really know? There's too much that doesn't ring true! You said in your note that he had agreed to pay off the apartments, but you had already done that! He swears the gun was disassembled and hidden, but was it?? My dad showed me his pistol: a .38 revolver, just the same. Neither of us could figure the first thing out about taking it apart, so how the hell did you put one back together — You weren't in the Army! and if Sam put it back together, answer me this: Why the hell did you waste that other bullet on the fucking CAR??

"Oh Fuck!" I choke and cough as the panic grips me; as the hatred rises. "No!" I say, and very quickly clear all the words from the screen again. My heart is racing.

I reach for my American Spirits, my hands shaking so badly three of them end up on the floor by the time I get one in between my lips. I'm holding the lighter in both hands to keep it steady enough to get it lit. I take a deep drag, I take another, now my heart is starting to calm and I say softly: "Enough Anker: you're a lover... you're a Sadge. One death was enough."

I haven't written my letter. I'm frozen again, staring at the blank screen. I'm going to read hers instead. I've lost track of how many times I have, but I'm going to read it again. I have to keep reading it, until my writer's block is cured. The cigarette is dangling from my lips. I leave it there as I reach for my briefcase, open the top and pull out Anne's letter. I leave the cigarette in my mouth as I begin reading, that way, if anything wet comes out of my eye, I'll tell myself smoke got in it: I haven't cried since I was 14-years-old; I'm scared of what might happen if I do.

My Dear Anker,

I'm sorry I have failed you as a mother and this farewell is the ultimate failure. I don't know why this deep depression began, too much stress for too many years, then the move and worry & lack of community and probably the biggest thing, a failure to reinvent myself when we came here. I was just done with the work on the house and feeling part of the "ridge community" when we reacted to a broker's request which led to the sale. Anyway, depression does run in our family. My father and brother Peter and your cousin Gary all had it, it is also sometimes accompanied by a manic component. I mention this so you'll be vigilant if you start feeling any signs. It seems to manifest in the 40s & 50s.

Frankly you appear to be a far happier person than I, I loved your little jokes as a child and your good laugh. You're a wonderful father and husband and son. I'm always delighted to watch you with the children. I'm so sorry I'm not well enough to be a good grandmother, but I'm just too depressed and anxious. Sam will give you a copy of the trust, and he has agreed to pay off the mortgage on the apartments so that should help and I believe he will agree to do more, I've asked him to. Get your father's help with it.

I have always loved you and tried to do the best for you but feel I came up short a lot. This may appear to be more of the same, but I believe I have gotten to the point where I will be institutionalized which will be neither pretty nor helpful for anyone. I cannot sleep & can barely eat and the medications I have been on combined with the stress have been deleterious to my brain.

I wish you a long and happy life. Please take care of problems early on, and please, please protect your daughters & teach them to speak up & stick up for themselves.

I love you all, Mom.

I put the letter back into my briefcase. I pull the cigarette from my lips and use the other hand to wipe my eyes: smoke has gotten into both of them. I realize the cigarette ash has fallen down the front of my shirt and into my lap, and look around trying to find a place for the butt. Jack walks out from behind his bar. He brings an ashtray and sets it in front of me, then bends over and picks up the three cigarettes I've dropped on the floor. He returns them to my pack, then places that next to my laptop and puts my lighter on top if it.

"Thanks Jack," I say: "Another whisky coffee, OK? I gotta write."

Jack ignores my request, pulls the other chair out from the table and sits down across from me. He doesn't say anything at first, just sits with me, filling the space with a very comfortable silence.

I'm the one that breaks it: "Jack?" I ask.

"What's on your mind, Anker?" Jack says.

"What's a guy supposed to feel, Jack, about the person who shoots his mother dead?"

He replies calmly, with no shock or surprise: "Hatred Anker. Hatred, pure and simple."

"But what about when that person is her?"

"Then I can only imagine that it must be much more complicated than that."

I keep staring at the glow of the computer as the comfortable silence continues. After a minute, he reaches forward and slowly pushes the MacBook screen down to close it, then runs his hand gently back and forth across its satin smooth top.

"I wrote a book years ago, Anker. It wasn't a big deal, but it was for me. I learned a whole lot about myself in the process."

"Oh, I'm not writing a book Jack. I'm just... I don't know what I'm writing."

"It doesn't matter what you're writing. But whatever it is, you have to know the story first."

"Yeah — I guess you're right."

"Anker, I want you to look around you for just a moment."

"Look around, Jack?"

"Yeah. Just look around. Look around you. What do you see?"

"Well... an empty bar."

"Yup. Now I want to show you something else. Bring your things."

"My things?"

"Yeah, your computer, your smokes, your briefcase: grab your things."

Jack stands and waits patiently for me to pack up my briefcase, then leads me to the back door of his bar. He turns the deadbolt to unlock it, which I think is strange, because he always leaves the back door open during business hours. You can tell the regulars at JJ's, because they always use the back door. He swings it wide open, and I blink my eyes as the bright sun streams in, and I see what a beautiful day it is.

I follow Jack as he walks down the three steps outside the door, and a few paces into the parking lot. "Anker, whatever part of your story involves sitting around a bar with a quiet old man smoking and drinking four or five mornings out of each week; I think you can write that now. And whatever part of your story you haven't quite put your hands on yet, well, I think you'll get a grasp on it faster if your fingers aren't wrapped around a bottle."

I stand and think about what to say to that for a moment, and realize the most honest answer is the simplest: "Thanks Jack." But when I turn to tell him, he's already at the steps, no "Goodbye," just there, then not there, just like my old friend Spencer.

It feels perfect to leave it like that, but as I watch the old man climb the short flight of steps, I look past his shoulder, and realize that the sign next to the door reads "Closed."

"Hey Jack." I call back as it hits me, and as he reaches the top of the steps and turns around I say: "Closed? You closed your bar for me, Jack? For three hours?"

"I felt like taking a break, Anker." Then just before he flips the sign back around and walks inside, he smiles kindly at me and says: "Why don't you try giving yourself one?"

And thanks to Jack, right then and there I started doing just that. I put my briefcase in the Volvo and left it parked, then walked out onto Porter Street towards Bay Avenue. With each step of my mile-long walk towards the water, I felt another layer of the distrust and suspicion that I realized I'd put up between myself and everyone else slip away. All it took was one caring gesture from an old man who had nothing to gain by it, who was willing to go out of his way to remind me of one simple, but essential fact: we're all in this together.

When I reached the beach at Capitola, I took my shoes off and walked through the sand, and a shiver of pleasure ran through my body as it sifted through my naked toes. When I reached the waters edge, I knew exactly what to do. Anne hadn't written with a return address. I didn't need to write her back. All I needed were three little words: "I am sorry."

Just three little words, spoken sincerely into the endless expanse of the rolling water. I said them again: "I am sorry." With no other thought in my heart, or words upon my lips, I let their cleansing power flow out, over the great waters of the ocean.

Epilogue

By the time I finally turned my back to the water on the last morning I visited Jack's bar, I knew that Anne's spirit had received my message, and forgiven me. Though my head was full of the sound of the waves on the shore, something deeper had quieted within me. The constant ominous *tick, tick, tick* of my mother's letter bomb had been defused. With a light heart I began walking back towards my home, and my wife, and my children, truly convinced that she had only been partially right: I *was* a happier person; a wonderful father, ready to get back to the business of being a good husband, and as for son... maybe two out of three ain't bad.

But explosives, once primed, are unpredictable. I hadn't stood long enough at the water's edge. Anne had forgiven me, that I know, but I left before receiving the most important forgiveness of all: that which I had not yet granted to myself. And as for Sam? There was still a lot of sting to come from that salt in my wound.

Within a few short years, Gia and the kids and I had a beautiful home in Santa Cruz (It's what Anne would have wanted, I told myself as I signed the closing papers.) I'd managed to land a good job as Director of Business Development with a marketing and design firm, and as each day passed, I racked up one more in a nearly five-year run of sobriety.

When it started ticking again, it wasn't Anne who reset the timer. Something deep inside myself, trapped where it knew it did not belong, reached up from the otherwise empty cell hidden deep within me and ripped to shreds the fake trappings of success by circumstance that I had wrapped around my life. I didn't need to re-read Anne's letter to keep hearing the words over and over, clawing at the back of my head: *depression runs in our family.*

When the clock hit zero, it was the promised manic component that exploded most violently. Instead of blowing me to hell, it swept us all away: away from the hastily sold home; away from our lives in California and everyone we knew — away from the past. When we discovered our new present, it was in a place that at first seemed a whole lot more like Heaven than Hell: *Mexico.*

I want you to come too. I want to show you a place where pure hearts still beat with ancient memories of how human animals were supposed to live on this planet, and true lovers bask in the rich spice of hot life and naked, sweaty passion. But before I sell the house, pull the kids out of school, bring you to one last bonfire on the beach with our old friends, and invite you to follow us on our long dangerous drive to Central Mexico, now that you've drilled through the tip of this iceberg with me, take a few deep breaths and get ready to plunge below the surface, when we meet again in the second book of the "Mexican Eskimo" trilogy: *Octopus Asylum.*

Note to Reader

As a first-time author working without the backing of a major publisher, the one and only hope I have of making this book a success is very simply, you. One of the most important lessons I have learned, is that with the exception of those extremely rare times that people like my old bartender Jack cross our paths, we do not receive, unless we ask. So I'm asking. Will you please help?

Here are a few easy things you can do:

Follow me on Twitter ~ @AnkerFrankoni ~ then tweet a message to your followers with a link to www.MexicanEskimo.com or the book's Amazon catalog page.

Follow me on Instagram ~ @MexicanEskimo ~ then share a photo of your print or digital copy of the cover of this book along with a few thoughts about it.

Visit www.MexicanEskimo.com and use the contact form or contest-entry button to add your e-mail address to my readers list. (Your address will only be used to inform you of my writing and book releases, and will never be sold, rented, given or loaned to any other party.)

Finally—and perhaps most importantly—if you can honestly recommend this book with a four or five-star rating, please take a few minutes to post a review on Amazon. If you can't, I would be even more grateful if you would share any thoughts or impressions directly with me, so that I can make the next book even better.

Thank you,

Anker Frankoni ~ anker@mexicaneskimo.com